8/12/17

To Ben,
Good luck with
your writing. Go for it".
/Joe Cohen

High
Gate
Health
and
Beauty

High
Gate
Health
and
Beauty

Joseph Colicchio

CREATIVE ARTS BOOK COMPANY
Berkeley • California

High Gate Health and Beauty
is published by Donald S. Ellis
and distributed by Creative Arts Book Company

For Information contact:
Creative Arts Book Company
833 Bancroft Way
Berkeley, California 94710

ISBN 0-88739-251-2
Library of Congress Catalog Number 98-83259

Printed in the United States of America

High
Gate
Health
and
Beauty

*To my wife, Pat
and my kids, Jack and Roy*

PART I

ONE

HERE IN HIGH GATE, LOTS OF GUYS HONOR THE old days and ways. They dress and walk in the styles, speak in the sounds and tongues that hold on to what used to be, or that create, like a group of kids playing Telephone, a never-was time that explains how they got to be here, how this happened. They talk out of the sides of their mouths and joke brotherly, even with pride, about being failures, lef'-behinds, boat men, and they refer to other white folk by the country they came here from—you seen the Irishman? . . . the old German? . . . the dumb Polack? . . . the dirty Guinea? There's no nasty intention. In fact, the words are affectionate. They show you're one.

So it gives an idea of the status of Uncle Mike's dog Prince that by us Bowers Street Park Regulars, Prince was referred to as the Dog, as though this indicated his ethnicity and not his species. "You think the Dog's hot with all that hair?" "You think the Dog'd want to take a walk to the saloon?" Because everybody considered the old man my mom insisted I call Uncle Mike to be such a prick, the Dog got more sympathy and attention than most people do.

Being the Dog was not only Prince's ethnicity, it was his diagnosis as well, like addictive personality, manic-depressive, identity disorder. It was the bottom-line explanation for his limitations, an explanation even the most bitter of the park-dwellers would have to accept. In our own little 1999 it-takes-a-village project, Prince got fed when he was hungry, petted when he was down, fanned when he was hot, and invited along when there was nothing to do. When the grown-ups and almost-grown-ups ended their card games and, safely, in numbers, were ready to show themselves outside the park, tromping up Griffith or Hutton for Central Avenue, "Where's the Dog?" they'd ask, looking around for the only outsider both welcome and willing to join them. "Maybe he wants to come. Where the fuck'd he go? Come on, Prince, you lazy so-and-so, keep us some company."

It was eight-thirty in the morning, June 24th, less than a week after I'd finished my sophomore year at Harry S. The sun at my back, peeking from behind the Twin Towers, I was sitting on top of a park table just outside the basketball court watching the eight-year-old McGuire twins race each other in dribbling. Freddie, the longer-haired kid, was in a Shaq Lakers jersey, Ty in an Iverson '76ers one. They had on the same baggy black Oh Boy! shorts that came three-quarters of the way down their cane-thin ghost-white calves. Neither Freddie or Ty had fingertip control of their dribbles yet and chased the balls this way and that, using only their right hand for bouncing. Their left arms, bent at the elbows, kept each boy balanced like the ring of a gyroscope as he lurched forward after his ball like it was a leashed dog chasing the right tree to piss on. Sitting on the tabletop, I was laughing easy, relaxed, happy for the early morning coolness, and I didn't notice Prince trotting over until I felt his snout pushing against my ankle.

Prince is a black dog but his snout and paws are tipped in golden brown. "Yo, it's the Dog. What's up, Princie?" I asked. He dropped his ball and pawed it around in some crabgrass then jerked his head in the direction he wanted me to throw. Though he's eight, a little more than half my age, Prince is always eager to play. Sometimes he brings his own ball—white skinned but pink sponge where the cover has been gnawed off. He's learned that humans are more likely to play with him if his ball's not all slimed up, so after he trots over, he drops his ball into the grass and rolls it around with his paw, a begging and cleaning action all in one.

The table I was on was just a few yards up from the Cliff Walk, the winding concrete path along the palisades that overlook Hoboken and New York City. Naturally, Prince jerked his head toward the downward slope, toward the Bowers Street end and the apartment where him and Uncle Mike lived. He'd figured out that running downhill was easiest but hadn't made the leap to realizing that downhill out

4

meant uphill back. There was a logical explanation, though: "What do you expect from the Dog?"

Me and Prince always got along great, even though we were different types. Prince was very affectionate—always a paw up in your lap, or licking at your ankles, or pressing against your leg. I didn't show affection like that, never even spoke of it— affection or any other emotion. In fact, sometimes I wasn't even sure if I was a feeling person at all. Prince, though, he wore his heart on his sleeve. Tail swingy or droopy, step springing or dragging, he didn't make a secret of his mood.

A lot of times I'd watch Prince around people and wish I could be like him, but since he was the Dog, a dog and only a dog, there was no reason to be resentful. I could admire the quality without being embarrassed by it, or by me.

I jumped down from the table and, like I did a lot when nobody was around, started wrestling with the fluffy mutt. I grabbed him under the armpits and flipped him over. Protecting my face with my arms and elbows, like a boxer covering up, I buried my nose and blew warm air where his neck met his chest until he got under me with his hind legs and knocked me off. "Hee-ya-ha." I faked him, karate-style. "You Dog. Me person. Hee-ya-ha, Doggie-man."

But Prince ignored my goofing. We rested and hung out— me on my back, hands behind my head, propped up on a clump of grass in the dirt around the table, Prince on his side, the breeze waving his hair, tickling his ear, his eyes opening and closing under the twinkle of orange sun.

When his eyes stayed shut, I petted him. I played with all the pieces of his paw—the concrete-roughed pads, the black nails, the wobbly knuckles. And when I fell asleep, he woke up and jabbed me above the ear. He got up on his fours as quick as he could and picked up his ball.

"It's gonna be hot later," I said as I sat up. I took the ball from him and faked throwing it. His tail started waving and his butt shaking.

Prince had gained some weight over the years and he ran with a huff and effort like he never used to. There were wiry grey hairs mixed in with the black, and the black looked a lot thicker and hotter than it used to. Still, Prince had always been a clean dog and Uncle Mike's overshampooing was probably the explanation for the fluffy hair.

Not that anyone would give Uncle Mike credit for truly caring about his dog. We all knew it was only because he saw Prince as a reflection of his own special self that he bothered. So Mike made sure to have Prince's teeth and nails done twice a year, and, because Uncle Mike hated stinks so much, Prince always smelled fresh, of flea powder and Octagon soap. He was never allowed out without his collar, and his dog tag was a special order from Don's House of Gold. My brother Brian said it was fourteen-karat and cost more than our mom's wedding band.

After two rounds of fetch, Prince's mouth was open. His tongue was slobbery and shimmering red. He dropped into the dirt and cozied up, resting his jaw on my sneaker. I petted his warm hair, the lump of bone on each side of his parted skull, the soft hollow spot in the middle where it felt like your finger was stroking his brain.

"Remember the bandanna?" I asked him, teasing. His head didn't move, just his eyes lifted. For a little bit of time, Prince had worn a red bandanna because, as Uncle Mike bragged, "My Prince is a dandy dog." But the bandanna had a different effect than intended and the bragging didn't last long. The only thing I could figure was that Prince connected the red bandanna with the biker guys who came into the park to work on their cycles Saturday mornings. These guys weren't dandies. And that bandanna got Prince bopping with their kind of swagger—head low and sagging like a heavy branch, balled-into-fists shoulders rolling, tail brushing the ground. Tired of life and all, a lef'-behind, a failure, so not like the real him. This wasn't any dandy's tippy-toed, nose-in-the-air, tail-curled swagger at all. Pissed that his foster child lacked the breeding he'd hoped for, Uncle Mike pulled the bandanna off Prince in three days. It was pretty funny. As a matter of fact, it was one of the best things that ever happened around here.

Prince jumped up, ready to play some more. He started nudging me and pawing at the ball. I took it from him, stood up—hiked my own Oh Boys! which were slipping down—faked two, three, four throws, Prince's fat fanny still wiggling and tail wagging like a pup's, barely able to keep his feet on the ground. I heaved it. But I heaved it too hard, clear out the far end of the park, half a block away. Prince stopped mid-gallop. He turned and shook his head. "Sorry. Sorry, Prince. I'm a fucking jerk. Get a drink while you're down there," I called, knowing there was always a bowl of water by the apartment building's cellar door. Prince slapped his tongue around and turned away, still shaking his head.

It was a long walk for Prince from where I was, near the basketball courts. The McGuire kids were slowly making their way through the park, throwing rocks over the cliff toward the Hoboken train tracks and projects. On the far side of the court was HouseRAD—House Row Arts District, a real rundown part of High Gate that a bunch of outsiders were moving into, trying to turn into something New York. The opposite end, the end I'd thrown the ball toward, was our end.

Ogden Avenue, the street I live on and that Uncle Mike's apartment house is on, runs through the park, just above the Cliff Walk. At our end of the park, there's a cutout where a road passes under Ogden and winds down the hill toward Hoboken, an old road, trashy, busted up and never used, still covered in cobblestones, a road we call Cobble Road. To reach from my bench to Cobble Road, I must have thrown the ball two hundred feet. That's a home run in Little League, and that's why I called myself a fucking jerk.

Once a ball bounced onto Cobble Road, it bounced down and down till God knew where you'd find it, if you ever did. Instead of hopping the fence, like he might have a few years ago, and finding himself on a mud and rock pitch down to the road, Prince took the long way around. That meant walking out of the park, from Ogden to Palisade Avenue, then doubling back. Prince stopped one more time and sat to scratch his ear. "I said I'm sorry. I'm a little jerk, okay?"

Prince was smart, but he wasn't smart enough to know the whole reason of why I considered myself a jerk. Like a lot of ninety-pound weaklings, to make up for my size, I sometimes overdid things. Just like I did then—instead of tossing the ball out onto the grass, I had to heave it as far as I could. That's my fucked up thinking—you never know who's watching, who's taking notes. But overdoing it just makes worse out of bad. There I stood, hands on my hips, a big little jerk.

I'm fifteen and a half, but someone hit the pause button on my hormones when I turned thirteen, and puberty still hasn't kicked in for real. I'm five-five, a hundred and fifteen pounds, and I don't shave. But I can make up for it! Throw Prince's ball two hundred feet.

At first, when Prince wasn't quick in showing himself with the ball, I figured that the thing must have rolled all the way out Cobble Road to the trolley tracks that used to connect Hoboken with High Gate, our section of Jersey City. I went down to the Cliff Walk and peered through the fence's high iron pickets. The skyline was grey against a pale blue sky. The Empire State was to my left, then came a dip and a low plateau, then a rise peaking with the World Trade Center, and finally, a heavy cluster at the Battery Park end. It looked like a giant transistor chip from my school's electronics lab. Way off to the right was the New York Harbor and the Statue of Liberty, near enough you could tell the direction the flags were whipping, the sun in the statue's eyes as she stood, her back to us.

Prince was taking a lot longer than he should have, no matter where the ball had landed. At his age, he had enough sense to know when a ball was lost for good, and so I started walking out toward Cobble Road.

Farther down Ogden, half a block past Uncle Mike's, I could see my mom and my Aunt Pat, alongside each other but staring ahead, slowly coming toward the park for what they called their morning work break. I gave a half wave, but concerned for Prince, not wanting to waste time, I kept moving, and they didn't notice me.

I followed Prince's route out to Palisade Avenue. When I made the turn back onto Cobble Road, right away I thought I saw him lying down below, in the shadow of the Ogden Avenue overpass, a hundred feet from where I stood. I walked over the bumpy grey stones, staring ahead but without words in my head, eyes steady on the still black lump. It was Prince, it definitely was. I whistled and called his name. As I moved closer, I watched for the rise and fall of his breathing. "This is fucked up," I said. I was close, just two car lengths from him. "Prince," I called, part shout, part whisper. The rusted hulk of a red and black station wagon set on cinder blocks tottered when I brushed it with my hip as I angled into the shade. I didn't take my eyes from Prince. His head was lifted, neck turned. He wasn't breathing.

I didn't start to cry. It didn't cross my mind. Only that this was fucked up.

His black body was shiny in the sunlight. The breeze circling up the road fluffed his hair. I knelt one knee on a rounded, silver-speckled stone. Prince felt warm as I brushed his hair with my hand. With one finger, I stroked his forehead, in the gully between the eyes. His nose was still wet and his eyes glistened, but they were turning gluey as I watched. He stared, but up off toward nothing. His head was really twisted funny, not flat to the stones. Part of his neck, from the right shoulder to the flap of his ear, was on the ground, but his snout was lifted, like when he used to sniff the air. Lifted and twisted, it was working against gravity, straining to see something, to peek back over his shoulder. Prince's neck was broke. I tried to push it down, but it wouldn't go. My heart let out a blast, pumping such blood that my fingertips began to throb. My hands, like a fright-night scream, jumped back, off of Prince.

I knelt next to him. I shut my eyes, but I came up empty, just pissed. The same words, "Fucked up."

I lifted one of his front paws, and I played with it. I bent and sniffed it—it smelled alive. But Prince was gone. I rippled the stiff golden hairs just above his paws. Before I got up, I tilted my head like his and stared up into the beautiful blue.

TWO

EVERY MORNING AT THAT TIME, BETWEEN NINE
and nine-thirty, my mom and Aunt Pat, each armed
with a beach chair and a long-handled straw bag loaded
with the day's necessities, took their rest break at the Park
House, an old splintering wood and cement bandstand. Even
though neither of them worked, for my mother, calling it a
"rest break" made some sense. She would already have managed to get me and Brian out of the house, to go to the A&P, or
at least have made up the list for me to go, to wipe down the
kitchen and bathroom and somehow push the apartment's
mess under cover. She'd come here, to the park, for an hour.
Then, like she'd been doing for more than a month, she'd walk
up to the library to do the Ed-Link computer grammar drills—
sound alikes, punctuation, possessives, parts of speech.

At age thirty-seven, she'd be starting Hudson County
Community College in the fall and, my mother being someone
who still kept her Saint Paul of the Cross Spelling Championship
trophy on her dresser, she wanted to do good on the placement
test. Brian, who's a student-tutor at the college, had told her that
if you didn't do good it could take you four years or more to graduate. "Time, I don't have," she said, but she always said that.

It was a year ago, after being there for three years, that,
following a state inspection, she was let go by Farsight Preschool
for not having any college credits. But even without a job to go
to, my mom kept organization in her life. My Aunt Pat, though,
she was different. Her life was without any sort of organization,
even when she did have a job, jobs that usually ended with a
bang and came and went a lot more quickly than my mom's. In
the years I could remember, she'd worked as a school-bus driver,
a consumer advocate, and a tarot-card reader. For a few months

she did volunteer work as treasurer at Loaves and Fishes Counselling and Rehabilitation Center. Her most recent job ended a year and a half ago. She'd been a liquor consultant at High Gate Pharmacy, but she was fired from there, with not so much as a full day's notice, when the store had its liquor and pharmacy licenses stripped and was downgraded to High Gate Health and Beauty.

Not that the unemployed life was easy for Aunt Pat. Exactly the opposite. Two years younger than my mom, thirty-five, just turned sixteen and going on eighty, she had an addiction to crisis. Maybe she wasn't always in a crisis, but she was always at least leaning toward one, as bored ("just friggin' empty feeling") when she wasn't in crisis as she was miserable when she was.

The empty feeling would lead to one of two things. She'd start feeling sick—intestinal pains, palpitations, migraines, dry mouth—and soon enough these pains, the pain they caused others as well as the pain they caused her, would lead to the crisis she needed. That, or she'd simply have an attack of nerves and have to retreat to bed. There, she might be overcome with the horrors and burst into the hallway screaming, "Shoot me, shoot me," or she might sleep for twenty-four hours. She could find a crisis in her past, present, or future, usually having to do with losing something—cigarettes, keys, equilibrium, pills, welfare benefits; her hair, her teeth, her looks, her phone card, her boyfriend, her mind, her reputation; a breast, a nail file, a pen that writes, a lighter that works.

June mornings, as the sun swung over Ellis Island, the bandstand was sliced, part in shade, part in light. From the top of Cobble Road, at the Bowers Street entrance to the park, I could see that my mom and aunt had settled there, right at the edge of sun and shade, facing the harbor.

On the back half of the bandstand, across a crack deep enough to grow its own hedge of grass, beyond which the concrete floor tipped like a piece of sandcastle about to topple off, their long beach loungers were directed toward lower Manhattan and the Statue of Liberty.

I hurried toward them, every half-dozen steps breaking

into a trot, huffing more from nervousness than exertion. I wanted to get done what I had to, and I was hurt, too, but not sad, still waiting to feel that.

It looked like my mom was sleeping, her head tipped over the recliner's backrest, her right cheek pink in the sun, her twinkling silver and blue earrings dangling plumb toward her stretched neck. Aunt Pat was hunched forward, her legs straddling the lounger. She was trying to do her toenails while smoking a nearly spent Carlton, the bottle of bubblegum nail polish unsteady atop the chair's webs. She saw me before my mom did.

"Hi, hon. What's doing?" she asked, waving with the nail polish brush between her thumb and finger.

I told it. Somebody had killed Prince.

"What do you mean?" asked my mom. She sat up, sidesaddle. One side of her face, the pink side, was all sweated, the other dry. "Prince is dead? What are you talking about? Are you sure somebody *killed* him?" She glanced at Aunt Pat. My mom, in her usual nerdy fashion, was wearing white leather cross-trainers, pressed Wranglers, and a tight, brand-new Hudson County Community College T-shirt. The way it was tucked in made her upper half seem big, like she'd been lifting weights.

The whole time I spoke, she nodded. One hand over her mouth, her fingers read her lips, like they were soft braille.

"His neck's broke. He's still lying on Cobble Road," I said.

Like my mom, my Aunt Pat was spun around in her seat, all but three bony toes painted. Her hair was brittle and frizzy, an orangeish blonde, fired when the sun hit it. She had a narrow face with big blue eyes, a sharp nose, a neck like a tortoise's. She wiped the already flowing tears from her cheek and the snot from her reddened nose. Bursts of sobbing, like glass bubbles, blew open her lips. Her shoulders trembled as she reached into her bag for her smokes.

My mother leaned forward, the padded outline of her bra showing beneath the white T-shirt. She put a hand on my aunt's shoulder and kept it there when she turned to me. "Look, nobody freak out, okay? Keep calm, please, huh? Okay?" pleaded my mom, who, like me, seemed to be having no trouble doing so. "Have you told anybody else yet?"

"No, it just happened. I just saw him—Prince, I mean. Who'm I supposed to tell?" I asked.

"Well, you got to find Uncle Mike," she said. Her eyes were darker than my aunt's, a color I couldn't name, and her face was rounder. Her straight brown hair was pulled back from her forehead and held by a pink hairband, a fashion holdover from her Saint Paul's schooldays. "Do you know where Uncle Mike is?"

"Oh, God help us. Poor Uncle Mike." My aunt's whole face seemed swelled with tears ready to seep through the pores. She started coughing and spitting, creamy yolks and clear saliva. She ran to the Park House railing, faced Manhattan. "Susie, I loved that dog," she cried, anticipating that my mom had about had it with her outpouring. "I can't help it." She was wearing a gauzy yellow shirt whose long tails nearly covered the bottoms of her dungaree shorts.

"There's Uncle Mike now," I said, pointing across the park.

My mom rose up in her white sneakers. "Oh, thank God. Hurry up, Uncle Mike," she said, the plea forcing its way out of her mouth. "Come on."

"Oh, thank you, Jesus Lord. You're always there," praised Aunt Pat, wiping herself up with a Kleenex from a handi-pack. "Poor Uncle Mike. God. God, what am I saying, fucking stupid me? You hear me? Poor Prince I should be saying if I had sense. I'm so stupid." She struck and lifted a trembling match to her Carlton.

Uncle Mike, in the cool shade of the maple trees that lined the zigzagging walks of the park, glided toward us, his upper body sitting on his hips like a prince riding an elephant. Even though he was seventy-two years old, it was hard to look at Uncle Mike and not think of a prick, especially in summer. You know the way some girls walk with their shoulders away and their chests out, just so they can ask, "What are *you* staring at?" Uncle Mike was something like that. He walked with his swaying shoulders held back and his crotch and belt buckle, a heavy polished steel cutout of his initials, MM, pressed forward. The belt buckle was the first part of him to enter a room, introducing itself, turning from his hips this way and that, "Hello, hello. How do you do?"

He wore very tight, very short cutoff dungarees, white or powder blue, and he either kept a couple of Ping-Pong balls in his drawers or he had the largest nuts in America because, I swear, they bulged huge against the underside of his zipper, optimists looking for a chance in the world. Sometimes, as Uncle Mike placed himself at the center of this group or that, listening to him I'd get the feeling that he was his prick and his prick a ventriloquist, his face just mouthing the words.

He had curly white hair growing along his shoulders and neck, and he was probably the cleanest man I ever knew. He took two baths a day and always smelled of talcum powder that I connected with another century. On top, he wore a sleeveless mesh shirt. Through it you could see his chest hair and brown nipples and a heavy piece of jewelry. For years I didn't know what the piece was. Just two weeks earlier, when he had been sitting barechested in the sun, he called me over for a close look. It was a glorified Med-Emerge medal, twice the regular size, twice the weight, sterling silver, not stainless steel. "See?" he said, holding it out like the Medal of Honor. Uncle Mike was a Czech who had escaped the Communists by immigrating here in the early sixties and had changed his name from something that started with an M and ended with a cz to Mayflower. He still spoke with an accent, and his sentences had stiff joints.

"Yeah, it's real nice," I'd said.

"I am a diabetic." He said it like "dia-beetic." "My blood is O-positive. I take insulin. My motha lost a leg, my father went blind," he bragged. "Wachoo gonna do, Joey? Me? Not so good. It infects your heart. How much time I got? A few months, a year-ahtoo. Not so good," he said, waggling his hand.

As he whistled past the park's WWII Memorial—a circle of ten-foot-tall flagpoles without flags around a copper globe on a graffiti-splashed pedestal—finally he noticed my mom waving.

"You're going to have to tell him," she said to me, arms folded across her bra-puffed chest. "It's your job, Joey. You were with Prince. You're the only one seen him. Come on, you're old enough."

"What's a matter?" Uncle Mike asked, eyes tipped onto me.

I glanced at my mom and aunt. Then, when I tried to, I

couldn't get any words out.

"Speak up, Joey," said my mom. "Come on."

"He's a little kid," said Aunt Pat. "Help him, Susie, for chrissakes."

"Shit. It's fucked up," I blurted. "Prince is dead, Uncle Mike, down on Cobble Road. Some fuck killed him."

Uncle Mike's chest swelled and he stopped breathing. He looked like he was going to burst. "Prince! My dog! Someone has killed my dog!"

"Yeah. He's in the middle of the road. Somebody *must* have killed him," I said, disgusted with the words I had to say. "I think somebody broke his neck." I pictured Prince and thought I was going to be sick. I had a terrible pressure, an aching even, through my chest, all the way to my spine, like two big hands were squeezing out the air. Every sentence I had to speak left me short of breath. "He's still down there. He's lying all by himself," I said. There was the sadness, right there, and I whispered the last words again.

Barefooted, Aunt Pat danced down the three bandstand steps. She reached out her hands, and her and Uncle Mike hugged.

"I'm sorry. I'm sorry," she sobbed. When she let go, Uncle Mike held on to her elbows and sat her down on the steps as he moved beside her. He had always been long with his hands where women were concerned, my mom and aunt included, but with my aunt moreso. He laid one hand on her sunburned neck—it tickled me just watching—and he began to rub her shoulders and, down inside her collarless tissue-thin shirt, her shoulder blades. "You're so tight, little girl," he said.

"Ooh," she said and stretched. "Friggin' tell me about it." She leaned forward. Elbows on her knees, her cigarette hand moved back and forth to her mouth. "These Carltons are *fucking* useless," she bitched, and she flicked the butt ten yards down the path.

"Prince. Gone," said Uncle Mike, one hand flattening his hair, brushing the white side wisps behind his ears. "I can't believe my Prince is dead. What a shame. A waste of time, a waste of money. But what's money," he said, eyeing us. "It's my dog. You, don't you worry about it," he said, tapping his hollow chest. "This fuck, I will get him. I will get this crazy fuck, I promise."

"When we seen you, that's exactly what I was saying—who could be so fucked up? God damn, you got to be really fucked up to kill a dog," said Aunt Pat. "Oh, shit, there it goes, my thyroid thigamajig," she said, two fingers to her throat. "See, it's starting up again. I'm fucked. Now, I'm fucked."

"Joey can help you out, Uncle Mike," said my mom, nodding at me as she spoke.

"Joey, call Buddy Resto," Uncle Mike ordered. "Explain to him what happened. He'll take care of this for me."

"Very good idea," said my mom. "Very good."

Buddy was a local, a few years younger than my mom and aunt, already a police lieutenant. He'd had weird relationships with both of them. There'd been a thing, a sexual relationship, with my aunt up until eight years ago, or four, or two. He was a lover or a boyfriend, a Saturday night good time or a scumbag cop, all depending on the day Aunt Pat told it.

Back when he was regularly screwing with my aunt, and I was just a little boy, he seemed embarrassed by the relationship, always picking something from his eye or staring off, or complaining about a headhache or covering half his face with a hand, embarrassed by it and annoyed, too, annoyed with my aunt for bringing their skin-to-skin out from the boozy light and vampire life of the Hi-Lo Club. Even then, eight summers ago, when I saw him a couple of times a week, I thought that my mom was the one he liked and that sleeping with her goofy sister didn't make him look that great, just certified him as another graduating police rookie—thick skulled, short sleeved, and Rolex proud. Over the past couple of years, those on and off times when he did pop up around the house, it was always my mom he came to see, no matter that she was five years older than him. Occasionally he'd still pop into the park to read a newspaper and be seen, maybe chat with my mother.

"I'll call him. Let me call up Buddy," said Aunt Pat, and she pulled a cell phone from her straw carryall. "Just let me do it. What's the number, Mike?"

16

"546-7007," said my mom. She stayed neat: tucked in the back of her shirt, used her pointers to push her hair under the pink band.

"Fuhf, Susie, I asked Mike. Can't you hear? Is that the right number, Mike?"

My mom took a deep breath, blew it out like I'd seen her do a thousand times before. I understood and I wanted to let her know that I did, that I understood what a pain my aunt could be, but my mom kept to herself, didn't look my way, pissing me off, and I had no chance to.

Aunt Pat, the thin phone pressed to her ear, searched some more through her bag. "Where the fuck?" she said. I didn't know if she was mad at something lost in the bag or at the precinct desk sergeant. Waiting for the pickup was frazzling her, stressing her all out, as though it made her look bad. She pulled a pack of Marlboros from her bag, fished out a cigarette, straightened and smoothed the wrinkly butt, let it dangle from her lips. Elbow deep, she continued to search the bag. "Where the fuck?"

"Maybe I should say goodbye to Prince," said Uncle Mike, his voice wearier, deeper. "I may never see him again. Oh, don't you worry. I'm going to kill the stinky bastard who did this to my dog."

"Don't *you* worry, Uncle Mike. Buddy'll do this for me. Where the fuck is that shit-ass thing?" Aunt Pat demanded, her teeth clenched, her hands digging deeper into her crowded bag like a dog digging into slippery sand. "Ah! *Here* the fuck," she said and showed her yellow Bic lighter to us, proof that she wasn't crazy.

"You go with Uncle Mike," my mom said to me, and she began folding up her chair. "We'll wait for the cops."

Uncle Mike held on to Aunt Pat, then reached out a hand to grasp my mom's shoulder, kissed the one then the other. Then me and him left. We were heading out of the park, two benches away from them, when I turned. My mom zipped shut her bag and lifted it onto her shoulder. She blew me a kiss and mouthed something, probably "I love you."

Aunt Pat was still on the phone, waiting for Buddy Resto, or someone, to pick up. She was sitting on the lounger, turned now to face the park, and she seemed in control again, too in control, like "I could sit here and let this phone ring all fucking morning until those pricks pick up. Burn their asses good." Leisurely, aimlessly, her right arm dangled, her hand soothingly playing with the paraphernalia in her bag, a pirate with her gold trinkets.

She noticed me and Uncle Mike walking away. Her lips all lopsided, Aunt Pat blew a stream of smoke out the side of her mouth. With her left hand, she held the phone to her chest. She took the cigarette from her mouth and held it in the air with her right. "He's with God now, Uncle Mike," she called. "He's in a better place and all. You know. Anything we can do, Uncle Mike. Anything at all. In your pain, in your pain, remember he's with Christ and the Virgin Mary, she's there, too. Prince is up there now with the best and greatest," she said and tipped her Marlboro to point it outside the roof of the bandstand. "Whatever and all. He's up above now. You and him, Uncle Mike, you're in our fucking prayers."

THREE

U NCLE MIKE LIVED ON THE THIRD FLOOR, IN THE
apartment directly above my real uncle's, my Uncle Vic's. And
so, even though I'd never been past the kitchen of Uncle
Mike's apartment, the layout was familiar, just reversed, reversed
because the flight of stairs from the first floor to the second, my Uncle
Vic's floor, zigs, and the flight from the second to the third floor zags.
From the street end of the building, you enter into Uncle Mike's
kitchen. The rest of the apartment is to the left, toward the back yard.
From the kitchen you go into a hallway, sided by a closet on the left
and the bathroom on the right. Behind that is a small dark living
room. In it there's a TV on a brass stand against one wall, a two-cush-
ioned corduroy couch against the other. Between the TV and the
couch is a shiny mahogany coffee table, a neat stack of magazines, and
a brass horse reared on two legs atop it. Behind the couch is a double
window covered by heavy red drapes worthy of a king's palace.
Finally, at the back of the house is Uncle Mike's much brighter bedroom.

Except for the layout, Uncle Mike's and Uncle Vic's apartments had nothing in common. Everything in Uncle Mike's was
slumbering— even the air was gentle and soft. In the kitchen,
the shades were half-drawn against the sun, the round table covered in a starched white, blue-trimmed cloth. The bathroom was
different from every other bathroom in the building—the ones I'd
been in and the ones I imagined as I shuffled past the apartment
doors—because Uncle Mike's didn't stink of wood rot, wet ceilings, and Raid. It was spotless and shiny, like a magazine picture. Even the rust around the sink drain, the rust that broke out
like an infection from the floor-to-ceiling white-painted pipes,
even the rust in the window screen seemed sanitary, not your
run-of-the-mill bacteria-mush rust.

I followed Uncle Mike and stood at the entrance to his bedroom. My eyelids dropped. The room struck me as a little princess's room. With the two back windows facing the skyline and the two side windows facing the Statue of Liberty, the four of them covered in thin, bridal-gown white curtains, the room must have been softly bright all day. Most of the linoleum floor between the bed and the doorway was covered in a white rug, soft and fluffy as Prince's shampooed hair. The bed was made and covered in a pastel-flowered spread. There was a white bureau to the wall on my left, and to my right there was a white dressing table with a framed mirror set on its round-edged top.

"Pull up that chair from da vanity there and sit in it by the window, watching for me. Let me know when the cops get here. I am going to take a bath," Uncle Mike said, pointing out each object he named with a stubby red finger. "I need it more than ever on a day like today is. Joey, I'm telling you, fuck the person who killed my dog. I'm swearing to you, fuck him, fuck him good," he boasted before muttering a four-syllable curse in Czech.

Lined up in a row on the dressing table, against the mirror, were opened velvet-lined boxes with jewelry and cologne and cosmetics, half a dozen one-ounce bottles, some of them clear oils, other beige lotions, and all sorts of grooming things in a black leather clip-case of their own—a teeny comb and brush, nail files, tweezers, baby-sized cuticle scissors.

I pushed back the curtain and sat at the window Uncle Mike had pointed to. A harbor breeze came through the screen. Uncle Mike whistled "Just the Way You Are." I turned and I saw that he was undressing, holding himself steady, one hand on the polished bedpost as he pulled off his short pants.

On the wall behind Uncle Mike was the room's only picture, an ancient one of what I took to be Mike as a teenager (blonde-haired and expressionless but defiant, one leg in motion forward), his sister (small and frightened, hands at her sides), and his mother and father (each holding a suitcase, smileless, unenthusiastic about their trip).

When Uncle Mike plopped onto his bed, straining forward to peel off a sock, I wrapped the white curtain around my back and turned my attention to the park. His whistling continued over the squeaking of the mattress and an occasional muttered phrase in Czech. Finally, with a limp caused by his undressing, he exited to the bathroom.

My mom was sitting on the bench nearest Cobble Road, her arms folded across her chest, her eyes closed and face in the sun. Aunt Pat worked the crowd that was gathering. Small groups wandered back and forth to get a look at the dead dog and offer opinions on the state of the world. I leaned my head against the window screen, trying to get back to that sad feeling I'd gotten when I told Uncle Mike about Prince lying on Cobble Road all alone.

At least forty-five minutes after Uncle Mike went into the bathroom and the window screen had become a part of my cheek, the cops finally showed.

I banged on the bathroom door. "Is Buddy Resto down there?" Uncle Mike asked after shutting off the water.

"No, it's two guys in uniform."

"No one you recognize?"

"Nope."

"Oh, I swear, Joey, I should have had your motha make the call. That aunt of yours, she fucks up everything. She's a real loser," he said. He turned the shower back on and spoke through it. "You go down while I'm almost finishing. Tell them cops whose dog it is. Try to get some action, would you, for chrissakes."

When I got downstairs, the cops had been joined by my mother and aunt. My mom was talking to them, explaining. Aunt Pat was back on the cell phone, waiting, again, for a pickup, talking to herself and massaging her forehead as she walked back and forth. "Buddy," she whispered, "I'm tapping my foot, yo. My fucking foot. You know what that means, Buddy!"

One of the two cops left the conversation they were having with my mother. He was short and egg-shaped and his uniform pants fit him low on the hips. Carrying a notebook and wearing rubber gloves, he slowly approached Prince. The one who continued the conversation with my mother was your more typical-looking cop. He was still in his twenties, an easy ten years younger than his partner. The metallic blonde hair on his neck glistened in the sun. His uniform fit snug over his Atlas Gym physique, and his short sleeves were rolled up nearly to his shoulders. He held a grey steel clipboard to take notes on what my mom told him.

"Who reported the crime?" he asked.

"My son told us," she said and glanced toward me. She nodded to Aunt Pat, whose back was to us. "She reported it—she called you."

Aunt Pat walked in circles. She held the phone under her chin and moved in a knee-bent shuffle, like she'd been slogging through the desert for a week. In the year since she'd bought her dungaree shorts, my aunt's waist had stayed thin but her hips had grown and, under the long, nearly see-through gauze shirt, the shorts swelled out in a funny way. "Why isn't fucking Resto picking up?" she asked in a voice loud enough for the cop to hear. She circled away and, in a more pleading voice, probably not meant to be heard, she said, "Come on, Buddy, huh? I hate you."

"What happened?" asked the cop. He avoided looking at us, looked everywhere but, even into the sun.

"You tell him," said my mom, unfolding her arms to nudge me.

I was angry with her, and I glared back.

"One of you tell me what happened, okay?" he said, staring at my chest. "Tell me what happened. It doesn't have to be a book."

"Go ahead, Joey. Like you told us."

It wasn't a book. I told it short and cold.

"Excellent, excellent," said the cop. He put the cap back on his pen and shoved it in his back pocket. "Very good job, son," he said, less for my sake, I thought, than for my mom's. She had her arms folded again, and one foot was more forward than the other. She had no socks on.

"What do you got, Stinky?" the pumped cop asked the humpty-dumpty one, who swaggered up Cobble Road like Sly Stallone in a funhouse mirror.

"I'm fucking tired and I'm dying of heat's what I got, partner." He reeked of asshole.

"Do you want to hear this?" the clipboard cop asked us as Stinky was about to read his notes.

Squinting and hedging, he had trouble making out his own handwriting. " 'The deceased canine,' " he began, rolling his eyes so nearly the entire pupils vanished. "The fucking dead mutt. 'The deceased canine was probably strangled with a rubber-coated cable rather than a rope. His neck is broken under the left jaw, possibly under the right as well, perhaps in a single jerking snap.' " The fear Prince must have felt before he died hit me, and the muscles around my mouth twitched. A feeling crept under my skin like ants running along live wires. " 'There are no bruises on the canine's body other than those caused by the strangulation. The canine in all likeliness,' whatever, 'was denied of oxygen from the first yank of the cable mentioned above, which is also what in likeliness prevented him from crying out,' or whatever the fuck a dog does," he said. He rolled his head on his neck and his eyes in their sockets. " 'It appears like said canine was frantic upon his loss of oxygen and the pain inflicted pursuant to the broken neck and that he lurched around or limped in circles. See stapled photograph of canine's sun-warmed body,' " he said and laughed. "There you go," he said. He tore the report out of his pad and handed it to the other cop.

"Was it your dog?" that cop asked my mom, his eyes forced to her face after they'd momentarily landed on her breasts.

"No," said my mom. She slipped both hands into her back pockets, tips of her thumbs showing on her sides.

There was little that was street about my mom, not much that showed, certainly nothing in the way she dressed. It was more little things—that she was missing back teeth on both sides, that she had a small scar partially hidden by her eyebrow, something about the too-conscious way she avoided curse words, something about the scrubbed cleanliness of her ankles and elbows.

"Was he hers?" the cop asked in Aunt Pat's direction.

"Uh-uh," said my mom.

When Aunt Pat realized we were talking about her, she snapped closed the cell phone like a card shark packing a deck and with one hand stuffed it into her back pocket. She fluffed her hair with her painted nails and joined us four.

"The dog belongs to the guy upstairs," I said.

"My son's helping the man out. His name's Mike Mayflower. Come on, step in, Joey."

"I'm hot, Becker," said Stinky to the other one. "Let's get in the air-conditioning. This is a dog we're sweating for."

"You spell it like the ship?" Officer Becker asked my mother.

"Fucking Mayflower. You spell it like the ship?" Stinky repeated, his hands on his hips as he stared at the ground, shaking his head. "This is a dog, Becker. It's ten-thirty. Remember, we worked overnight last night. We didn't have no supper."

"I asked do you spell it like the ship?" Becker asked again, as though it was my mom who was irritating him.

"I think so," she said.

"Did you look for the cable?" Becker asked Stinky. Becker was looking in a tree, at squirrels running through it along a wire.

Stinky was looking at my aunt's legs. "Yes, I did," he said.

"Did you look thoroughly?"

"I'm ready to leave, Becker."

"Just answer me," said Becker, taking a quick glance at his partner.

Jowls formed as Stinky's mouth turned down. "Fuck you," he yelled. "I looked on the ground. I looked this way, I looked this way, and I looked this way," he said, pointing out left, right, and center. "I saw no friggin' cable."

"Well, you'll have to come back and look thoroughly—all the way down the hill. I'm putting that in the report," he said and took out his pen.

"Fuck your report. Put whatever you want in it. It ain't shit to me. I'm ready to leave, okay? You understand?"

"Yeah, I understand," said Becker. He swivelled his head, lifting his eyes from his clipboard to meet Stinky's. "And I'll keep you here all goddamn afternoon if you don't shut your ignorant fucking mouth."

"Yeah, like horseshit, Becker. Up your ass. Becker the Pecker showing off because two broads are watching," Stinky said. He turned and, as the smell of asshole faded, he bopped off to the car, rolling his shoulders and shirking his arms like a rap-per. "Tootootootoo-tootoo-tootootootoo. Uh-huh, uh-huh."

"Give this to Mr. Mayflower," Becker said, doing nothing more than wiping the corners of his mouth with two fingers to show his aggravation. He sucked the bit of scum from his fingertips, then handed me a yellow carbon. "Read it. All of you should," he said, directing his words to my mom. "It's pretty straightforward. If you have any questions, my number's on there. Okay?"

"Okay, thanks," said my mom, her hands still in her back pockets. Crooked at the elbows, her arms flapped like bellows handles, pushing her breasts in and out. I could read her better than she could read me, and it embarrassed me to an ache to see her like this, all in front of a man.

"Yo, do you two work out of North Station?" asked my aunt.

"Me and my friend in the car? Yes, we do. Why do you ask, ma'am?"

"Did Lieutenant Resto—he's your boss, is he not—he's the one who sent you down here?"

"Yes, he did, personally. Why again?"

"Oh, nothing. Nothing at all. Lieutenant Resto will hear from me, though, rest assured," she said in a whisper, hoarsely, through her nicotine-burned mouth and throat. She touched her finger to her nose before wandering over to a crowd of seventeen- and eighteen-year-olds checking out the scene—shoving one another, giggling, posing.

"Whatever," muttered Becker. He turned to my mom. "You got to take care of this dog."

I could see my mom's tongue playing in her mouth, swinging left and right along the back of her teeth as she thought. She lifted one finger in my direction. "Joey, you heard," she said.

"Son, you got that? You got to move the dog out of the street, put him in a box or something. And call the Animal Control Unit."

I'd already done more than my share. I complained to my mom. "I got to do it?" I whined. "What about Brian? Why do I have to do it?"

"Hey," the cop said, a finger in my face. "Just get the dog out of the street, okay. Now. Move the goddamn dog." Then he turned to my mother. "If he's not moved, you *and* Mr. Mayflower get summonses."

My mother took the punch pretty well. Her face went droopy and her elbows stopped waggling, but she aimed a stern look, not a hurt one, at Becker.

"You don't have to be such a prick," she said seconds later as Becker finger-read his report.

It took him another few seconds to make sense of her words. When he realized what she'd said, his face flushed. His eyes opened wide then shrunk. "I'm sorry. Look, I'm sorry. Really. We came on midnight yesterday. It's been a long . . . I need a drink," he said, and for the first time, I smelled the alcohol on his breath. "Ay, I need a bed more than I need a drink."

"Plus him you got to put up with," my mom said, motioning to the cop car.

"You wouldn't believe it if I told you. He's a goddamn nightmare."

"Hey, we need good cops, you know," said my mom. "Like you."

She'd crossed some line and embarrassed him. This wasn't flirting, this was personal.

"Hmmmph. Good cops," he said. "Right." He put his pen back in his pocket and his clipboard under his arm. "I'm sorry about being rude, but you got to move the dog. We'll get back to search better. But really, do you care who killed the dog?"

My mom didn't hesitate. "Sure we do. We're trying to maintain the neighborhood. Don't want it rotting."

He thought she was nuts, I could tell, but caught his grin before it spread.

"Yo, Officer Becker," called my aunt, front and center in the crowd of teenagers. "Tell Buddy—I mean Lieutenant Resto— that Pat Scadutto's pissed at him."

"Yes, will do," he said with a wave of the hand. "And what are you pissed at him for?"

She laughed even before she said anything. "For sending you two assholes down here."

Hunched and hiding their laughter, all the kids turned away, except for one, Lefty, tall and bony, his frame a year ahead of his muscles. My aunt locked her arm around his chest. There was no turning away for him. He pulled his Marlboro cap over his eyes. "Shit. Ho-ly shit, yo."

Becker looked at her and nodded—maybe you're right, maybe you're not. He smiled, amused, I think, at his own weary reaction. My mom, though, sudden sweat dripping from her scalp onto her forehead, looked like she wanted to throw my aunt over the cliff.

"See you," Becker said to me and my mom. Then straight to me, he said, "I know having to put the dog in a box sucks, but I'd rather be you, out here, than me." I knew what he meant. Anything would be better than getting into that air-conditioned car with Stinky. You could be there for years.

Becker opened the car door. Led Zeppelin roared out, "Stairway to Heaven," but Stinky looked asleep in the passenger seat.

From my blind side, "You're a damn disgrace," my mom yelled at my aunt.

"Oh, fuck you," said my aunt. "Come on, give it over. Who's got reefer, boys and girls?"

Me and my mom stood at the wall overlooking Cobble Road. She still hadn't gone down for a look at Prince.

"Joey, go up and give the police paper to Uncle Mike. Come on, go ahead. Please."

"What about Brian?"

"When he gets home, I'll make sure he helps you."

"And with Prince, too."

"Yes, with Prince."

"What time?"

"It depends on how busy tutoring is. He said Clay might let him go early. I promise I'll send him as soon as he gets home."

"Mom, you can't *send* Brian anywhere."

She looked into my eyes. Her own were sad as she reached to stroke my neck. "It's hard for you, huh."

My mom was on a roll. Like with the cop, she'd crossed a line with me. This was getting personal. "Bye, Mom."

"See? When I am loving and all, what do you say? 'Bye, Mom,'" she said, laughing at us both. "Love you," she said.

"Yeah, love you, too," I said, neither of us able to say the "I" part of the sentence.

As my mom went in the opposite direction, where she could loop back onto Cobble Road, I marched through the park toward Uncle Mike's. The teenagers were tromping up Bowers Street, toward Central Avenue. Aunt Pat was sitting alone on one of the curbs at the edge of the grass, her knees up. She was sobbing and her face, all red, was hanging between them. Her forearms were tucked under her knees and her hands were cupped beneath her face, collecting her tears to have something to remember this by.

FOUR

FTER I GAVE UNCLE MIKE HIS COPY OF THE police report, I had to come right back downstairs to box up Prince. When I was done with that, it was noontime and I returned to Uncle Mike's to babysit until Brian showed up.

Uncle Mike was at the kitchen table in a burgundy robe and knee-high white socks, his hands folded on the starched tablecloth. The radio was on.

"What happened down there?" he asked.

I gave him the story, first what had happened with the cops, then a version of boxing up Prince. "Stay by the window," he said. "Tell me what happens next." He fine-tuned the radio and raised its volume to make me leave the kitchen. He was listening to opera. A man and woman were bellowing away in Italian.

Back in his bedroom, I looked out the same window. My cheek pressed against the screen, which by this time was shady, as the sun had slid behind one of the park's healthier maples. Below, a crowd of eight from the Animal Defense League—all in green and gold ADL of Hudson County T-shirts—had marched through the park from the HouseRAD side and gathered around the box Prince was in.

Each time I peeked into the kitchen, there was Uncle Mike, back to me, working on his fingernails, silent and still in the throb of his music, leaving me trapped in the bedroom.

It had taken a full hour to find a box for Prince, not too big and not too small, and to finish the job. I hadn't had it in me to bend and squeeze him, so a case-of-beer box was too small, but that was the size of most of the boxes where I looked—in the back garbage of Ruby Z's Liquors, Groceries, and Favors. The smallest of the bigger boxes was a Bounty towel box, big enough for four three-packs, and that's the one I used. The Bounty box was as long as the other big boxes but not as wide, only the width of two rolls, and once I got Prince in, it wouldn't leave him room to do so much sliding and bumping when moved. Getting him into the box was awful, though. Because the box had to be loaded from the top, I had to pick Prince up by his four paws, like a pig you're going to roast.

I couldn't help but look at him as I lifted. His legs, when I first grabbed on to them, felt warm, but that was just the hair, from the air temperature. When I squeezed hard to lift, I could feel the cold underneath. His eyelids were glued where they'd sunk half shut. His neck, pressed by gravity but not dangling, was at a sideways angle. That bothered me, so I let go of the paws and pushed down on the side of his head a little bit. His neck bent but didn't give—like neither muscles nor bones, but something like half-cracked popsicle sticks were holding up the weight.

Lifting him to eye level so his sagging spine was above the edge of the box took all the strength I had. Still holding his weight, I had to let him slide to the bottom and then fold his legs so they weren't sticking straight up. I petted him a couple of times under the chin, where a beauty mark sprouted a pair of wiry hairs. Then I folded the top shut.

Picking him up and putting him in the box had been the hardest part. My heart swelled and I started to cry—no sobbing or trembling, just tears.

I tipped the box onto its side, tried my best to keep the top shut, and pushed it bumping over the cobblestones, till it was under the Ogden overpass, against the parkside wall, where it would be in the shade all day long. On top of the box with a PaperMate I'd bought at Ruby Z's, too thin for the job so that I had to retrace the letters half a dozen times, I wrote—"Prince (the dead dog) is in the box."

I walked away, proud that my heart ached, that I'd at least thought the words "I love you," even if I couldn't whisper them to him.

Every ten minutes, I checked in on Uncle Mike. He'd put away his manicuring stuff. The leather case was closed on the table. From my back view, I couldn't tell if he was bored or thoughtful.

Loud as ever, the music blasted. The only thing I could think of when I heard that thundering music was of God killing people, but as end-of-the-world as the music was, the announcer who spoke between the songs was worse. He was twice as eerie, even though I think his comments about diseases coffee causes were supposed to be funny. I don't think Uncle Mike heard him at all.

The ADLers stood at the park wall overlooking Cobble Road and Prince. Their leader was a Geronimo-looking guy in high-waisted Levi's and silver-tipped cowboy boots. He led the group of nine—which now included my Aunt Pat, who had elbowed her way in—through some prayer in which they didn't fold their hands but held them up in a double "How" sign as though they were touching the air together.

From the far end of the park, my Uncle Vic and brother Brian were walking our way. When they got halfway into the park, to the path, around the WWII Memorial, Brian split off, heading away from the group and toward Palisade Avenue. Uncle Vic stopped him. It looked like he asked Brian where he was going, but Brian just nudged him forward, in our direction, with a little push to the back of the shoulder. The obvious fact that something was up not only didn't interest Brian, it sent him off in the opposite direction, but this was typical of Brian, pissed at everything, tired of the world at nineteen. Right then, though, what bothered me more than his dead, all-is-bullshit personality was the fact that his veering off would also mean I'd be stuck up in Uncle Mike's that much longer.

Uncle Vic, on the other hand, was game, yanking up his belt as he approached Aunt Pat and the rest of the group, a mix of HouseRADers, dark foreigners new to our part of the neighborhood, and park failures, lef'-behinds, and junkies. Aunt Pat had tied the tails of her yellow shirt up above her belly button and, from her straw bag of tricks, she'd pulled a black-with-red-ruby-sparkles bandanna, which she tied around her forehead.

"You make ten," said Aunt Pat as she pulled my uncle over by his pants pocket. "This is my wonderful Uncle Vic," she announced. "He's known Mr. Mayflower for . . . how many years? Thirty is it, Uncle Vic?"

Seventy-six-year-old Uncle Vic is a little guy, just five feet three inches tall. Some say I take after him, but with Uncle Vic the only older-generation male in the family, that may just be something to say for comfort's sake—somebody's comfort. I hope that's the reason.

Hands in his deep pockets, Uncle Vic stood a few feet outside the semicircle. "Thirty-five years," he answered.

The ADL leader reached a hand out to shake and Uncle Vic's slowly rose to meet his. The Indian slipped the greeting into a double-handed upright clasp. Uncle Vic stepped back like the guy had kissed him. He spread his legs and slipped his thumbs inside his pants waistband.

Uncle Vic wore pants by Haband which I believe the company had stopped making a quarter of a century ago. There are still some of them at Dolph's, the last men's clothing store on Central Avenue, where they've been sitting in plastic in the back room through six generations of stock boys, fading at the knee fold, disappearing one a year for the past decade, whenever Uncle Vic goes in there to buy. ("Thirty-two waist. I may need them hemmed. You got any new colors in?")

He began to unbuckle his belt.

"You looking?" Uncle Mike called to me as I looked down.

I turned around. He was poking his head in the doorway. He could see me. It was obvious I was looking. So I dealt with it the way I always deal with stupid questions. I didn't answer. I turned back to the window.

"No Buddy Resto?"

"No. He ain't coming."

"This is bullshit. I'm telling you, someone's to blame for something," he said, and he slammed the bathroom door. "Nothing done right around here."

The crotch of his brown pants comes halfway down Uncle Vic's little legs. Under the pants, he wears boxer shorts, blue, yellow, or white, never checked or striped, and they get all tangled up with his shirttail. Like anyone would be, he's very fussy about the way everything lays down there. He tends, though, not to just reach in but to unbuckle and to unzip and to drop his brown trousers almost to his knees. Then he spreads his knees to hold the pants while he does his housekeeping.

From the window, I couldn't make out their exact words, but the leader and a HouseRAD-type, hair-to-the-waist woman in sandals who was taking notes were asking lots of questions of Uncle Vic. Uncle Vic's teeth were working his stogie, moving it from side to side. The woman note-taker, maybe thirty, maybe a little older, stared at my uncle the whole time, even as she wrote. She was very skinny and had small tits that pulled and creased her tight ADL shirt like drops of paste had dried there. She'd cut the sleeves off her shirt and had hair under her armpits. She seemed to mesmerize Uncle Vic, who kept his knees spread and hands busy in his drawers much longer than usual, reminding me of a kindergartner who doesn't realize he's sucking his thumb.

"What are you doing here?" I heard the voice behind me. Halfway into the room was my brother Brian.

"What am I doing here? You know what happened, don't you?" He stared at me in one of his odd ways, waiting for me to tell but not curious. "Didn't Mom tell you what happened?"

"No, I didn't see Mom. Just tell me and get it over with, okay, Joey?"

He came to the window and looked out just for a second before he turned away. He's a few inches taller than me, five-eight, but has a soft body and must weigh one-sixty, forty pounds more than I do. He's got a sort of moon face—that's what my mom calls it, especially when she fawns over old pictures of him and his father. He's got a small nose, high, flat cheekbones, and eyes so half-closed they make him look Oriental. He's also got a different last name from me. I've got my mom's name, Scadutto. Brian's got his father's, Lorre.

I told him the short version of what happened with Prince, with the cops, with the box, and with the ADLers. He sat on the edge of the bed and listened patiently, like it was a school lecture.

Brian's hair is medium brown compared to my light brown, and making his face even more round are the Caesar-style half-inch bangs that come down onto his forehead, sidewalls that are swept forward, and a strip of beard that doesn't stray far from his jawline, barely dirtying his cheek.

"What are you doing here if Mom didn't tell you?" I asked.

"I've got to talk to Uncle Mike," he said.

If I showed little emotion, Brian barely showed life.

"About what?"

"Who are you?" he asked dully, unwilling to argue. "You my priest now?"

"What do you got to talk to Uncle Mike about?" I persisted, though I thought I knew the answer.

"About business," he said.

"Business. I know what business."

"Goody, goody for you," he said, waggling his head.

The bathroom door opened. "Boys," yelled Uncle Mike, "don't debate this. Now's not the time. Brian, Joey told you what they did to my dog?" His robe belt was hanging loose. He had nothing on underneath. "Joey, there's no action down there?"

I looked out. "No. There was a group, but they're leaving."

Aunt Pat had joined the ADLers, skipping like a schoolgirl alongside the leader. Uncle Vic stood alone, saying a prayer over the death box.

"Then okay, Joey, you can go if you please," said Uncle Mike. "Tell your mother you were a wonderful helper. Me and Brian have to talk now."

Their business was no secret to me. Brian was the one who set up the visits between Uncle Mike and the college girls.

FIVE

THE NEXT MORNING, A SATURDAY MORNING, AT TEN o'clock, I was sitting in the park at one of the steel-pipe tables, reading the *Jersey Journal* and drinking a pink lemonade. It was beautiful out, cooler than the day before, chilly even, but the sky was deep blue and there was barely a haze around the New York skyline.

Sparrows hopped from the grass to the concrete walkways, picking at candy wrappers and Blimpie rolls. Moms in sweaters pushed their strollers. A group of fifth-graders told stories on the bandstand steps, and there was the constant swoosh-swoosh of the breeze in the full trees.

Even though I knew my Knicks jersey, sleeveless like it was, was too skimpy for this park morning, I wore it anyway. I'd worn a basketball jersey every morning since school ended. I loved the silky way it brushed me and the way the breezes would jet down the openings, brushing my back and chest and belly.

My *Jersey Journal* was opened to page ten, the continuation of a front-page article about Prince and the cops and the ADLers. Setting on the paper was my carton of pink lemonade, the straw just a lean from my lips. My hands were moving around inside my shirt, my palms pressing against the cool skin. I tipped forward for a sip. Out of the corner of my eye, I spotted Lieutenant Resto walking toward me. In his hand was a flopsy black canvas briefcase, more the sort a teacher or student would use than a businessman. He wore wire-rimmed sunglasses, an orange knit shirt, pleated white pants, and grey-brown Nikes, more boot than sneaker, the logo matching his shirt. He had a stiff left leg but walked with lots of confidence despite it, there being something athletic even about the slight limp.

I closed the paper, but there was no hiding it. The front-page headline read, "Police Leave Park Dog to Rot; High Gate Precinct Commander Cited for 'Insensitivity.'" The precinct commander, that was Buddy Resto. Making worse out of bad were sentences like this: "Animal Defense League Spokeswoman Pat Scadutto explained that the police had been called to the scene, but rather than caring for the dog and its owner, seventy-one-year-old Michael 'Uncle Mike' Mayflower, the police threatened to arrest the grieving Mr. Mayflower if he didn't immediately load the dog into a cardboard box and push him to the side of the street. 'As supervising commander, I hold Lieutenant Resto responsible for this travesty of justice and accuse him of extreme insensitivity to man and dog alike,' charged Scadutto."

"Your aunt's a piece of work, Joey," said Resto as he plopped down across from me and dropped his heavy bookbag onto the table, rocking my lemonade.

"I know," I said.

"I know she did this because she's out to get me, but really, she needs help," he said, his big hands lifting off the table. "She's crazy. You know what I mean? She's delusional."

Buddy Resto was thirty-two years old, three years younger than my aunt, five years younger than my mom. He was a handsome guy in a jockish way. The lumpy bones of his forehead rippled like muscles. The skin over his cheekbones shone, always a little pinkish. He had a scar at the point of his chin, sort of lightning shaped, which made a bare spot in his whiskers. When he smiled he looked like an eighteen-year-old posing for his high school picture and seemed to be able to turn the light in his eyes on and off like a penlight by just lifting his head the slightest bit. Everybody liked him except us, people who disliked anyone who everybody liked.

"How's your mom been?" he asked as he unsnapped his bookbag, pulled loose the Velcro. He took out a fat book, a Police Administration Civil Service Arco Test Guide, the kind of book like they keep at school for preparing for the SATs. "The captain's test's in less than two weeks. Get a load of this freaking thing," he said and looked at me like I was supposed to sympathize. He kept pulling books from the bag. "And this one, and this one, and this one," he said, showing me three more books, textbooks, twenty years old or more, with dull cloth covers and grey page edges. "That's what I'm concerned about. This test, not your friggin' aunt."

From his perspective, their long-ago romance didn't amount to much, was something he'd rather forget altogether. "Romance" was a word he'd never used to describe it. Not even "affair." He called it "the thing," like it was out of a horror movie. Once before, when Aunt Pat was on his ass, he'd said, "Sometimes you stay in a bar ten minutes too long and have one drink too many. That's your aunt's domain."

Who knew the truth or who was to blame. Buddy talked about it only when Aunt Pat forced the issue, and he made her out to be a madwoman. Aunt Pat spoke about it a lot—she'd had no kids in her life but had three abortions and, in nostalgic moments, referred to Resto as the father of her middle one. She always tried to damn Buddy to hell, but generally her talking about their thing had the same effect as when Buddy did—it made her seem crazy.

"She's a vindictive witch," said Resto. One of the things about him was that around me and my mom he always changed curse words to softer ones he knew we'd see through—bitch to witch, fucking to freaking, scumbag to dirtbag, nigger to negro.

On the one hand, everything Resto said about my aunt was right, but on the other hand, I disliked him. He was a phoney, I thought, a tough guy, a street guy who knew every bottle of cologne at Health and Beauty. I saw him as a yuppie, not one of us, somebody who wanted it both ways—wanted nothing more than to get out of Jersey City, out of High Gate, but also to be loved, honored even, as a great guy when he came back. He lived on one of the top floors of the twenty-five-year-old Saint John's Arms, right where the original High Gate had stood.

"Is your mom going to be around this morning?" he asked. His hair was light brown and wavy, except for the buzzed sides, which were shorter than they used to be. His eyebrows were a shade lighter and they were brushed up at the temple edges like airforce wings.

"Yeah, she's trying for a job. She'll be back."

"I thought she was going back to school. A job, too?"

"Yeah. She's motivated," I said as though I was apologizing. "There's my aunt," I said, pointing her out with my thumb. I folded up the *Journal* and tossed my empty pink lemonade carton under the table.

Buddy turned slowly toward my aunt, either like he didn't know what to expect or he knew too well. She was just crossing into the park from our end, carrying her straw bag in both arms like a bundle of groceries, the back bar of the beach chair hanging from her bent elbow, clanging against her hip and knee. We were a good twenty yards in from Ogden, halfway between it and Palisade Avenue, and as she passed, she wouldn't look at us, her nose in the air and lips pursed for whistling. When she got to the bandstand, she put everything down and, her back still to us, stretched into a *Y*.

"Your aunt's big mistake is that she thinks everybody thinks like her. She doesn't know how freaking unique she is," he said, shaking his head, his eyes down toward the books, but his winging brows lifted. "There comes your mom now, too. What was she doing in HouseRAD?" he asked, pointing the Arco book in her direction.

"That's where she was looking for work."

"What kind of work's there in the RAD?"

"There's a new restaurant. They had a sign for waitresses."

He gave an approving little snort. "Hey, I give her all the credit in the world," he said, and he dropped the book from his fingertips, letting it thud onto the table. Then he tapped the Arco. "This one I can study," he said. "But these? In ten days? No freaking way."

Our eyes turned to my mom. She was cutting across the grass, a direction that would take her away from Aunt Pat. "How was the interview?" I asked when she crossed from tree cover to sunlight, though she was still a distance, on the other side of the new plastic playground, yellow and red and green, that Recreation had plunked down.

She wagged her hand, fifty-fifty.

Her hair, dark brown in the shade, became reddish in the

38

sunlight. She was dressed a lot like she'd been the day before, and the day before that, and the day before that. Only difference was she'd put on a pair of white sweatsocks, and instead of an HCCC T-shirt tucked into her black Wranglers, it was a pressed short-sleeved peach blouse that had a military look, with epaulets and pocket flaps and pleats that only my mom could iron.

She was smiling. It was obvious she didn't know about the *Journal* article.

"Hi, Susan," said Buddy, the yearbook photo on his face, his eyes turned on.

Back behind my mom, Aunt Pat, sunglasses up and down, up and down, checked out the conversation.

"Hi, Buddy," said my mom, and she tucked her hands into her front pockets instead of her back. This made her look not like a thirty-eight-year-old woman, but like a beaming farm girl happy to be noticed by a manly hand.

"You got a minute?"

"A minute? Yes, I think I do." She sat next to me. I was all squeezed up, hands under my thighs to keep warm. She touched her hand to my shoulder and tut-tutted me when she felt my cold skin.

"Susan, you remember we talked about this captain's test, right?"

"Captain's test?" she said like she was deciphering a foreign language. "Gee."

Buddy had big plans—"pig plans" Brian called them. That's a part of why I disliked Buddy, too, and that's why Brian despised him. Brian hated anybody who had plans, the bigger the plans, the bigger the hate.

"Talked about the captain's test?" She squinted. "When did we talk about it? Two days ago? Three?" she asked, teasingly.

"No, no. More like two months ago, or three. Sometime in April."

"Yes, I remember. It was the day after Easter."

"That's right."

"Oh, you remember, too?"

"Susan, come on. Stop."

My mom put on an obedient "no teasing" face and leaned

JOSEPH COLICCHIO

forward on an elbow.

"The test's in ten days," said Resto. "*Ten days*," he repeated, nodding his head like he was agreeing with everything his own words suggested. "You know, Susan, after that test a lot of things happen real quick. They'll make three captains in September. There'll be the mayor's election in November. Things are gonna happen quick." My mom stared back blankly, making him work, her mouth in a "duh" shape. "Look, you know all this. I don't have to tell it to you."

Her elbow still on the table, her chin in her palm, she nodded, studious and sleepy at the same time.

"Susan," Resto complained, "listen, all right? Please," he pleaded, widening his eyes and giving more lift to his brows. "Come on, gimme a break."

In another little change from the day before, my mom had replaced her pink hairband with a tortoiseshell one, a good move considering the HouseRAD interview and all. A few brittle hairs, greys with browns, were straight up in front and loose above her ears, waving in the breeze.

"All right," she said, straightening herself on the bench. "All right, then after the election the mayor makes a new police chief."

"Correct. From the captains."

"Yeah, and if you don't pass the captain's test," she said, widening her eyes to mimic Resto, throwing open her hands, "no luck."

"That's where these come in," he said, lifting the four heavy books. "I need help studying. Outlines, study cards, you know, whatever. I can't read all these. So that's what I'm asking."

This couldn't be going over well at all with my aunt. Like Godzilla passing before the skyline, she was pacing the bandstand floor, talking to herself, her shoulder turned to us, over-the-shoulder glances coming one every ten seconds.

"I'm a busy woman, Lieutenant Resto," said my mom.

"I know, I know. You're a mother and a working woman *and* I hear you're gonna be a college girl, too."

"That's right. I got to study for my own test. I don't want to have to take the Basics. How'm I supposed to read those fat, ugly things? Like I have nothing to do?"

"All right, all right," he said, palms up in surrender. "All right. I didn't know you were getting a job. I didn't know for sure you were going to school. I take it back. I'm sorry if even asking you was arrogant, thinking that you might. But at least I was going to pay you, Susan. I didn't assume you'd be jumping at the chance."

"Buddy, that's crazy. *That's* arrogant. Don't think about paying me."

"Shoot. Let me go before I dig a deeper hole," he said. He held his nose with one hand as, cautiously, like a man holding a rotten fish, he flipped the books back into his bag. "Well, if you decide to do it, that would be great. But it's not like I expect you to," he said. He pressed down the Velcro straps and snapped shut the clips on his bag. He turned to me. "But either way, though, Joey, you've got to come and see me."

My mom cocked her head and stared at him. She didn't have to ask a question.

"Because he's the only one knows about the frigging dog," Resto said. "The 'deceased canine' I'm treating so insensitively."

My mother didn't get the whole of it.

"Can't you talk to him here or at our house?"

"No, he's got forms he's got to fill out. There's forms I got to fill out. Now we got to treat this like a full investigation. Hey, thank her, not me," he said as he stood and tipped his head toward the bandstand.

My mom closed her eyes and shook her head. "I don't want to know, not now. Joey, tell me later," she said and looked at me. "Are you cold?" she asked.

"No," I said and took my hands out from inside my shirt.

"Look how skinny he is," she said, squeezing what passed for my bicep. Her hands were stronger than mine.

"You have to eat, Joey," said Resto. He stood, hands in his pockets, looked at my mom, who kept her eyes on me. "You want to grow, don't you?"

I don't think I showed how pissed I was. I swirled round on the bench and freed my legs, stood up.

"You got mail from Mr. Rodriguez," said my mom. Looking up at me, she shielded her eyes from the sun. "It was postmarked

West Virginia. Did you tell Buddy about that trip?"

"No," I said, meaning I'm not about to either.

"Well, go see what the letter says."

"I'll read it whenever. I'm not going on any trip," I said and started to back away.

Mr. Rodriguez had been my history teacher the past two years. This summer he got a grant to take kids on something called a Wagon Train, part of the state's Vision Quest Program. I'd turned him down on Wagon Train One, but he'd said there might be a Two, just a couple of weeks later, in July. That's what I figured his letter to be about.

"Make sure you let Mr. Rodriguez know what you want to do."

"I said I'll look at it whenever."

"He likes you. He's nice to you," said my mom, still looking up, shielding her eyes. "Talk to some of your school friends, see if they're going."

Buddy stood on the other side of the table, canvas bag in hand, respectfully listening to my mom. He looked like a taxidermist had just finished with him.

"Right," I said and walked away. "Like I'm gonna jump at the chance."

SIX

NORMALLY IT WAS SATURDAYS, LATE AFTERNOONS, that we went to Uncle Vic's for dinner. But that late-June week, what with the time taken up by Prince's killing and my mom being so busy, the three of us, me and my mom and Aunt Pat, didn't make the trip down the block until Sunday. Brian came along with us a lot of the time, but he'd been missing since Friday afternoon, when I'd seen him at Uncle Mike's, and didn't know the dinner'd been switched from Saturday.

Each weekend, we'd bring Uncle Vic his week's essentials. That Sunday, a shopping cart pushed by my mom and a rusted red wagon pulled by my aunt were loaded with clean laundry, one bag full of the groceries we hadn't bought during the week, a *Sunday Star-Ledger*, a twelve-pack of Old Milwaukee, and all the bottles and cans and rags and towels needed for the night's apartment cleaning. I carried the ingredients for supper, as usual a meal built around sausage. All we needed was the mule team.

In my back pocket was the letter from Mr. Rodriguez about the *other* Wagon Train.

There were lots of different parts to the NJ Department of Human Service's Vision Quest Program. The one that Mr. Rodriguez had gotten his grant for was called Wagon Train: An Impact Project. Wagon Train One had left the Tuesday before. The letter he'd sent to me was addressed to five other kids, too, all, like me, going into junior year at Harry S. There was a little bit in the letter about how the trip was going as of day two, mostly what it was like getting everything packed for eight staff and thirty kids. But I figured Mr. Rodriguez's real intention was to let the six of us know that the second half of the grant, the part for Wagon Train Two, had come through (Mr. Rodriguez had written,

"Now you six pussies will have another chance") and to make each of us know who the other five were and to make us feel like a team. One of the other five was a girl named Marcy Harrigan, a half-Irish, half-Filipino girl, tall with dark curly hair and an athlete's legs, the nearest I'd ever had to a girlfriend. Just before spring break, we'd talked about doing the Train together, but then didn't have much to say to one another once we got back to school in April.

Wagon Train Two would be leaving in less than two weeks and would follow the same trail as this one, from Harrisburg, Pennsylvania, to Charleston, West Virginia, where they'd get one night's sleep at a hotel, and on to Cincinnati, ten days in all. He also included a hugging and laughing picture of the current group, taken at their pre-trip orientation. I knew more of the boys than girls, but I noticed the girls more—their hair all pulled back, arms dirt brown, T-shirts sweaty and loose. Though at first it seemed pretty goofy, it had been a good idea for him to include the picture.

As me, my mom, and my aunt marched down Ogden, from 208 to 175, the Wagon Train tromped in and out of my mind. I let myself imagine it—being on a dirt road that cut through high grass, chasing down a stupid bell-clanking cow, scooping up horse poop, soaping myself in a wooden tub, soaping Marcy, cooking over a campfire, laying out, resting my head on Marcy's belly, looking up, seeing her and the bright moonlit sky, waking the next day, everything cool, watching her hike up a mountain road.

I imagined, but the idea of doing it was another story. Leaving High Gate to go on a wagon train? It seemed too weird, too ridiculous. I made sure the imagining was just that and nothing else. Just imagining I'd keep to myself.

We got to the apartment house, clanked over the broken outside steps, pushed open the foyer door, and huffed up the inside steps. At the top of the stairs, Uncle Vic, as usual, was waiting with his door open. "Come on, where you been? You're late," he said, waving us forward.

I'd barely set the grocery bag down on the table when I was sent by my mom on up to the third floor, to Uncle Mike's. We always had leftovers—not having enough food would have shamed my mother—but since Brian wasn't with us, there'd be even more than usual. I knocked on Uncle Mike's door but got no answer. Ten minutes later, when we thought we heard him coming in, no one had the inclination to run out and invite him. For one thing, Uncle Vic never liked Mike. Dead dog or no dead dog, to Vic he was a nasty, show-offy bastard who liked women *too* much. Uncle Vic, I suspected, was a lifelong virgin—celibate might be a better word—and each time somebody brought up how similar me and him were, or worse, when my Uncle Vic warned me that I was going to turn out like him, a life of smoking cigars, getting my pants hemmed, and only watching love was the first thought that came to mind.

Reason number two for not inviting Uncle Mike was that so far my mom and Aunt Pat were okay together. It had only been a day since my aunt had watched the chummy conversation between my mom and Resto, and so far their don't ask/don't tell deal was working. But in the bottom of the shopping cart, in a canvas Hudson County Community College bag underneath the laundry, was one of Resto's books, and so far only goes so far.

Third, I'd personally had enough of Uncle Mike, white underwear and pink legs and all.

Uncle Vic sat across from me at the kitchen table and relit the White Owl he took from the glass Pep Boys ashtray. My mom, at the counter between the stove and the sink, worked on supper —sliced tomato, kielbasa, baked beans, and string beans. Aunt Pat was in the bathroom working her ass off, grunting and groaning as she bent behind the four-footed bathtub to reach corners that not even the linoleum did.

Saturday's cool had been replaced by a steamy Sunday, the temperature over ninety even as the clock hit six. The sun, just a week past equinox, white in the steel-grey sky, glowed above the treetops. It shone through the kitchen window's pink and white curtains and beat on the buzzing air-conditioner in the window's lower half.

But the AC couldn't keep up with the humid air and the heat of the sun and the oven. Every time it kicked into a higher gear it would rattle the window frame and vibrate the whole room. Its back part was tipped toward the ground, the two-by-two behind it no longer enough to bolster the mushy frame, and, from all the groaning and creaking coming from it, I was sure that if air-conditioners had living wills, this one would have been a goner.

When Aunt Pat came out of the bathroom, her face was flushed and her bandanna sweat-soaked. Blue veins pulsed against her tissuey neck. My mom took a glance and concentrated on her work, pinning herself to the stove and counter.

"I need a smoke break," said Aunt Pat. She lit a Carlton and took a Busch beer from the refrigerator. She collapsed onto the table's third chair and rested her head on her folded arms. It was nice and cool there, right in front of the AC's blow. Beyond the table, the cool barely penetrated at all.

Me and Uncle Vic continued the game we'd been playing. I had the almanac out, a Christmas present from me to my uncle two years ago, and was quizzing him on zip codes. We played for nickels and dimes, my dozen on the vinyl red-and-white table-cloth protected by raised cigar-burn bunkers and blisters, Uncle Vic's hidden behind his beer can and White Owls pack.

Having been born in 1922, Uncle Vic was good not just with zip codes, but with a lot of twentieth century questions besides—gangsters, saloon songs, war dates, radio shows, train lines, horse racing, boxing, famous Italian-Americans—just about any event or personality you'd imagine in black and white. But to him there was a year, different in each category, after which nothing mattered—no TV show since *Bonanza*, no singer since Connie Francis, no war since Korea, no horse since Kelso, no ballplayer since Willie Mays. It would irritate the hell out of him to ask anything past the cutoff.

Aunt Pat peeled her cheek from her arms, peeled her arms from the tablecloth. She had worked hard, we all knew it, but she couldn't leave well enough alone. "My ass is whipped," she gasped and fluffed her T-shirt, a scissor-cut *V* at its neck. She put the Busch to her cheek. "Come to the mountains," she said. "Phooph, I can't get my breath."

My mom wouldn't turn around.

"That smells scrumptious, Susie," said Uncle Vic. She pressed the kielbasa. Like a geyser, grease-splattered smoke rose.

"Uhuh-uhuh," coughed my aunt. "Uff, it's cho

"Tampa, Florida?" I asked.

"Main P.O., 33606. Dime, please."

Aunt Pat bit at the nail of her raw pinky and leaned to get a peek into the bottom of my mom's HCCC bag, where she had Resto's book.

"Who's setting the table?" she asked, gnawing away like a rodent, her uneven teeth trying to latch on to a split of cuticle.

"Whoever," said my mom, turning away from the stove, toward us, with her spatula in the air like she was posing for a job on Nick at Nite. "Would you mind doing it, Patty? If you don't mind?"

"Of course not."

My aunt rose and drained her beer, giving the eyeball to my mom, who'd turned back to her cooking. "Geez," she said and she placed the can on the table. Yeah, it was awkward the way my mom asked—"Would you mind?" "If you don't mind?"—but she was just being nice, too polite, too formal is all, and my aunt didn't have to react by showing off how out of place it was. She could have just let it go.

"Get me a beer, Joey, while I set the table," said Aunt Pat, holding up her empty. "Then that's it, two's my max, otherwise I go all wacky. Uncle Vic, will you *please* take the coins off the table. Haven't I told you before, coins carry disease."

As I pulled the beer from the refrigerator, I heard someone knocking at Uncle Mike's. We all heard the knock but we couldn't hear any voices. I figured it was the liquor store, if the White Knight was open on a Sunday night, or maybe a college girl. I didn't know what the others knew about Uncle Mike's guests. Aunt Pat probably knew. My mom, maybe. Uncle Vic probably didn't know but imagined something worse.

Aunt Pat wanted our attention. She held a Coca-Cola glass up to a sliver of window light, twisted it, looking for smudges, then wiped it with a dishcloth. "So, Susie, what's the book you're carrying? More stuff you're studying for going to college?" she asked.

"No," said my mom, turning from the stove in battle mode. "Actually, it's Buddy's. He's taking the captain's test in less than two weeks. He asked me to help him."

Aunt Pat continued to study the glass held to the window light and my mom turned back to the stove. When my mom turned, my aunt turned. She gently put down the Coke glass. She tipped back her head and took a hard drag on her Carlton, like she was sucking from it the courage to endure.

"Oh, well, that's great news. Just what I should have known," she muttered before the rest of her words crumbled, the most meaningful syllables popping from her lips in smoke-signal puffs.

"Go to hell. You're freaking crazy," said my mom, so suddenly it surprised even me. "You're pathetic. You're more pathetic than you could even guess." I wished she hadn't said it. Even though all of Aunt Pat's blows were low, it seemed cruel to hit her back. That's how she survived—pity and guilt.

Holding together, "Talk about pathetic," Aunt Pat said, glancing at me and Uncle Vic to see how she was doing. "Look at you, falling all over such a jerk."

"Fuck you. I'm not even gonna talk to you."

"Good, don't talk. This beer's flat, Unc," said my aunt. "You got any white wine?"

"I got red wine. There, behind the vinegar."

Aunt Pat pushed back her chair, stood, and nearly toppled, her back foot not following quickly enough. She looked down and blamed a sneaker, looked at it like it had said something dumb. "What the fuck?" She scraped her tennis sneaker across the linoleum, little chips of mud scratching off. To get a closer look at the linoleum, she bent, feet spread like an old woman, floating cigarette smoke burning her eyes—maybe a pebble or tack had scraped off, maybe the linoleum was ripped. She laid her cigarette in the ashtray. "What the fuck?" she said, shaking her head and blowing smoke.

Forget it, I wanted to tell her. Aunt Pat, just go get your wine, for chrissakes. Drop it.

She leaned onto the table with her left hand, held onto her sneaker with her right. She was fucked up from the beer plus whatever pills may have been in her system plus her condition—her thyroid problem, her low blood pressure, her high blood pressure, her idea of fun. When she caught my mother checking her

48

out, she faked being more stoned, began swooning. She stumbled forward, the back of her hand against her forehead, and she brushed past my mother on the way to smashing against the refrigerator. She hit it harder than she'd intended, rattling the grease-grimed glasses and smiley face lemonade pitcher on top.

My mom shook her head. Aunt Pat sagged against the refrigerator, unmoving, like a rag doll. "So fucking pathetic," whispered my mom.

Aunt Pat put her fingertips to her lips and doubled over in laughter. With one hand, she held herself up by the corner of the refrigerator. That tipped the whole thing. It rattled and wobbled the glasses and pitcher even more. With her other hand she hid her rubber-band-lipped mouth.

"Ooh, shoot. I think I twisted my inner ear," said my aunt.

"Oh, Christ," gasped my mom. "You're bad. You're really damn sick."

"Susie, I'm kidding," said Aunt Pat, lurching forward but her hand still holding on to the refrigerator like it was a life preserver. "I'm just goofing, honey. That's all. Just messing around. Jesus Christ, some people take themselves so seriously."

"Hey, you two, come on," scolded Uncle Vic. He rose up from the table, all five-three of him. He began to unbuckle his pants. "Did you come here to drive me crazy? You're doing me a favor, Susie? This is company, Patricia? My God." He tightened the belt a notch and rebuckled it.

"Oh, I love my sister, Uncle Vic. I was only kidding. Boo-hoo-hoo," she said, breaking out in play tears and burying her face in her hands. "Boo-hoo, why am I such a bad, bad girl," she said, slobbering the words into her hands. She lifted her face and shook her head. She stared at Uncle Vic, her lips smiling, her eyes nearly clear. "Really, Uncle Vic. I'm just joking, you know me. I'm just trying to have some fun, okay? Can't a person have a little fun anymore?" She stepped toward my mom. My mom watched her but didn't turn from her cooking. "I love my sister. Right, sissy?" my aunt said as she put an arm around my mom's shoulders. "You either laugh or you cry. What are you gonna do?" she asked, tapping my mom's arm. "Cry every time someone does something to hurt you?"

"I didn't do shit to you. What I do in my life has no fucking thing to do with you at all," said my mom, and she smashed the spatula on the stove. She paused a minute. Aunt Pat took a step back, like she was alarmed. "You do enough to hurt your own goddamned self. You don't need nobody to do it."

"Prrrrrph." Laughing gas split my aunt's lips like they were the lips of a balloon with the air rushing out. "I'm kidding, I'm kidding. I'm teasing. We're just playing, Uncle Vic, don't get upset," she said as she headed back to the table and lifted her Carlton, barely more than a warm filter, from the Pep Boys' ashed-over faces.

Sections of Bowers Street Park were still bright with long, twinkling light, but from our window view, the sun had sunk behind a cluster of trees, and with this a darkness penetrated the apartment's heat. Aunt Pat turned on the radio, played with the dial, moving it from end to end so quickly the stations blurred. My mom, her back to us, stared down at the three cooking pots, still, like she'd fallen asleep there. Uncle Vic sculpted his cigar's ash along the lip of the ashtray. I reached behind me and flipped on the overhead fluorescent light. As it flickered, I paged through the almanac, switching categories from Zip Codes to Academy Award Winners.

A sudden nasty sound came from upstairs. First, an "Uhoorooh," a person's voice, like someone pushing with all his might. I didn't know if I was the only one to hear it, but the next sounds were much softer, and I was sure no one else heard. There was another "Uhoorooh" sort of sound, higher pitched but very quiet, like a kitten in the wall. A thump, then the squeaky sound of bed wheels across linoleum, then another thump, the mattress shifting over the frame, and another thump that I had to squint to hear, maybe a tumble onto the bed.

"Come on, Joey, ask me," said Uncle Vic.

"Yeah, uh, Best Actor, 1974."

"Come on, come on," he said, fidgeting his fingers as though he were rolling his cigar though the cigar was in the ashtray. "Why you asking me about the seventies? What's the seventies got?"

"Well, guess."

"Joey, come on, come on. Vic Scadutto don't guess. The Scaduttos don't guess."

My mom wiped her hands on a dishtowel and took a step toward the table. "Why don't you go up and invite Uncle Mike for dinner?" she suggested.

"No," I said. "I seen enough of him."

"Go ahead. Maybe the old bastard'll liven things up down here," said Uncle Vic. "Tell him he can come down for one hour."

"Just invite him, Joey. Don't say for an hour. Hurry, okay. The beans are ready."

I shut the door to Uncle Vic's behind me and stood at the bottom of the staircase that led to the third floor. It was even darker and hotter in the hall than in the apartment, and with each step up the air got smellier, like the odors rose with the heat.

The apartment house had changed a lot in just the last two years, and the hallway smelled of all the unfamiliar dinners being cooked that Sunday night—new tenants meant new foods, and new foods meant new smells.

The third floor was lit by a pair of flickering orange flame-shaped bulbs screwed into plastic candles, giving the hall a turn-of-the-wrong-century feel. The mustard-colored walls were bulged and buckled in parts. The bulbs' light spread over them in shadow and shine. Overhead, there was a black skylight surrounded by a ceiling turned grey-green from a hundred years of cooking.

From the top step, Uncle Mike's door was just a corpse length in front of me. I was scared, partly because it had been less than five minutes since I'd heard the noise. I stepped forward and knocked. Got no answer. I balled my fist for another knock, but before hitting the door I thought I saw the crystal knob quiver. I was squeezed with fear and I jumped back, staring at the knob like it was alive.

"Uncle Mike? Uncle Mike?" I whispered as loudly as I could, but I couldn't do that shift in my throat that'd give the whisper the gravelly sound of spoken words. I knocked again. "Uncle Mike? Uncle Mike? It's Joey."

I took hold of the doorknob. It was cold and dead as could

51

be, but it was loose in its setting. I jiggled it every which way, including in and out, but gently, afraid to jiggle hard, afraid it would come off in my hand, break like a skeleton bone, and the jiggle was more to make noise than open the door. I let go, but my jiggling had freed the latch and the door pushed back to the edge of the casing.

Shit, I thought. Just my luck. I called louder, and when I knocked harder, the door backed off, but it was held by the inside brass chain. I peeked in, but I saw nothing, able to glimpse only a narrow slice of the kitchen—the tablecloth hanging still, the clock ticking, the radio silent, a black boot mark on the floor.

I'd done my bit. Maybe he was in there with a girl. Probably they'd both passed out. Who knew and who cared.

Behind me, a foreigner, a Korean or something, a big man in his thirties, fat-footed in sandals, climbed the stairs. He nodded without smiling as he passed me, then he turned to his apartment at the other end. He kept his back to me and I watched him insert his key, slip inside his apartment, close the door behind him.

I started back downstairs. I'd just tell them nobody was home.

SEVEN

THE NEXT MORNING AT EIGHT-THIRTY, WITH BRIAN and his friends Sonia and Clay, I sat on the steps of the House-for-Sale, just off the edge of the crowd that had gathered in front of Uncle Mike's and Uncle Vic's. The day's *Jersey* lay across my knees, my attention split between it and the cops hustling in and out of the apartment house. The article and picture of a nineteen-year-old black kid who'd just been sentenced to twenty years for a murder—an article by the Hudson County Prosecutor's daughter, Joy Kenny, in which Resto got a big mention—and a story about a cop-on-cop killing had knocked Prince off the front page, but only to the first page of Section B. Talking to the press brought out the worst in Resto. Things like this: "Contrary to the Animal Defense League's claims, we've been taking this crime very seriously, relative, of course, to our concern with human victims. Officers Becker and Costello are fine patrolmen. Nothing this department has done is in any way inappropriate or insensitive, though I'm sure all reasonable-minded people recognize that this is not our only priority. We're continuing to actively pursue the matter."

Except for the hubbub left and right, nothing much had happened yet, but what was more important to us sitting on the bench and the crowd in the street was what had happened the night before and caused the morning's commotion.

Uncle Mike's body hadn't been found until seven, when someone on his way to work had noticed Mike's door cracked open and, when he pushed it clear, discovered Uncle Mike on the floor. Nobody was sure yet who it was who'd found him, but the way the cops were interviewing the guy who'd passed me on the stairs, "The Chink who lives with his mother and sister," our guess was it was him who'd made the find.

53

We waited, knowing nothing more than that Uncle Mike was dead, killed, everyone said, strangled. I felt fear, especially when I pictured myself in the flickering heat of Uncle Mike's landing, and I felt worry, two killings, some sort of maniac on the loose. But like with Prince, I didn't feel sadness.

With three patrol cars, two unmarked police cars, and two black sedans with Hudson County Prosecutor's Office shields in their windows, plus one hearse from the county coroner's office, the police had blocked off the street, and, as if directed by instinct, like ants in an ant farm, they were busy in and out of the building. All the teams of them—the uniformed Jersey City Police, the detectives, the blue T-shirts from the prosecutor's office—whether hustling with their guns wagging, or pointing out this or that, or sipping coffee, a hand on a buddy's back, seemed very happy, as though they'd just been released from jail themselves.

The crowd outside must have been a hundred, less than half of it white. There were so many newcomers—Indians, Arabs, Asians, a couple of blacks—that they almost made the Hispanics seem like us. A scraggly cluster of HouseRADS, like Doonesbury characters, had wandered this way but stayed inside the park. JCPD detectives and Hudson County Prosecutor's Office investigators moved through the crowd, chatting people up, taking phone numbers, reminiscing, occasionally bossing around some foreigner or teenager or drunk. But early on no one bothered us.

Me, Brian, Sonia, and Clay were on the steps of what used to be the Caruso house. The old man, Mr. Caruso, had died a year ago at eighty-four, and the week before this past Christmas, Mrs. Caruso was carried out of the house, still seated in a kitchen chair, and taken to MLK Nursing Home. The Carusos had two sons, both older than my mom, but they were long gone from here, didn't even show when their mother was taken away.

Since then, since Christmas, the house whose porch we sat on had been empty, left to the effects of vandals and nature. With some damage it was hard to tell which of the two was the cause. It could have been nature, it could have been the vandalism that caused the broken windows, the chipped steps, the fallen wires. Other things, it wasn't hard to tell at all. On the one side, there was the knee-high itchy grass, the shin-high crabgrass, there were mice and worms and roaches, a family of possum in the attic. Then, on the other side, the vandalism side, there was the graffiti—"Kill All Niggers," "Arabs Are Fags," "White Boys Suck Dick"—there were the hammerholes in the doorway, the soda cans, plastic cups, and whiskey bottles in the grass.

I sat on the third of the five slab-stone steps. Brian and Clay were on the top. Sonia stood, leaning her belly against the fence. I was sure it wouldn't be long before one of the detectives strolled our way since all three of them were involved with the girls coming to visit Uncle Mike. Clay recruited them, Brian introduced them, and teeny Sonia was one of them. I knew they'd want to talk to me, too, as soon as the fat-footed Korean told them I'd been up at Uncle Mike's door.

Clay, Brian's boss at the tutoring center, was neither thin nor fat. He was always tan and had a coppery tint to his wavy hair. Clay had moved here less than two years ago from Belmar, a town on the shore, what he called "down state." He'd moved to Belmar two years before that, after he graduated from a little college in Massachusetts. He had grown up in Florida and moved north on his own when he was nineteen, so the story goes. It seemed like everywhere he lived he had great friends—oodles of friends and money—but the fact that he talked about them so much and had none here, none of either, made you wonder.

He's twenty-seven now, a part-time teacher and master tutor at Hudson County Community College, where he'd met Brian. Sonia Lopes had started HCCC in January, and not long after that she wandered into the tutoring center under the orders of her basic algebra teacher. She met Brian and Clay. One thing led to another, and there sat the four of us, waiting for Uncle Mike's body to be carried to the hearse.

Clay was spinning a beat-up white Frisbee between his fingers; Sonia, her skinny butt in carpenter's jeans, was holding on to the fence, rocking back and forth; Brian was closed for business—like a pudgy corpse, his lips and eyes seamlessly shut. I was finishing up the *Journal* article about the black kid convicted of murder, the part about Hudson County Head Prosecutor Ed Kenny, who, on his last day heading the office before he left to commit full time to his run for mayor, wanted to thank Police Lieutenant Buddy Resto "for his team cooperation with the prosecutor's office and his relentless tenacity in apprehending this heinous criminal."

Silently, no horn honking, no siren on the dashboard, Resto arrived driving his own car, a red and black Cherokee. He parked at the far end of the block. His hands were in the pockets of his khakis and his head was bowed, wagging a bit, his chin scratching against the collar of his pink shirt. He headed for a group of four cops—two plainclothes detectives, a sergeant, and a uniformed black lieutenant—who, together, controlled who did and didn't get into the building. Brian had opened his eyes and was blankly staring at the group. He ran his fingers over the scraggly beard at his jawline.

Resto stepped into the circle and immediately became its center. The same way as he'd approached, hands in his pockets, head down, nodding now more than wagging, Resto listened attentively to what each had to say. He patted the lieutenant on the back before heading up the steps and disappearing into the dark foyer.

Not half a minute later, Spanish music blasted from the building next to Uncle Mike's. It was a beige brick building with a ground-level garage that stood out for its newness, fifteen, twenty years old, but that had no curtains in the windows, just raised white shades, and still had Christmas lights around the second-floor picture window.

All business, a young head-shaved black cop trotted out of Uncle Mike's building like a football player coming out for pregame introductions. He tilted into the arc his charge made and, without a lost stride, jumped the steps next door onto the first landing, took two more leaps to the front door. He lifted his rubber-soled shoe and kicked in the door. Inside someone yelled in Spanish and the music stopped.

"Watch this shit," said Sonia, just half turning to us, keeping an eye on the building. "Watch this nigga."

Through the picture window we could see the cop yelling at a chubby, brown-skinned teenager, who, while trying to explain or apologize, held his hands up as though a gun had been pulled on him. A shirtless, flabby-breasted older guy, looked forty or fifty, probably the kid's dad, came into the room to defend the teenager. But as though he were grabbing a shirt, the cop grabbed the man by the chest, by his bread-dough breasts, pushed and pulled the man before shoving him against the wall. The cop yelled something. What I heard was just the end of it, something like "—enfuckin-ganow!" The kid opened the sliding window next to the center one. Next thing, a boombox, red and black and big as a crib mattress, came flying out. In a pop and spray of plastic, the box landed on the unlidded garbage barrels inside the gate, split in half and dangling.

"You see that shit?" said Sonia, turning around, looking at Brian. "Fucking niggas, man. I'm telling you." Brian nodded, just enough not to piss her off.

I'd met Sonia for the first time in late March along the Cliff Walk when I ran into her and Brian on their way to Uncle Mike's. It was a windless but freezing cold blue day, so clear you could count the windows in the skyscrapers across the Hudson. That day was really the first day I was sure what the girls were going in and out of Uncle Mike's for. Nobody had to spell it out.

It was Sonia's second visit. Brian, a dozen steps back, was more tagging along than leading the way. For awhile we walked silently, me alongside her. Sonia kept glancing at me, pretending she didn't want me to notice. Finally, the first words out of her mouth were, "I can't believe you're Brian's brother. You know why? I bet you couldn't guess why if I gave you all year. You know why? Because I thought you was a chick," she said and laughed into the bunched neck of her hooded sweatshirt.

Over the grey sweatshirt, she had on a big, army-green vinyl coat, unbuttoned. The fur-framed collar was loose and, with the sweatshirt hood, made a cradle around her small head. Her beige corduroy pants, so wide-legged they looked like a skirt, hung loose from her hips and long over her untied boots. Everything seemed ready to slip off.

"I swear it. Your name's Joey, right? I swear I really thought you was a chick. No shit."

"Yeah, why'd you think I was a chick?" I asked, hoping that the cold had already turned my pale cheeks pink and my blushing would be hidden.

"No, nothing, little man, don't be so embarrassed. It's just the way you look. I saw you once when you came in to the tutoring center. I was there. You was talking to Brian and I thought you was his girlfriend. Don't tell him, man, but I was jealous," she said, one hand half covering the lick she gave her lips. "How old are you anyway?"

"I'm fifteen," I said. I looked back at Brian. I hoped he'd hurry up. He was dressed awful—cheap sneakers, Wonder Store jeans, more like thin cardboard than denim, a shiny black jacket a size too small. His hanging back didn't make any sense, was more like hanging around. It made no sense unless he liked her, and Brian didn't *like*.

"No," she said out of nowhere. She laughed and used her hands in her pockets to open and close her coat. "Man, I swear, man, you would be a good-looking chick." Her small head reminded me of a coconut.

"Fuck yourself," I said, squinting at her, brushing my hair off my forehead.

"See that, man, you are so cute. You got nice cheekbones, a puckered kind of little kissing mouth. Sad little junkie eyes. You're skinny, too, like the chicks with no tits in the Calvin ads. Man, I bet if you had the balls to try you could be in one of them. You really got it, man."

"Yeah, and you sound like a lesbian."

"Wow, man, you could make me one," she laughed, flapping her coat open, keeping it there as she stopped walking. "No, I'm teasing, man. Aw, I'm sorry, Joey. I mean it, though. Your bone structure it's called, it's excellent. I'm sincere, man. I'm jealous."

Running along the Cliff Walk, there's a knee-high wall topped by a six-foot iron-spiked fence. Sonia stepped up, lifted her arms, and, except for her hands on the spikes and her thumbs over the points, seemed to disappear inside the coat and pants and boots as she swung back and forth like a ghost sailor on a mast.

"I live down there," she said, nodding toward the Hoboken projects. "I grew up there since I was eight. Ten years, man, a long time. See that building next to the last one closest? That's my building. We take a lot of shit from the niggas. I get along with Spanish and I get along with white, but not them. They don't want to. They won't let you. All I tell you is thank God for my moms, man. She raised me and my brother all by herself. She raised us good. Everything I do is for her. College, you name it." Her skinny arm poked up through the coat sleeve as she waved. "I love you, Moms. I love you so much."

She jumped down from the wall and took a hand mirror and lipstick from her coat pocket. Like her hood, the pocket was trimmed in fake fur. In the background, an opened paperback in his hands, a cigarette between two fingers, Brian, now seated on the ledge, rocked his knees to fight off the cold.

Sonia handed me the mirror and raised my hand to the right height. Her lips were full but pale and slightly chapped, tender but rough, like an orange under the peel. Her lipstick was as brownish as it was red and, except for a slight sparkle in it, blended with her skin. As she looked at herself, she did some exercises with her lips, then took back the mirror.

"Come on, huh?" said Brian, walking toward us, hands in his jacket's high pockets and elbows sharply bent. He motioned with his head toward Uncle Mike's.

"We're going, man, we're going," said Sonia.

"Let's just do this shit, okay?"

"Oh, it's 'shit' now. It wasn't shit two weeks ago."

"Let's go, all right?" said Brian, his mouth smirky, disgusted, probably with himself. "Sonia, let's just go. The old bitch's waiting."

She jumped back onto the ledge. This time she didn't hold on, just used her feet to lock herself and waved with both hands. "Bye, Moms. I love you. I tell you it every night, Mommy, I love you, babe."

The bald black cop came trotting out of the building the same way he went in, like the incident had meant nothing to him. Only when he got outside the house's gate, two strides toward the apartment building, did he slow down. All the cops, leaning on cars, talking to old buddies, tried to hide their high spirits. Looking into the building, I could see two guys in navy blue slacks and yellow coroner's office T-shirts carrying Uncle Mike's body out of the building. A doctor from that office, a man who looked like Huckleberry Hound, followed them, and Buddy Resto followed him. Coming down the stairs, Uncle Mike's body, saggy at the waist, bent almost in half, was in a zipped black bag, which the two carriers placed on a stretcher just inside the entranceway.

His eyes droopy and his white shirt untucked, the coroner's doctor scratched his five o'clock shadow. He explained something to Resto, who was again the perfect listener.

"That's your man, ain't it?" said Clay to Brian, pointing out Resto. "Everybody's buddy."

"I can't stand him," said Brian, and he shut his eyes and leaned back like his head was killing him.

"He's a super wanna-be," said Clay, trying to egg Brian on.

"Be quiet," said Brian, eyes shut, a man being bothered while he was trying to find some peace.

"Wanna-be," that was Brian's most used word. It wasn't a wanna-be-anything-in-particular, just a wanna-be, period. It didn't matter to Brian what a person wanted to be. Wanting to be something, anything, that's what was fucked up. And a wanna-be was Resto exactly.

Uncle Mike was loaded into the back of the hearse. Resto and the worn-out doctor shook hands. The hearse rolled away and Resto called two sergeants to him. One to his right, one to his left, Buddy had a hand on each of their shoulders, the quarterback in the huddle.

"Right. Right, okay," they said. Then, whispering to one another, they left Resto, one of them, the Hispanic one, wiping his hands on his pants, the other, white, checking his watch. The first went over to the two prosecutor's office cars and must have told the three guys there to leave because that's what they did. The other one gave orders to the uniformed cops standing around. Like Boy Scouts at a car wash, they were eager to do a good job—at least for Resto they were.

Four cops got into two cars and left, two stayed to disperse the crowd, and two more started to set up the crime scene. Two detectives went into the building.

Resto finally noticed us and headed our way. Clay began laughing, for no reason as far as Resto could tell. But Resto didn't seem to care. He pulled a black string from his pink shirt and shrugged with his winged eyebrows. Brian leaned forward and hid his face in his hands. Resto ignored that, too.

"You guys, hey, we got to talk. You know anything?" he asked loudly, one hand on the gate. We muttered no. Sonia turned away from him. Brian just shook his head. "Prince and this, in two days, unbelievable." We still ignored him. "Well, I'm gonna have to talk to you, you know. Come on," he said, his palms out to us, half cupped like holding water. "If not now, later then, all right?" he asked. "Well, I guess it's all right. Do you have a choice? No, you don't. So long, guys and lady. Have a nice day," he said as though we'd just had a pleasant little conversation. I wasn't sure if he was being sarcastic or not. "See y'all later."

Clay snickered when Resto left. "Wowee, what a tough interrogation by the lieutenant." But I don't think Resto could have cared less what Clay said. He was busy with his own thing.

PART II

ONE

I N SUMMERTIME, THE HCCC TUTORING CENTER IS basically a two-man operation, Clay and Brian. The center is located on the fourteenth floor of the Jersey Journal Building, Fifty Journal Square. The college rents five of the office building's floors—the sixth, ninth, tenth, and fourteenth floors, which had been converted to classrooms and labs, as well as the ground floor, an open but dark and airless lobby used for college registration, blood drives, and student orientations, the old shops and stands around its perimeter turned to college offices and stock rooms. When the building conversion was done, though, things hadn't worked out perfectly.

The tutoring center was the back room of the Manhattan-facing side of the building. There were only two windows in the center. The window at what you'd probably call the front of the room, flush against the blackboard, had been part of the original stairwell, and so was sort of a mutant. Small as a prison window, it was a single pane of plastic with no way of being opened. The other window, at the back of the room, was a real window with a latch that could flap it in and out. The problem was that the window was split in half by the renovation's false wall, which divided a big room in two and now separated the tutoring center from the data processing lab. This left the window just a foot and a half wide in each room, clouded with spackle and impossible to open, latch or no latch.

Clay Nanuet was a master tutor, a job that earned him eighteen dollars per hour and the right to train other tutors, a job he'd gotten the same way he'd gotten his part-time teaching job at the college, by lying: forging his transcripts and recommendation letters, claiming to have a master's degree and teaching experience, denying his criminal record, Possession with Intent to Sell and Impersonating a Police Officer. But that was Clay. Scam your way through life, and he who dies with the most hustles wins.

Clay had hired my brother. Brian's title was math peer tutor. He earned eight dollars per hour, a dollar more than he was supposed to earn. He got the extra dollar because Clay liked him from the start. He recognized someone who, like him, had a superiority complex, only Brian was too cynical to use his in the open. The friendship was perfect from Clay's point of view. One big intellect finding another, the one who never shut up meeting the one who never spoke. But I didn't know what Brian saw in Clay. Knowing Brian, I figured it must have driven him crazy to sit and listen to that windbag all day. Clay, the rebel yuppie, was as big a wanna-be as Resto. Still, Brian never talked about him, good or bad, about Clay being a great guy or Clay being an asshole.

When I walked in that Wednesday, two days after Uncle Mike had been found dead, it was just the two of them. Clay's long six-two frame was oversized for the scratched grey metal desk he sat at. On top of the desk was a *Vanity Fair* magazine half out of his briefcase, a messy pile of white and pink tutoring forms and schedules in a plastic In/Out box, and, pointing right at you when you entered, so there'd be no mistake who ran this place, Clay's baby-powdered brown plastic sandals. Except for his heavy red jogging pants, Clay was a pile of browns. He wore a rust and chocolate rugby shirt, and around his neck was a braided brown choker. His wavy hair was straight-from-the-bottle copper brown. His face, which was a pockmarked spongy texture, like the inside of Prince's ball, and his thick neck and his arms all seemed saturated with tanning oil that had turned him the color of a nearly new penny. He was reading a paperback, *Chicken Soup for the Soul*, and sipping from a twenty-four-ounce Dunkin' Donuts cup.

Brian was asleep. He was sitting alongside one of the six cafeteria tables that made up the center's work space, his feet up on a yellow molded-plastic chair. Unlike the building's muggy lobby, elevators, and halls, the tutoring center was cold as an icebox. The tip of the room's thermostat had snapped off at the low end, and knowing how things worked at the college, Clay was afraid to make a report, figuring this extreme was better than the opposite, the likely outcome of a work request. Brian slept with an aqua and orange Newport-cigarette beach towel wrapped around his shoulders. Under the dim light of the center, where more of the ceiling's fluorescents were out than worked, he looked bad, practically homeless. He'd slept at the house only one night of the past five. He hadn't shampooed in a while, making his Caesar haircut even flatter and greasier, and he hadn't shaved in a while either. Since he was growing a beard, not shaving didn't matter too much, except that the thin whisker patches across his cheeks looked extra oily and grimy when he was unwashed on top of unshaved.

Under the Newport towel, he wore a green and grey polo shirt, and he was wearing the same type jeans he'd had on the day I first met Sonia, the type that never got worn in, just went from cardboard to tissue.

"Hey, Joey. What's happening?" asked Clay, perking up at the sight of company, even me. "Check it out. We got a new refrigerator. Hey, not bad work for eight dollars an hour, is it?" he asked, pointing out the Shangri-La him and my brother found themselves in. I guess I didn't seem impressed. "My man, that's forty dollars your brother gets for sleeping for five hours. In the service, I'd dig for a month and a day before I'd make what I'm making today for sitting on my ass."

Without turning toward me, Brian opened his heavy eyes, letting them peruse as much of the room as possible without moving his head. I took my cue from him and tried not to respond to anything Clay said.

The center's furnishings were a crowded mess, made up either of castoffs from other school departments—a beige water-cooler, a pair of almost-matching metal bookcases, a photocopy machine, six cafeteria tables that formed the student-and-tutor work space—or different things that tutors had contributed themselves—a grease-splattered microwave, a coffeemaker, a clock radio. The room was made even more cluttered by the debris and materials left over from the renovation—the ten-gallon tubs of spackle, the refrigerator-sized boxes of Pink Panther insulation, the four giant spools of orange and black cable.

I sat at one of the tables, two away from Brian.

"You guys," I said, "we all have to go to the police station tomorrow."

"To be interviewed?" asked Brian softly. I traced back the sound of his words, but looking at him gave no clue he'd spoken.

"Yeah."

"Oh, so are we suspects?" he asked, hissing the last word.

"I don't know. Not according to Mom," I said. "She says Resto's interviewing everybody who might know anything."

"Resto's doing the interviewing, or someone else?" asked Clay. He swirled his coffee, watched it spin, lifted the cup and posed.

"Resto, I think," I said.

"Figures. He wants to be the big man, the man in charge," said Clay. "That's where the glory's at. Headline Man, Buddy Resto."

The tutoring center's ceiling was made up of sixteen foam tiles, four translucent lighting panels, and four more holes where panels were missing. Behind the four missing tiles, three of them together in an *L*, was a narrow black space. Aluminum vents and steel electrical boxes hung from the hard ceiling behind, a space where bare wires and black, orange, and white cables dangled loose.

"Hmm, hmmm. Hmm-hmmm-hmmm," mused Clay, tipping his head this way and that, listening to voices. "Interviewed by Lieutenant Resto. Hmmm-hmmm. Yeah, okay. That's okay. That's cool, that's very cool."

"Yeah, and what's very cool about being interviewed for a murder?" I asked.

"Nothing—if I was guilty, my man. That would not be cool, but me and Resto, head to head, that's what's *very* cool. That'll be a challenge, son."

As I processed this fool's words, I looked over at Brian, but he was closed up again, in his death-over-life pose. His body was stretched out across the two chairs, head tipped to the ceiling, rested hands on his belly, eyes shut. I looked for a twitch or a tightening of muscles or a hard swallow, but there was nothing. I knew that having to do an interview would disgust him, having to deal with the world, answer questions about himself. Worse, the questions would come from Resto, that asshole, the epitome of Respectability, the guardian of Morality, Brian's two archenemies, R 'n' M.

"Let's get it on, Lieutenant, you and me," said Clay.

"I got to be there at nine," I said. "Brian, you're nine-thirty. Clay, ten. He's talking to people all day."

"You first, then Brian, then me?" asked Clay, a finger tapping his lip.

"Yeah, so? What's your big point?"

Brian opened his eyes and turned to face us. I'd delivered my message, but my agitation was showing I couldn't deal with Clay like Brian wanted me to. It was time to go.

"Why do *you* think it's in that order—you, Brian, then me?" asked Clay.

"I have no fucking idea," I said slowly.

"No? Well, you think about it, Near Man."

"It's probably because you and Resto are the main event," said Brian to Clay. I laughed. I took the comment to be sarcastic and so did Clay, though he was unsure. When I looked back at Brian, I could see he was angry at me for reacting.

Now, thanks to me, he had to go out of his way to reassure Clay, to get on the guy's good side. He had to explain, speak in complete sentences, sentence after sentence.

"No, honestly," said Brian. "I mean it. Why else would he schedule it that way? He probably figures he can get whatever he wants from Joey. So him first," said Brian. The monologue was sucking from him the little breath he had. "Me? I think he just sees me as a fucked-up kid, figures, well . . . whatever. You, though, are different. Like you said, it's going to be a challenge and he knows it. Resto can see that."

"He ain't stupid," said Clay.

"All right, so you understand. That's all I meant, Clay."

TWO

T HE NEXT DAY MADE SIX DAYS SINCE PRINCE HAD
been killed, four since Uncle Mike had that Sunday night.
Early in the morning, it was pouring rain outside. Dressed
an hour before we'd be leaving for the precinct, me and my mom
sat in the kitchen. The yellow ceiling light against the dark windows gave the apartment a feeling of nighttime.

Our house was the second floor of an attached two-family.
All the rooms were narrow, and the kitchen, because the stairway from the first floor came up alongside it, was the narrowest.
It was squeezed and long and, since the ceilings hadn't been
dropped like the ones in the living room and bedrooms had,
seemed especially tall. It was an old-fashioned kitchen with a
black-knobbed stove, painted steel table, speckled linoleum, and
blue paint above grey, white, and blue salt-'n-pepper-shaker-pat-
terned wallpaper. It smelled always of coffee and Pine Sol and,
whenever Aunt Pat was living with us, of cigarettes, too, and
sometimes of a clothesline-and-bus-exhaust breeze that ruffled
the white curtains at the double windows. Old-fashioned it was
and that's the way my mom wanted it, having turned down the
Iranian who was landlord two landlords ago and was willing to
remodel the whole thing.

I was wearing jeans and a Goosebumps T-shirt I'd bought
three years ago but that still fit. My mom, smelling more of Ivory
soap than of her going-out perfume, was dressed for work in a new
pair of white Wranglers and a new Native American-style belt—
brown with patterns of blue and white and desert-colored beads.
The pants, with her blue denim shirt tucked in, fit tight, made her
zipper bulge. Her hair was different, sprayed into a stiff but fluffy
unparted wave that let her skip the hairband but did nothing to get
rid of the nerdiness. She had an extra dose of pink on her cheeks

and an extra stroke of black eyeliner. Only my mom would take her first day of work as a waitress this seriously.

She had to be at the restaurant for a training shift by ten o'clock. She'd have to hustle there from the police station. From work, she'd have to hustle again—to Uncle Mike's afternoon wake.

I sat at the kitchen table, watching her. She was in two worlds at once, one on this side of her eyeballs, one on the inside. When there was a riot going on in the inside world, like there was this morning—me, Brian, Resto, the interviews, Aunt Pat, Uncle Mike, work, Prince—she seemed with you, but not with you either. A sleepwalker. The only way you could get a peek into her head was through her eyes, where the two worlds met, and now and then by a tilt to her head—"Oh, that's an idea I hadn't thought of," it would say in response to her braintalk—or maybe by a twitch or a grimace or a smile that would rise from her face but that she wouldn't be aware of and wouldn't erase, would let linger too long until it melted in a creepy sort of way.

But the eyes, though. Her eyes would harden and shrink back in their sockets, and in them you could see the chemistry of a chirpy conversation going on inside—apologizing or explaining or predicting or debating. There'd be shifts in her eyes, little dilations, rods then cones lighting up in kaleidoscope patterns. The voice her eyes reacted to was too nervous ever to settle, a Jiminy-Cricket Superhero leaping from neuron to neuron, sucking out the fear or worry in each one, leaving behind unlasting assurance.

But on the outside, all her worrying showed up in the opposite way. Mess? What mess? Problem? Huh?

For almost a whole hour in her reliable kitchen she took what was already in order and made it more orderly. If it was clean, it could always be cleaner. If the room smelled fresh, it could always smell fresher. And who was to say a straight curtain couldn't be made straighter?

"What time do you start at the coffee shop?" I asked.

"No, it's a cafe. It's not a coffee shop. It's called the Pioneer Cafe," she said. Her answer was half her own words, half Jiminy Cricket's. "I start at ten. I train for two hours. Don't worry. It'll go fine."

71

She wiped down the tablecloth with a scrubbie.

"But Brian's interview's at nine-thirty."

"Yeah, I know. I'll have to go right from there, quick. I don't think Buddy'll keep him long," she said, and there went her pupils, the black growing toward the edges, the brown shrinking to a thin rim.

The job was in HouseRAD and that didn't make it any easier. A woman in her thirties, from this side of the park, serving tables. I felt bad for her, white Wranglers and tucked shirt and all. I hoped she wouldn't have to make up some humiliating lie for being late her first day.

My mom brushed away the rainwater that had leaked in through the windows. Head tilted, she straightened the blinds, a job she took way too long to finish, like she was putting the final touches on a work of art. She set the pots perfectly square and balanced on the stovetop. She sniffed the hallway leading to the bedrooms and sprayed it.

At ten past eight, Brian wandered in from the bathroom, hair wet and neck soapy, dressed in the clothes he'd slept in, his sneakers in one hand, balled-up army-green socks in the other.

"You're coming to the police station?" he asked my mom before dropping into a chair, bending and straining to get his socks on, an unwilling hump in his back.

"Of course," she said cheerily. "You know me. I know there's no need to, but I really want to. I have a personal need," she said, trying to joke.

She knew what I knew: to communicate with Brian, all the effort had to come from her. So, she shut down the voice inside and brought her whole self out to play. I could see it was a strain. "You know, we'll look like three drowned rats if we walk. Joey, why don't you call the taxi," she said, broom in hand as she studied the clock, calculating, "in, say, four minutes, okay?"

The time was eight-fifteen. Outside, a perfectly vertical rain fell like strung beads. The grey that hid everything but the nearest trees and clotheslines deepened and pressed harder against the window.

"Uh, eight-twenty would be a round number," I said.

"That's what I mean. Between dialing and them picking

72

up, that's another minute anyway." She looked at Brian, smiled with loving sadness. "Oh, it doesn't matter—three minutes, four minutes, five minutes. It doesn't matter."

"Live it up," said Brian.

My mom laughed at herself, covered her mouth, looked at me as she bent then, for a second time, pulled a can of Glade from the cabinet under the sink, looked at it, rejected it, put it back, wiped her hands on a dishtowel.

In the silence, the nervous chatter inside her head picked up again, and she kept at her straightening routine. All her movements were smooth, no breaks, nothing awkward, no abrupt shifts from one angle, one action to the next. Pick up the towel, make the wipe, fold the towel, fold it more evenly, lay it over the rack, straighten its edges. Reach with the left hand, brush the crumbs, catch 'em in the right. Brush your hands, don't mess your pants. Smile and spin. Reach for the Fantastik, spray the refrigerator. Slow down. Draw a paper towel. Rub in circles, check, get the missed spot. Slow down. You're happy. Toss out the towel.

"There," she said. She smoothed the tuck of her denim shirt, pushed it to the back of her white jeans. "This'd probably be a good time to call," she said, glancing at the clock.

"We're gonna be twenty minutes early. Who wants to sit there?" complained Brian. He touched his fingers along his forehead like he had a headache he was trying to interpret.

I hesitated on my way to the phone.

"Has Sonia called?" he asked.

"No," I said softly, waiting for a cue whether or not to dial the cab.

"Go ahead, call," he said, and I continued on into the hallway.

"Does Resto say anything about how the investigation's going?" Brian asked my mom.

"Oh, he's not saying too much. He shouldn't, you know. He's not allowed."

"Are there any suspects?"

"A lot of people, I think. I know there's one girl Buddy's looking at real close."

There was a three-count pause.

"Natasha Matthews?" Brian asked.

Someone picked up the phone. "Taxi," said a hillbilly woman.

"Yeah, how'd you know? She's in it pretty deep," said my mom. "And Brian—I know how you know her," she said, her voice cracking in fear of him. "You know what I mean, her and her whole crew. I know what you and Clay were up to with those girls, them and Uncle Mike," she said, but that was as far as she dared to push it. "We're gonna have to talk about it, okay? Sometime."

"Yeah, okay. That's fine."

When I came back into the room, she was looking at Brian, trying to form words in her mouth, but she said nothing.

"Five minutes they said at the taxi," I said. "Are we suspects or not?"

"Joey, you're supposed to be helping Buddy with the investigation, and that's what I expect you to do. If he asks you a question, please cooperate. Don't just sit there like a lump, stick him with a bunch of yes's and no's, the two of you. Help him, okay? Yes? Is that a yes?"

"It's a yes," said Brian, and I nodded along. "Natasha, or whoever killed him, robbed Uncle Mike, too, didn't they?" he asked.

"Yeah," said my mom. "He had his money in fifty-dollar bonds. Nearly twenty thousand dollars' worth."

"He always bragged about his money," I said. "He bragged about everything. Nobody liked him."

"Joey, it was still terrible. And it's terrible you even think that."

"I'm not thinking anything," I said.

What I'd said about him was true. No one liked him and he did brag about everything, even the diabetes he said was killing him. The higher his sugar count, the more he bragged. "More than four hundred today, too much ice cream. There goes my foot swellin', the bastard."

"He told me he was losing a foot, maybe a leg," said Brian. He looked up from the table. "Dia-be-teez," he said drawing out

74

the "teez" ending in imitation of Uncle Mike. My mom smiled, proud and bashful both, like this joke had allowed a glimpse of the old Brian, of his love for her.

"He already had a heart attack," I said. "He told me he only had a year left."

"So what?" asked my mom, her jaw dropped and her hands out, waiting for a reasonable answer to fall into them. "Murder is murder. No explanations, no excuses. It's wrong, it's immoral, it's sick, Joe. Murder's murder."

Brian's face went like someone had stuffed dogshit up his nose. He looked at my mother like she'd said the dumbest thing he'd ever heard. "No," he said, looking into the window's fog. "Murder ain't murder. It's not simple."

"Mom," I said, smiling to keep the two of them apart, "nobody's making excuses."

"You really think all murders are equal? Murder's murder?" Brian asked, talking down to my mom. "You really think that?"

"Mom, nobody wanted him dead," I said quickly.

"What would be worse," asked Brian, "somebody killing Uncle Mike or, like was in the paper yesterday, in Union City," he pointed through the apartment, north, "somebody killing a nine- and a ten-year-old?" he asked, sneering.

Lame as could be, "They're both awful," was the best my mom could do.

"Oh, God. Of course they're both awful," I said, looking back and forth at them, searching for the little island the three of us could stand on.

She thanked me in a little way, a quick glance, embarrassed for needing one son's help with the other.

"Oh, where's the taxi?" she asked. "They're usually so quick." She looked around the kitchen for something to clean, but when she came up with nothing, she patted her cushy hair. "I hate my hair," she said and turned away, zombie-like, heading for the bathroom.

Alone with me, Brian quickly upped, too, and headed into his room. On my way to the front room, the living room, to watch for the cab, I passed his open door. That side of the house was attached. Brian sat on his bed, head tipped back against the windowless wall.

Like the rest of the apartment, our living room was narrow. Against one wall was the couch, above it a pink and white painting, *The Minuet*, against the other wall, two armchairs. Between the front windows was the TV. I stepped between the couch and the TV, pushed back the curtain, and leaned on the windowsill. A wind had picked up and the rain, whipped into spinning gusts, smacked the glass. The thinning fog allowed a blurred view of the red-white-and-blue-capped Independence Day light floating at the top of an otherwise invisible Empire State Building. Inside the park, darkness kept the streetlights on. Beneath them, a police car, its cherry lit and spinning, sat in the park on the grass, between the wall alongside Cobble Road and the new plastic playground. Coming through the park, creeping toward our house, even slower once it crossed the Ogden overpass and it had to check for addresses, rolled a long white Chevy, our cab, no roof light, no name, just a peeling phone number on the door.

THREE

AS WE RAN ACROSS CENTRAL AVENUE, MY
mom tried to squeeze the three of us under her black
umbrella, but it didn't work, and we sat in the police station's domed steam-bath lobby with our heads the only part dry, me and my mom on a mahogany wood-slat bench, Brian on a shorter, matching one sideways to us. Soothing, I guess, to the cops, the building smelled of lead pencils, fresh paint, shoe polish, and Burger King wrappers, of dry cleaning in plastic bags, and of cigarette smoke—even though there were No Smoking signs on every wall, sometimes two or three.

A female officer, Sergeant Kitty Paluski by nameplate, sat at a contact-paper-covered front desk that was as big as a church altar. She pressed an intercom button and told Resto we were there. Sergeant Paluski was about forty years old, with a cartoonish face—big cheeks, fat nose, sunken eyes. I remembered seeing her picture in the *Jersey*—she'd been the first woman on the force, and three years ago had been made the first female sergeant. She'd outgrown her uniform shirt, had to wear a T-shirt under since she couldn't button the top, and she kept her JCPD baseball cap bobby-pinned to mound-on-mound blonde hair.

Some officers went out into the rain, others came in from it. They smelled of Old Spice and rubber, their yellow and black raincoats dripping, their curses of good cheer echoing off the walls. That seemed like their job, to go in and out of the rain, making sure Sergeant Paluski kept track of their comings and goings, cheering one another up.

Me, mom, and Brian avoided one another. I pretended to be curious about the surroundings. My mom, smiling a painted smile of peace and confidence, avoided contact with everyone in the room by gluing her eyes to the small schoolroom speaker high

on the opposite wall, in love with the music coming from it—
"Rock around the Clock," "I Wanna Hold Your Hand," the one
that went, "It's a little bit funny, this feeling inside." Brian
slumped on the shorter bench, his eyes fixed in judgment on the
squeaking feet that came and went.

I was the only one with a good view of Resto's office, down
a corridor that had been squeezed to a single lane by paint cans,
brushes and rollers, a ladder, and a crunched drop cloth.

Ten minutes after we got there, just at the end of a Classic
Sports promo for Marciano-Louis, Resto's door opened. Sideways,
with his slightly stiff left leg locked, he walked past the paint
mess toward us. The officers watched him. Part admiration, but
part resentment, too, I thought—their eyes soft with the first,
lips tight with the second. Resto winked and nodded his hellos,
then came straight over to where we sat, to my mom first. She
laid her hand out there and he grabbed hold of it with two.

"I've got notes for you," she whispered. "Chapters nine and
ten. I didn't know if I should bring them."

"No, keep them for later," he said, his back to the other
officers. "Thanks, though," he said, lifting his eyebrows for
emphasis. No matter that I'd smelled it before, his cologne, cin-
namony, almost rum-smelling, sending a little burn up your nostrils, caught me by surprise, especially in that place.

He was in a police casual uniform, khaki pants, a blue
three-button knit with a gold JCPD seal on the breast, no cap on
over his glistening side-buzzed brown hair.

He stepped toward the corridor. "I'll see you at the wake
this afternoon," he said to my mom. "Well, Joey. You ready?" He
stepped aside so I'd walk first. "Freaking smells, doesn't it?" he
asked as we walked past the paint stuff. I felt his eyes on my
neck and nodded without turning around. Guys like Resto made
me think about my littleness. He made me realize I wasn't a
man, and I was suddenly worried about the interrogation.

"Have a seat. You know why you're here, right?" he asked
as he walked around the desk, his limp more noticeable as he
made the half-circle.

Three bright lamps were on in the room, but there was no
overhead, and the room was a mix of dark and light patches.

"Yup."

"To see if you can help me solve this thing."

"Mmm-hmm."

Resto's office, set back from the action and with an air-conditioner that didn't so much cool the air as draw out the staleness and humidity, was filled with all sorts of things you'd never expect to find in a police lieutenant's office, which I took to be exactly the way he wanted it. His desk was real old, older than the standard, maybe an antique, a red wood. The top was covered in black leather attached to the desk by a border of steel tacks. There were no files or papers on its top, except for the folder he was preparing on me. Other than that, just a very bright lamp and a couple of brass thingamajigs that looked like stuff from a nautical store. All his folders, long and marble green, were on a darkwood narrow table sided by an orange-shaded floor lamp. Next to this table was a big shoeshine chair, old as hell but shiny as an archangel.

"I wanted to talk to you for only a few minutes," he said, too gently, like talking to a little boy. It wasn't meant to be mean. He was just as confused with me as I was. "Pick your brain. You know, you can be a big help in solving this crime."

On the most obvious bookshelves, right behind him, there weren't the kind of study guides and police procedure books I'd expected, the kind of things my mom had been outlining for him. On the top one of the three shelves there were no books at all. There was just a yellow and maroon record player and what must have been four feet worth of little records, smaller than albums, standing next to one another in single file, like he'd ripped the guts out of an old jukebox.

His phone rang.

"Hello. Yes, Director. Yes, fine. And how are you?" he asked, making eyes at me, his winglike brows lifting as another section of his brain lit. "I'm fine. Yeah, yeah. Sure, sir. . . . I'm listening."

The books on the second shelf were brand new, a collection of the classics: Socrates and Sigmund Freud and Malcolm X and Thomas Aquinas and Bob Dylan, maybe twenty in all. The shelf's empty space was filled with more nautical and weather things. The books on the third shelf were all old: a red set of encyclopedias, a set of Children's Golden Book Encyclopedias, their spines ripped, an even older set of military history books. They left just enough empty space for the only photograph in the room, one of his black and white dog, Rover, autographed.

Buddy Wanna-be. When he looked away, I made a sour puss with my mouth, like I had to spit. I wouldn't give him a second break.

"Director, I understand that perfectly. I know we got a new county prosecutor. Oh, I don't need to be told that, sir. Well, sure, sure," he said and gave the director the finger. "Yes. No, go ahead. I know that. Know what? That homicides are investigated by the prosecutor's office. But I know," he said, rolling his eyes, rolling his head. "Ours is a support role and whatever they ask, we help. Whatever the people from the prosecutor's ask, it's theirs. Of course, Director Santana. Of course. No problem. No, not from my end. Well, according to the paper, they valued the help, sir. Yeah, I know it's a new guy," Resto said and tucked the phone under his chin. He held up his hands, palms out, like he was under arrest. "Hands off, hands off, okay. Whatever they ask me to do, I do. If they don't ask me to do anything, then I don't do anything. I know, I know, they got their staff they want to promote, help out, whatever." He folded his upheld open palms into fists, showed them to me, let two middle fingers slowly rise. "No, it's your job, Director. Yeah, no—thank *you*. No, I wouldn't do that. Sure. Yeah, thanks again. Thanks for the call."

Holding the receiver with just his thumb and forefinger, he hung up with a gentle touch. "Damn Puerto Rican," he said softly. "Joey, that's an example of bullshit. This new director, Santana, an affirmative action boy. Freaking Puerto Rican. All this Hispanic shit now," he said, shaking his head. "I don't like to talk like a racist, but that man does not like white people, plain and simple," he said, pointing a loglike finger at me. This was the first time I'd seen him angry. He didn't seem to like being that way, unusual for a cop. "Joey, that's an example of a Hispanic racist for you. It's stupid to look to cause problems. Sometimes you get more flies with honey. Santana, though, he got no tact. The idea of me getting his job after election burns his ass, and now he's got a pal over at the C.P.'s."

He pulled open his right-side drawer. "Everything's race with him. Ah, the hell with him. The world's a complicated damn place, you know?" He laid a red and gold box of candy on his leather blotter. Each candy was wrapped in gold foil. "Take a couple," he said, gesturing with his chin. "These are from Switzerland. You won't get candies like these on Central Avenue."

He stood and went over to the side table where his folders were, and I stuffed a couple of chocolates into my pocket. He brought four more green folders and a notebook back with him. He shuffled the folders and put them on top of the one already there. "Okay," he said. "Down to business." He took a red mechanical pen from a drawer and set himself to write. His arms and his hands, popping with vein ridges, were muscular—to me, more weapons than tools, even though, like they'd spent the previous hour in hot water, the flesh was soft and clean as Pilate's, the fingernails like seashells. "You're a great kid, Joey. Your mom's real proud of you." He looked at me with a warm smile and friendly, encouraging eyes. "Now, tell me what you know about these girls who visited Uncle Mike. That's where you three guys can come in the most helpful."

"What do you want to know?" I asked, uncomfortable with his warmth.

"Well, basic stuff. How many of them were there? Who were they? What do you know about each of them? Any of them nasty?"

"Brian and Clay could tell you a lot better than me. I guess there was almost ten. Maybe not that many. I only knew, like, three or four. Not any of them real good."

"Well, you know Sonia real good."

"Pretty good." I shrugged and slouched, scooting my butt forward in the slippery polished seat. "Not real good. Only a month or two."

"So, who were the other ones you knew?"

I told him as he laid out three chocolates for himself and put the box away, trying to keep his eyes on me as he did.

Natasha Matthews was the one he was interested in. "Tell me what you know about her—when you met her, your impressions, who her friends were, her activities, hobbies, any of that kind of stuff, how many times she was up at Mike's, if anyone ever went with her."

I had my legs spread and my hands in my lap. I pretended to be looking down, but really I was staring at his hands. They got larger and larger. Even though his voice and his face, each time I glanced up, were reassuring, friendly, almost loving, those arms and hands were threatening, what Mr. Rodriguez used to call the stick behind the carrot, what my Aunt Pat used to call the fist behind the kiss.

I barely knew Natasha, and nothing I told him could have meant anything.

"Did you know she was a second cousin or something to that boy we just locked up for homicide? They lived in the same building in the projects. Mr. Buddah Hayes."

"No, I didn't know," I said.

"Well, she was," he said. I looked up and he nodded, seemed to be making a lot out of the connection.

"Yeah, okay," I said, lifting my eyes. "They were second cousins."

Even though I'd never really had a conversation with Natasha, I'd known her much longer than I'd known Sonia. I'd been up the park lots of times when she was there, talking to guys older than me, Brian for one. She had gone to high school and graduated with him. In fact, up until three or four years ago, she was the only black person hanging up the park. She seemed comfortable around us. She grew up and still lives in Hudson Gardens. That was the last project where there was a lot of white people, and when she was a little girl, there must have been plenty of us around, though now, ten years later, out of a hundred-and-something families, maybe half a dozen are white.

"Did you know . . ." he began, scratching his temple with one finger. "Well, let me ask this way. Do you know whether or not she's got a criminal record?"

"Yeah. She was arrested for selling drugs in the park."

"That's right. She was selling heroin. Do you know of anything else? Any other offenses?"

"No. Nothing. I don't know about anything else," I said, shifting in my chair. I could see he was making a point.

"So you don't know about any other criminal activity?"

"No. Nothing."

Natasha was very tall and thin, maybe six feet tall. She liked to wear cutoff T-shirts, grey ones especially, that showed off her belly button, and jeans that hung from her hips higher on one side than the other, like a holster. She had shiny, looping bangs that practically blinded her and a double blob of hair atop her head making her look like a Supreme. She smelled like she'd added an incense packet to her laundry detergent. I didn't tell the physical stuff to Resto. I was sure he knew what she looked like and didn't care how she smelled.

"I know she had corny taste," I said. I didn't know if he'd care about that either, but I remembered my mom telling me not to stick him with yes's and no's.

Resto laughed as he made a little note. He looked like a high-school jock.

"What does that mean?" he asked. "Corny taste?"

"I mean she used to listen to corny music. Mariah Carey, Michael Bolton—what's-her-name—Whitney Houston."

"I thought she listened to jungle music," he said. I wasn't sure what he meant. I thought of Tarzan movies. "I mean *rap*."

"Yeah, she listened to that, too, but that wasn't so weird."

"Michael Bolton and Whitney Houston. And she's a drug dealer and worse. That's coloreds for you—some of them. I bet she'll tell you how she spends Sundays in church, too."

"I know she wanted to start her own business."

"The card thing?" asked Resto.

"Yeah."

"That's a flop," he said.

Our eyes got caught on one another's. Resto didn't like Natasha, that was pretty clear. "You're right," he said, though I hadn't said anything. "I should give her credit. I do give her cred-it. She's still trying."

When she hung up the park she was always talking about starting this greeting card business. A lot of times she brought a little sketch pad with her. She had a whole thick book on greet-ing cards, too, not how to do them, but where to sell them.

Since her park days, she'd even taken a course or two in New York. But that corny taste of hers always got in the way—white cats with big eyes, a black Jesus busting through the clouds, little brown babies in a black Virgin's arms, castles, uni-corns, Martin Luther King. I heard the teachers didn't like her work and she got pissed and quit.

I told Resto what I knew about all that, but he wasn't very interested, concentrating more on unwrapping the last candy on his desk than on anything I said.

"Did she use drugs herself? Not necessarily heroin. Anything?"

"Probably. I don't know."

"Do you know of any reason she'd be frequenting the neighborhood recently?"

"No. I haven't seen her."

"Just a couple more on this. Do you know Hardy Cummings?"

"Just the name."

"What does the name mean to you?" he asked as he savored his chocolate, sucking it more than chewing it.

"He was a bad dude." I shrugged, unimpressed.

"Him and Natasha'd make quite a team, wouldn't they?"

"I don't know," I said, shrugging again. "I don't even know her good."

"Right, right," said Resto.

He asked the names of the other girls, and I gave them to him, but they were even less interesting to him than Natasha's corny cards. All his notes on them, the other three girls combined, took up less than a page, whereas Natasha got a whole page to herself. For a minute, I thought we were through.

He leaned back but held on to his pen, tapping it against his knee.

"How well did Brian and Clay know these girls? Better than you, right?"

"Yeah. They knew them pretty well. I don't think they knew them real well."

"How did they work this? This deal with the girls and Uncle Mike?"

I told him. Clay did the setting up and the appointments, handled the money. Brian brought them there.

He asked me when Brian's relationship with Sonia started. I told him I didn't know what he meant by "relationship."

"Okay, scratch that. Clay was more or less the mastermind?" Resto asked. He flexed his left bicep as he held it with his right hand. He winced like he'd hurt it working out. He loosened the JCPD knit from his shoulders.

"Well, I mean, it seems that way."

"And you've known Clay how long?"

"Just over a year."

"What do you know about him?"

I huffed and told him what I knew, where Clay was from and all.

"No, I mean what's he like? For instance, does he talk about his plans, that sort of thing? He seems like a person who would."

"Plans? I guess. I mean, he has a lot of plans. I mean, I don't spend a lot of time with him."

Resto laughed his king-of-the-prom laugh, the one he figured no one could resist. His eyes shone on me. "Yeah, neither would I. He ain't my cup of tea. But any plans specifically?" he asked and rolled his hands through the air like I could pick from this kind of plan, that kind, whatever. "For instance, about money? Having money, needing money, anything like that?"

"No, nothing like that." I didn't like it and decided that I'd been cooperative enough.

"Do you like him and find him trustworthy?"

"I find him to be okay. He's okay."

"All right, all right. We're about done, Joey. You've been terrific. Last thing," he said and he leaned forward and folded those hands on top of an open folder. "Take me through that night from your point of view, the night Mike was strangled." Did he have to say strangled? "Just tell it, go ahead. You were downstairs at Uncle Vic's. It was you, your mom, your aunt, and Uncle Vic," he said, counting on his fingers.

"Yeah. I think Brian was at Clay's," I said, and as soon as I said it I was sorry I had. "I'm not really sure, though."

"No, that's okay. I'll ask Brian about Brian. You tell me about you."

"Don't you already know all this from my mom?" I asked, half in pleading, half in aggravation.

"It's better that you tell me. That's the way I got to do it," he said with his gentle smile, not his jockish one. "Just take a breath, Joey, relax, and tell me the story. Tell me simple, step by step. Come on, you'll be done in two minutes."

I told him the tale just the way he wanted me to, describing step by step. I left my uncle's and went upstairs. I made sure to mention that I saw the Korean and he saw me. I knocked, I got no answer, I came back down. He nodded throughout. His questions weren't that hard, and my voice never cracked. I was thankful he wasn't as tough on me as I was sure he'd be on others—on Natasha especially, and on Clay and even Brian. I was thankful and relieved but still trembly inside. I don't think I could have held up if he'd decided to push me around. I would have made myself sound guilty when I wasn't. At the end, when he thanked me for helping, meaning I could stand and leave, I said okay, you're welcome.

I opened Resto's door and the heavy smell of the paint made me dizzy, tipped the floor sideways. I touched the wall as I walked through. Brian watched me. When I got out to the end of the hallway, his elbow touched mine as we slid past each other and my relief turned to guilt.

My mom watched Brian all the way down the hall. I caught the end. He knocked on Resto's door and opened it. My mom turned to me. She smiled proudly and bent down, her face in mine. She winked and kissed me on the shoulder. "One down, one to go," were her first words. "You're no little boy anymore, my Joey, are you? You're grown up," she said. I shut my eyes. I almost cried.

FOUR

WHEN I LEFT THE POLICE STATION, ALONE, THE rain had slowed to a drizzle, and by the time I made the walk down the hill from Central Avenue to Palisade, it had stopped. The park was empty, though, and everything wet, the tables puddled, the tree leaves dripping, the cats still hidden under the bandstand. I went home and lay in bed. I read and reread Mr. Rodriguez's letter, or at least tried to. Soon as I got horizontal, my eyes rolled and I slipped into and out of an anxious sleep, worrying each time my neck rolled and my cheek fell onto the pillow that if I passed out I'd be late for the wake. But I was too exhausted to get out of bed and check the kitchen clock. Finally, I fell into a solid stretch of sleep, dreamless and cloud grey, needed but too short, more tied up than covered by my sheet. When I pulled myself from the sleep and lumbered, barefooted and ankles cracking, into the kitchen, it was already ten past one.

As quickly as I could get my socks and sneakers on, I walked back up Hutton to Central, where Himmel's Funeral Home was across the street from High Gate Health and Beauty. Uncle Mike's wake was scheduled for just that one day and for only two hours, one to three. I entered the funeral home through the parking lot, up an outdoor flight of cigarette-butt-littered steps and through the back screen-door entrance. It turned out that even though I got to Himmel's by one-thirty, I was the last one to arrive except for Buddy Resto, who got there a few minutes later. My mom, straight from her training shift at the cafe, was there, and so was Uncle Vic and Aunt Pat and Brian and Sonia. They were all near the front, but the very first row was empty. On the chairs against the side, an old man and an old lady from Uncle Mike's building sat shoulder to shoulder in grey cardigans, experienced enough in wake-sitting to know the room would be cold as an icebox. There were a couple of card players from the park—Walter and Bill Stanis, an uncle and nephew, and a park retard, Chucky, all three of them in Gentlemen's Club black and grey zippered windbreakers—leaving when I got there. That was it. No one else came, and no one, except for Aunt Pat, shed a tear. Even for her it seemed like work, the price of her reputation. No priest or minister ever showed, and so it was up to the old funeral director, the original Himmel, I think, to say a few words about Mike's soul, this brief time on earth, the importance of good deeds, everlasting peace and the kingdom of heaven and all.

The old man's weak words, which came clawing up his throat and fell from his mouth without going very far, only made me think of how alone and unknown Mike really was, at least for these last years when I knew him. For a minute, I got mournful. I thought about the old family picture in Mike's room and of him growing up in Czechoslovakia, and I wondered about the suitcases in his parents' hands. I remembered what I'd been told about his wife and daughter, that they'd both committed suicide less than two years apart, nearly half a century ago, and I remembered Mike telling me about the thirty years he'd worked for Erie-Lackawanna, collecting tickets— "Thirty stinky, son of a bitch years, all of them, every one, Joey." Aunt Pat caught me pondering, and she broke into sobs, but the aggravation of looking at her and her sad-eyed response, like me and her were sharing the moment, put a quick stop to the mourning business.

At 3:05, we headed down the corridor that led to the front porch, where, overhead, the sun had busted through the mixing grey and white clouds. As though he hadn't been allowed in, Clay stood, one foot up on the bottom step, waiting. My mom invited everyone over to our house to have lunch and share some memories of Mike. Resto and my mom and Uncle Vic and me walked down the steps and past Clay. He smiled and nodded sympathetically, but like something was truly funny, too, about the somberness, the clean shaves, the neat clothes, the shock. We turned, backs to the sun, toward Bowers Street. In a group behind us, Brian and Sonia, staring down at the gutter, and Clay and Aunt Pat, lighting Carltons from a shared match, were slow to follow. And there it was, obvious. There were two teams.

Himmel's is half a mile from our house. We came down Bowers past Cambridge, Hancock, Sherman, and Webster, all the way to Palisade. We cut through the park past the WWII Memorial to Ogden, then along it until we crossed the overpass to Uncle Vic's and Uncle Mike's. It's another half a block to our house.

According to my mother, our side of the street, the side that faces Manhattan—though most of the skyline is blocked by the buildings on Uncle Vic's side—was always known for its maples. Since the street's so narrow, trees were only planted on the one side. But in the ten days since school ended, city workers in orange jumpsuits have taken down two more. In the past year, it's been four. And in the past five years, at least ten. Now there are just two maples left on the block. One, down the far end of the block, at South Street, is huge and old, leaves only at the very top, more like a monument than a living thing. The other tree is two doors down from us, toward the park. It's all by itself, but who knows how long it will last. Some of its main limbs are blackened and dry, a few grimy three-year-old leaves still clinging to them. Other branches still look spry enough, though their leaves came late and died young.

At eye level to me, the tree had a football-sized wound where something like Coca-Cola was oozing through the spongy bark. I was expecting the red *X* to appear any day.

Through the whole walk, down Bowers, through the park, along Ogden, the Brian-and-Pat group had been falling further and further behind, like their will to make it to the house was fading with each step. When I turned around, halfway between Uncle Vic's and our house, a few steps behind my mom and Resto and Uncle Vic, they'd disappeared. But there, coming out of Uncle Vic's, was Natasha Matthews. I think I was the only one to see her.

In sandals, tight jeans, and a sleeveless grey T-shirt, she stood on the top step, counting something on her fingers. Tall and lanky and with that hair piled on her head, she looked like a totem pole. She stopped counting when her thumb reached the pointer finger of her second hand and whispered to herself. She ducked back, partly inside, read something off the doorbells, and when she stepped back down to the landing wrote a note in a little assignment book that I imagined had a picture of a white kitty or a corny religious saying on the cover. Rightful as a meter reader, she stood on the landing gathering her thoughts. I figured that no one from either the police department or the prosecutor's office had spoken to her and that, as far as she knew, no one suspected her as the killer. I walked a few more steps, watched my mom and uncle and Resto climb our porch, and turned again to look at Natasha. She tucked her pad into her back pocket and danced down the steps, her arms jangly and long. She skipped like a little girl across the Cobble Road overpass and into the muddy park, shuffling her feet and slowing to a walk as she neared the war monument. There, bulging arms folded across his chest, Hardy Cummings paced back and forth.

Our house, 208 Ogden, is a drab one made even more sad looking by the new "Reduced for Quick Sale, Call Mr. Henry" sign and phone number that was pasted across the "House for Sale by Owner" sign that had been wired to the fence for the past four months. It is a yellow two-family house with brown-painted concrete porch steps and columns and a malt-brown-painted iron fence. To the one side, the house is connected to another exactly the same. To the other side, the Bowers Street side, is an alleyway before another pair of identical houses. Four of these pairs of different-colored vinyl-covered houses make up the center of the block.

Our house, like all the paired houses in that stretch, is narrow, like the builders had cut off a few feet from each one so they could fit in four pairs instead of three. Fortunately, ours is the side of the pair that has the sun all afternoon, as much of the sun as can slip down the four-foot-wide alley. Even for High Gate, it's a beat-up and embarrassing little strip of neighborhood, leaning each year a little more toward the slope and a tumble down the hill.

We'd gotten pretty used to having the house to ourselves since, in the eight years we'd been there, the downstairs apartment had been empty more than half of the time. You couldn't blame the current landlord, who was pretty average. He didn't bother you if you didn't bother him. The only tenants I really got to know was the family that lived here last. They had an Italian name, Greco, but were from somewhere in South America. The mother could speak three languages, and the daughter, Allina, could speak good English, pretty good Spanish, and curse words in Italian. I never met the father, Giac, pronounced Jock, because he was in jail. Sometimes, according to the way Allina told it, the reason for the tough sentence was the drugs, sometimes it was the guns. The main reason I knew them so well was because of Allina. I was thirteen and a little bit of fourteen when they lived here. Allina was good looking. With a dark complexion and eyes that could change color and puffy red lips, she looked like she was always about to cry and was probably even shyer than me. But I'd known Marcy, Allina's best friend, longer and had always had a crush on her. Because of Marcy, I never knew how to act around Allina, who I'd see practically every day, and mostly wound up ignoring her. Then the Grecos moved out suddenly, right after my Columbus Day birthday, before I ever had a chance to act on what I was thinking and imagining in terms of the girlfriend thing. Allina rang our doorbell and asked me to come down to the porch. She had on a grey sweater with pink flowers embroidered across the chest. She was the same size as me. She had catlike eyes and brows that nearly grew together above her nose. Her eyes were a grey-green that day. She gave me a card that said "Goodbye to my dear friend" in three languages and three colors of ink, and she had dotted the "i" in friend and Allina with a colored-in red heart. I swallowed the lump in my throat. "Thanks," I said and smiled, all fucked up.

FIVE

SETTLED IN OUR SHOEBOX SHAPED KITCHEN, ME, Uncle Vic, and Resto around the table, we all picked Coke when my mom gave the choice. She set down the cans after wiping them dry with a dishtowel, then dumped a whole bag of Cheese Doodles into a white plastic bowl. She turned the oven on and went to the freezer, where she pulled out a tray of Stouffer's Baked Macaroni and Cheese, an aluminum tray that was the size of a painter's roller pan.

Me and Resto sat across from one another. Uncle Vic was between us at the table's end, the refrigerator close enough behind that when he tipped his chair back he could lean against it. He tugged up his pants legs, bunching the material at the knee and showing more of his white socks, then squished out his cigar in the NY Giants Superbowl XXIII ashtray on the table.

"So what do you hear, Buddy? What do you know?" To make up for being a miniature man, Uncle Vic always boomed his words, his questions even louder than his statements, and when he asked those two of Resto, his voice was big enough to be heard anywhere in the house, empty downstairs included. Sometimes the words started coming out more quickly, too. "You got it solved, Buddy? What's the status of the investigation?" asked Uncle Vic, biting down on his unlit White Owl, folding his arms across his chest, tipping back his chair. "Come on, Mr. Lieutenant. What do you hear? Status?"

"The status? Jesus. Everything's still possible, but, you know, nothing real solid. Not just yet."

"Someone he knew or a stranger?" bellowed Uncle Vic. Bent and stiff, with the skin stretched to a shine around his swollen knuckles, the first two fingers of his right hand curled as if a cigar was still hanging between them.

92

"If I guessed, I'd say someone he knew," said Resto, crunching a Doodle after he tapped off some orange.

"One of the girls visiting," said Uncle Vic. "One of the girls and her friendies, ain't it? You know what I'm talking about."

"Maybe, Vic. It's possible," Resto said and he folded his clean, strong hands on the table like a schoolkid.

"Uncle Vic, leave Buddy alone," said my mom. As she turned away from the stove, she brushed ice crumbs from the Stouffer's box off the counter and into her palm and wiped her hands dry on her butt. "He's restricted. You should know that."

"It's a dirty business, ain't it, Buddy?" said my uncle.

"Yeah, Vic," said Resto, laughing.

My mom checked the macaroni and cheese so soon after putting it in the pan that it hadn't even begun to thaw. She took the chair from out by the phone and brought it to the table. Me and my uncle pushed aside to fit her in. Because the kitchen was so narrow, squeezed by the stairway, we had to set the table longways against the window wall.

"I guess they ain't coming," said Uncle Vic, looking toward the front of the house.

"No, I guess not," my mom said. She looked at Resto and made a gesture toward her mouth, thumb and pointer together, like smoking a joint.

"They're too lazy to walk up a flight of stairs," said Uncle Vic. He'd said that many times before.

"Hey, how was your first day, Susan? God, I didn't even ask you," said Resto.

"Great, but it's not over yet," said my mom. "I go back in a couple of hours. Everything was great." She touched her round, schoolgirl-styled hair with all ten fingers. It all moved at the same time. "Everything was great except for this hair," she said, and she frowned like the sad sack in a Revlon commercial. "I hate it!" she screamed out of the blue, her face tight and her nails poised above the 'do, ready to dig and yank.

Resto leaned back and laughed. Me and my uncle just leaned back.

"You got to work a regular shift tonight?" I asked.

"Yeah. They asked me to. Five to nine."

"They liked you and you liked them?" asked Resto.

"Yeah," said my mother, showing surprise and enthusiasm. "I really did. They're not that different. Some of them are funny." She pointed at Buddy, then stood up. "I got something for you," she said. On top of the refrigerator, next to the chips and pretzel bags, were the two books Resto had given her to study and, under them, a spiral notebook, the thick kind that are for three subjects. She took down just the notebook, laid it in front of Buddy, and opened it to the first page, a red number one in a black circle in the upper right.

"Wow!" he screeched like someone who's just opened up his first copy of *Girls Behind Bars*. But it was the work my mother had done. "God damn, Susan, you're unbelievable. How did you do this?" he asked, his voice high in amazement.

"I guess my insomnia's paying off for you."

There were at least twelve pages of neatly written notes, mistakes whited out, each page so perfectly outlined that the words could have sat steady atop one another even if the paper'd been pulled out from under them.

"This is so much. It's *so* much, Susan. With everything else— work, Uncle Mike, your college test. What about that, your test?"

"Oh, don't feel guilty. That's the way I do everything. Anyway, I enjoyed doing it," she said, tapping the notebook like a new but dear friend. "I only missed a couple of days of my studying. I should do fine."

She got up from the table while Buddy was in the middle of looking at her and took the half-empty bowl of Cheese Doodles with her. Stepping in behind Uncle Vic, she opened the refrigerator to get a shiny bowl of red grapes. She put them on the table.

One-handed, like he was showing off a skill, Uncle Vic plucked a few and shoved them in his mouth three at a time. "Come on, Buddy, tell it. What's the motive? Robbery, you think? That's what I think." Buddy just stared at him, dumb and blank. He'd keep staring until Uncle Vic changed the subject.

"Eh, he won't talk," Uncle Vic complained to my mom. He grabbed a book of matches from beside the ashtray, held them in one hand, the cigar in the other. Him and Buddy stared at each other. "Come on, I'm alone in this apartment building," said

Uncle Vic. "I got my worries, too, you know. This killer could strike again."

"We know, Uncle Vic, believe me. We know and we haven't forgotten about you," said my mom, head tipped, eyes gentle.

Uncle Vic lit the cigar and eyed my mother, troubled that this thought had crossed her mind, too.

"We can't say what the motive was for sure," said Resto.

"It's got to be robbery, don't it?" demanded my uncle. "All those bonds gone."

"You're probably right, but whoever went up there went up prepared to kill him."

"Meaning what?" asked Uncle Vic, his face whitened, his eyes glancing from person to person.

"Meaning it wasn't an incidental killing. The killer wasn't carrying around cable to hook up Mike's TV."

"Hmm. Strangled the bastard. Had to be a man, strong enough to strangle a man. Had to be a man, Buddy," Uncle Vic said, his hand turned over so the lit end of the cigar was pointing at himself, the mouthed end at Buddy.

"A man or a very strong woman, or any two people."

"A maniac, man or woman, is what I say."

"Yeah, to kill a dog," I said, shaking my head as I remembered finding Prince dead, his neck twisted.

I knew what I said sounded fucked up, a man and a dog killed and me thinking that killing the dog was weird, but I said it anyway. It was true. It did seem weirder. I shoved some grapes in my mouth to keep from saying anything else retarded.

"I think the person was testing on Prince, to see if he, or she, could actually do it," said my mom. "Do a killing. Prince was the test."

"Hey, I got money in my apartment, too, you know," said Uncle Vic, tipping his chair against the refrigerator, holding up a grape for us to see as though there were something true inside it.

"We know, Uncle Vic," said my mom, nodding at Resto. "We know," mouthed Resto.

"Susie, what do you mean you know? *You know?*"

"Buddy and me talked about it," she confessed. "I told you long ago you should put your money in a bank."

95

"Oh shit," said Uncle Vic. "Don't be a worrier like me when you grow up, Joey. Be happy. Smell the roses for once."

Uncle Vic's money wasn't nearly as much as Uncle Mike's, three or four thousand in twenties plus another couple of hundred in change and loose bills. But his was cash, not bonds, an open invitation.

Coming over to him, "Oh, Uncle Vic, we'll take good care of you," my mom said. "You got me and Joey and Buddy and Brian. We're all looking out for you. You're safe as can be," she said and she rubbed his shoulder like he was a toddler.

Uncle Vic stood and unbuckled his pants, straightened what needed straightening like a man's man, spit in the sink as he passed it, ran the water to wash it down. He disappeared down the hallway and into the living room. My mom went back to complaining about her hair, how after thirty years of the same haircut it might be time for something new. Probably because he agreed, Resto changed the subject. He opened up the notebook, shook his head admiringly. "I really can't believe it," he said, smiling, turning the light on in his eyes.

"Look at this," called Uncle Vic from the front room. "Look at this and tell me I'm not seeing what I think I'm seeing." We walked into the living room. Uncle Vic was standing at the right side window, the one that was aimed at the park. "I hope I'm wrong on this one, but I don't think so."

The living room was shaped like a stop sign, except squeezed, narrower. On the wall, above the two armchairs, was a long mirror framed in gold-painted wood with shelves for knicknacks—a picture of my mother's mother and father, a picture of me and Brian, no picture of my mom but an award she'd gotten as the best student when she graduated grammar school, Saint Paul of the Cross, and lots of swans and such with nets of hard candy that my mom had brought home from friends' weddings. On the opposite wall, above the couch, was a framed picture of a colonial days man and woman dancing in a pink and white room. They were dressed in ballroom outfits, their arms arched, hands held together high, by the fingertips. The title, *The Minuet*, was on a brass plate screwed into the bottom center of the frame. At one end of the couch there was a small table with a lamp and another, almost the same, between the two windows. On a cart at the room's front, set in a bay made by the three windows, was the TV, the remote, and the *TV Guide,* with the CD player and the CDs, all ten of them, underneath.

Uncle Vic stepped back. I looked out the window and my mom squeezed in against me.

"If they're doing what I think they're doing, so help me," warned Uncle Vic. "If she's introduced that boy to drugs, don't let me get a hold of her."

I squeezed more to the side, off my mom's hip. In the still-wet park, around the table nearest Cobble Road, were Brian, Sonia, Clay, and Aunt Pat. Natasha and Hardy were gone.

Sonia, the bloodless thing, was always cold and had on an oversized flannel shirt. Aunt Pat was in the sundress she'd worn to the wake—a strapless powder blue number with an elastic top, all pleats and ruffles from the waist down. Clay was sitting on top of the table, and my aunt, her back to us, stood behind him, running a brush through his luxurious hair. Brian was sitting opposite them on a table bench, Sonia resting her head on his shoulder. He was puffing on the remains of a joint and snapped his fingers like he'd burned them. Just as I stepped away from the window, he reached out to hand the joint to my aunt.

Uncle Vic was still muttering about drugs and Aunt Pat, but when Resto took the spot next to my mom, he gave her a look like it was no big deal.

"That's pot, Uncle Vic, marihuana," said my mom without turning. "Believe me, everybody does it."

"Oh, is that so? And that makes it okay? One thing leads to another in this world. Am I right, Buddy?"

Resto stepped back from the window, lifted my mom's hand from the sill to bring her with him. "Vic, it ain't the drugs. Like Susan says, it's all over. You ain't gonna stop it. You just gotta watch it. It ain't the drugs so much as it is all the things around it," he said and pointed his finger at the ceiling and spun a circle around it with his other hand. "They know the rules—keep it in the park, leave the little kids alone, no robbing, no harassing, no begging, and no noise. And *don't* start bringing in a bunch of you-know-whats from the outside."

"Aw, come on," said Uncle Vic. "This is hard drugs. Ain't you heard?" He flopped down into a chair, his feet tipped forward so his toes reached the floor. "What happened to this neighborhood all of a sudden? Drugs in the park. All out in the open. Nobody's safe," he said, his hands on his lap, his eyes tied to the floor. Resto and my mom headed for the kitchen. Uncle Vic's words got louder and louder. "What's becoming? Buddy?" he called. He glanced up at me. "A dead dog. A dead dog, Joey. Prince," he said softly, pleading. "Joey, you know what I mean. Prince. Prince, Joey, Prince. We loved that dog, didn't we?"

SIX

MY MOM GOT IN LATE THAT NIGHT FROM HER FIRST shift at the Pioneer—must have been past midnight when I heard her and saw the kitchen light flick on—but she was up early and out of the house before I woke the next morning. I got dressed after my shower, and, when I came out to the kitchen, Aunt Pat, who'd spent the night on the living room couch, under *The Minuet*, was sweeping the floor, barefooted and wearing the faded nightshirt she'd slept in. On the table, there was a beer mug with an inch of Coke next to another mug filled with orange juice. "Go ahead," said Aunt Pat. "I poured it for you."

Also on the table was a note from my mom in a sealed envelope. As I ripped it open, my aunt stopped sweeping to catch eyes with me and smirk at my mother's secrecy. "Joey," the note said. "They asked me to come in again this morning, eight until noon. They get a busy morning crowd and then a late-at-night crowd. Great tips! Here's a list of what we need from the Acme. After my shift, I'm going to Uncle Vic's to put in a new door lock. Come by to help if you want. Mom."

Aunt Pat was sweeping with her back to me, the thin, pink nightshirt barely covering her panties. "There's a message on the machine, too," she said. "Tell your mom I didn't play it. Obviously I'm not welcome to." She wiped her forehead dry with her bare shoulder and reached to fluff her nightshirt from her sticky back. "Phoo. I'm pooped." She bent and grabbed low on the broom handle to push the schmutz into the pan. I hit the message flasher.

"Call for Joey Scadutto, all points bulletin for Mr. Joseph Scadutto. This is Mr. Rodriguez. I haven't heard from you, yo. I told you in my letter we have another Wagon Train planned very soon, very soon. Little more than a week, baby cakes. Hello, earth to Joey. Move your butt, now, just do it, man. Oh yeah, Marcy is definitely coming. She'll be disappointed if you're not there. Also Felix, Kerri, and Lanniqua. You coming or what, gringo? Or is it gringa maybe? Call me, Joey. Call me at my school number. I'll get the message, man. Don't wait, it'll be too late."

Leaning on the broom like sweeping had been her proud profession for fifty years, "Ooh, boy, sounds fantastic," said Aunt Pat. "Don't you have any white friends?"

"I hardly got any friends. They're just kids I know."

"Did that guy say Wagon Train? I could hardly understand his English. What's he, Puerto Rican?"

"Yeah, Rodriguez. And, yeah, the thing's called Wagon Train. It's a program." I pressed the flasher again to erase the message. "Don't worry, I ain't going."

"I know, honey. I know you wouldn't. What you doing this morning, babe?"

I told her about the Acme and she said she'd walk with me. We'd stop for breakfast at the Al'n Mo. Happier than she should have been that I accepted the offer, Aunt Pat quickly changed clothes and washed her face, came out of the bathroom with a bloody tip to the chin pimple she'd scratched at. We went downstairs, me first. I opened the outside door before the inside one was shut and the blow-through pushed open the door to the downstairs apartment. I peeked into the staleness and eerie still behind it and pulled the knob until I heard it click.

Sonia was sitting on the porch, finishing off a buttered roll and coffee, her knees together, a magazine resting on them. There was something New York about her and it wasn't just the magazine—a thick, glossy one, *Soho Interiors*, that must have cost ten dollars and that I was sure she'd ripped off. She heard us and turned, shut the magazine, smiled big, raised her arms for a hug. Aunt Pat wiggled forward to her, bent, and the two of them embraced. "Sony," like the electronics maker, my aunt called her when she invited Sonia along to the Al'n Mo. Too thick to roll up, Sonia tossed the magazine into our hallway.

Aunt Pat first met Sonia after I had, not more than a month or two ago, and back then, not so far back, they couldn't stand one another, Sonia seeing my aunt as white trash, Aunt Pat seeing Sonia as a skinny Puerto Rican whore. Or maybe it was the other way around—Sonia seeing my aunt as the whore, my aunt seeing her as trash. But now those impressions had changed. They'd opened their hearts to one another and bonded big time, a little showy with it but genuine, the way only drug addiction or twin nervous breakdowns can make men bond. By the time we'd begun the walk up the Hutton Street hill, they'd shown me just how powerful sisterhood could be.

Barely past nine o'clock, it was still cool, just seventy degrees, and we stayed on the sunny side of Hutton. Until you crossed Sherman and reached Saint Paul of the Cross church, this stretch was mostly commercial garages and empty lots patrolled by guard dogs that loped through the weeds and the debris and their own shit like starved wolves.

All the way up the hill, Aunt Pat delivered to Sonia a history of our neighborhood, which was really her history of white America brought down to square-mile size. Even though Sonia and her mom's apartment in the Hoboken projects was walking distance from ours, she had never hung out with a mostly white crowd before, and even though Aunt Pat had had plenty of dealings with Puerto Ricans, here was one who'd actually listen.

"The people on these two blocks here, where we're coming to," said my aunt as she pointed down Webster Avenue, "I don't know what it was, maybe just the twinch of fate, but oh my God, they were really, really stupid. Ignorant *and* dumb. They always got left back, every one of them. Fifteen, sixteen years old in eighth grade. I bet their kids are like them, too."

"No shit," said Sonia. "We had the same kind of block where I was growing up, uptown, before we moved to the projects. Really dumbass people. And nasty. Why dumb people have to be so nasty, too? I hated them people."

Sonia and my aunt could have been mother and daughter, except that there was too much goodwill and elbow-rubbing between them. Like me, both of them were on the little and skanky side, Aunt Pat not so little and not as skanky as when she was younger. In addition to the now-balloonish butt, her shoulders were beefy, her legs fat in the thighs but still skinny below the knee. Sonia was built like a twelve-year-old boy—ankles nothing but joint and tendon, shapeless legs, boney shoulders, always those raspberry nipples pushing against her shirt—but inside her there was something wild and urgent as a fire under attack that made her real sexy.

At the next corner, Aunt Pat spoke: "Twenty-five years ago, Sherman Avenue used to be nothing but doctors' and lawyers' offices. Shingle Row, we called it. And beautiful trees. I would go up and down this block for no reason, go out of my way," she said with a Puerto Rican-style hand gesture, a sort of maestro's quick loop and a line drive. "It was oaks and elms and what else, chestnut trees, apple trees. They had an orange grove and whatnot down there, where all those tires are stacked."

Uh-huh. Whatever you say.

We stayed on the sunny side of Hutton on up past Saint Paul's—the church, the rectory, the convent. We were just about to Central, which looked not so bleak as usual on such a clear and clean morning, when Aunt Pat grabbed hold of Sonia's hand and explained what had happened to the avenue, what the malls had done to it, how it had happened all over New Jersey. She said, "That's why to this day I hate malls with a passion. This here was the heart and soul. Man, what happened to the trust, to looking out for each other's kids? Why? You know what I mean?"

Yeah, and what had happened to helping old ladies across the street, to dropping some change in the March of Dimes can, to fighting clean, to picking up after yourself? They'd been fucked. Why? I didn't know. I'd never been there.

We were in front of High Gate Health and Beauty—yeah, Aunt Pat, and what had happened to High Gate Pharmacy—waiting to cross, when from the diagonal corner, a woman called. "Hey, Scadutto. Yo, Patty." It was a meter maid. She'd stopped in the middle of writing out a ticket for a taxi double-parked outside Pitboy Subs and Salads.

"Hiya, April. Hey, girl," waved Aunt Pat as she steered us in the other direction. "Fat bitch," she mumbled.

April moved to get the plate number off the back of the car, and she glanced over to check my aunt's reaction, though the white foam brace on her neck made turning a whole-body chore.

April walked with a limp. She couldn't bend her right knee and was able to tip her body just enough to pass her right foot over the street. As she tried to mount the curb, she had to drop her hand onto the cab's hood. She leaned her weight that way, rocking the car, and swung her right leg onto the sidewalk. Cool out as it was, her face and neck glistened with sweat. The foam brace looked like it was choking her and her wraparound sunglasses were pressed into her swollen face. She wrote out the ticket and, with the butt of her left hand, knocked off the sweat bubble dangling from her nose as if she was chasing away a mosquito.

"Fat bitch," laughed my aunt. "She was lucky to get that job. That job should have been mine, fifteen years ago. But I wouldn't get on my back for it like her. April was a beauty contest runner-up when she was a kid. What a body. And tits!" Right, and the neighborhood used to be built on trust and we all looked out for each other's kids.

"Then a month after she gets the job—I still had my license then and *I* wasn't bad looking either—I'm double-parked and talking to this guy who had a tryout with the Jets and whatnot. April's in one of the hotdog-wagon-type things they used to drive," explained my aunt as we crossed Central, away from April. She must have known we were talking about her and had turned her back to us. "April starts beeping the goddamn shit out of me. I look in the mirror and the bitch is giving me the finger, yelling, 'Move it, move it. Let's go, move it *now*!' It was the '*now*' that got me, the way she said it. April was a very shrill person in everything like. So I got out of the car, nice and slow, and when she recognized me I put the death stare on her 'cause we both knew full well if we fought I'd leave with her eyeballs." A few steps short of the Al'n Mo, she grabbed on to our hands so she could finish her story. "So she sees it's me and her tits shrink. I'll never forget it. It was one of my great days. All of a sudden, she's sweet and embarrassed, giggling and apologizing, as if we ever really liked one another. Fuck you, I said to myself, and just made her wait in that hot wagon until I made my date with Willie." Aunt Pat put her hands on her hips and shook her head with all the nostalgia she felt for her old self. "She knows me, she knows I haven't forgotten. Look at her, look. Sweat. Sweat, you fat pig."

Probably because changing their prices would mean getting a replacement for the front window's paint-on-white-metal sign, the cost of an Al'n Mo breakfast hadn't gone up in years:

2 EGGS ANY STYLE
W/POTATOES AND TOAST $1.30
FREE COFFEE REFILLS
ONLY AT THE AL'N MO GRILL
OPEN 365 1/4 DAYS PER YEAR
YOUR SATISFACTION IS OUR BUSINESS

The owners, Al and Mo Grammachi, were a pair of sixty-ish doo-wop fanatics with thick, silvery grey hair and moustaches. They seemed to think that the world hadn't changed since the day Elvis went into the army, the same day that they got discharged and bought the restaurant. Al and Mo lived in the second- and third-floor apartments above the restaurant, and, up until I was twelve, my mom had me believing that, except to walk to the corner to buy a newspaper, in all those years they hadn't left the building—the restaurant, or the apartments upstairs, or the tiny yard in back that had not just chain-link walls but a chain-link roof, too, set even with the base of the first-floor windows, making a cage of it.

"Duke of Earl" came from the silver cassette player and radio set next to the little cereals on a shelf behind the counter. I held the door open for Sonia and my aunt. Everybody in the place, owners, cooks, and customers, turned to make sure I firmly pushed the door, all the way shut. Al Grammachi was sitting at the cash register doing the *Daily News* Jumble. Mo was trying to explain to the cook what eggs florentine was though it was pretty clear that he wasn't too sure himself. Al's oldest daughter, Flo, was the waitress. Flo was my mom's age and lived two blocks away from the restaurant with her boyfriend and their combined four kids. She had a younger sister, Betty, who'd gone to college and moved out of Jersey City when she was through, and moved not to Bergen or Monmouth County either. She had moved to Cambridge, Massachusetts, was still unmarried at twenty-eight, and dressed, they said, like she wanted to stay that way. Betty never called, only wrote postcards. There was a younger brother, too, Phil. Phil was a year younger than Betty, ten years younger than Flo. He was 19-11-5 as a light-heavyweight. He lived upstairs with his mom and dad and boxed, I figured, because he'd rather get his brains beat than work in the restaurant.

At the front tables, facing Central Avenue and the police station directly across the street, were four elderly white couples dressed in Atlantic City rainy-day gear. At the counter were four men, evenly spaced, two white, two black, two in their thirties, two in their sixties, eating from plates smeared with ketchup and eggs. Of the five booths opposite the counter, two were taken. At the first one was a scroungy-looking guy in green Converse and a worn white T-shirt, probably the eggs florentine customer, probably a migrant from HouseRAD, writing notes in a half-sized spiral pad. Two tables behind him, waiting for the A.C. bus to arrive and the front tables to open up, was Boy Evans.

Boy was from a local family, the fourth of six kids with a range of ages that stretched from my mom's to mine. One of Boy's older sisters, Terry, used to hang with my aunt. Now she practically lived in the psych unit of Christ Hospital. She seemed to have found a balance in her life, following several months of heavy drug use with two or three months of electroshock-therapy stupor, the EST being a good fallback, much better than counselling, since its cost was covered by Medicaid, and besides, Terry had come to think of it as a kind of high. Boy had his own problems with booze and drugs, speed and angel dust especially, later on with LSD. When he dropped out of high school at sixteen, it was only a matter of months before he was mainstreamed into detox and detention, and the only work he'd ever been known to do in all the years since was panhandling along Central Avenue. It was during those panhandling years, four or five or six years ago, that he got booted out of Bowers Street Park for pulling a lot of dumbass stunts that involved owing people money and lying to his friends. Not being allowed in the park was a hard thing for Boy, making him the leper the lepers wouldn't touch. He still walked around staring at people, all paranoid, like he expected any minute to have his ass kicked or to be humiliated some other way for something he was sure he was guilty of but had forgotten about.

"Tell Terry I love her," said my aunt as we passed Boy on our way to the back table. "Just tell her, 'Ever Together.' She'll remember."

"Truly. Sure will, Patty. Truly will," he said, a clenched fist in the air. Boy's light brown hair hung in strings to his eyebrows. He had light blue, acid eyes with swirling funnels for pupils, a sharp, once-broken nose, teeth of all shapes and colors, and a greasy cleft chin.

Boy's life was made more miserable because he was broke most of the time, and so, even when he didn't have that expecting-to-have-my-ass-kicked hunch to his shoulders, there was still a more general ashamed something in the way he carried himself, a something that came along with being dependent on a handout, from family or welfare or a stranger on the street, a handout to get him by day to day. Boy still panhandled along Central Avenue, except now it was for nicotine, caffeine, Instant Lottery, the occasional quart of Miller, not hard drugs.

"Hi, Joey," he said as I passed and he held out a hand, making me stop and turn back to shake. "Say hi to Brian and your mom."

Boy no longer had much in the way of scams going on either. The only one I knew of was that he'd get rid of handguns for a group of cops when they needed a few extra bucks. Just over a year ago he was charged with selling a confiscated pistol to a thin-haired egg-shaped cardplayer named Bobby Harding, one of the guys responsible for getting Boy thrown out of the park back when. The case was dropped, though, when it became pretty clear that Boy hadn't sold Harding the gun, that he'd given it to him as a gift at a time when a bunch of seventeen- and eighteen-year-olds from Union City were looking to kick his ass. Ripping people off to give away his profits, you couldn't say Boy had a soft heart. More like he had a torn one, the two parts never speaking.

I left Boy and slid into our booth, across from the two of them, me facing the front. No sooner had I sat down than Aunt Pat pointed a wicked finger at me. "You," she said. "You know what I want to talk to you about."

SEVEN

Y EAH, I KNEW. AS SOON AS SHE POINTED HER FINGER,
I knew. If Aunt Pat held such a grudge against shopping
malls and April, what real hate must she feel for Buddy
Resto.

From the coffeepots behind the counter, Flo called to Aunt
Pat and held up one finger. Aunt Pat looked at Sonia. Sonia nodded her head. My aunt called back to Flo. "No. Two," she said and
held up two fingers.

She wiped some corn muffin crumbs from the table,
dumped them on the floor.

"What did Buddy Asshole have to say?" she asked. "You
know, that's supposed to be the prosecutor's case, not his."

"You know why he wants the case, don't you?" said Sonia.

"Yeah. He wants the credit for solving it. Buddy
Headlines. Buddy Big Plans. Creep," bitched my aunt. "What did
he ask you?"

"He wanted to know a lot about Natasha Matthews."

Sonia and Aunt Pat knew as much about the case against
Natasha as I did. They knew about the Buddah Hayes connection—that he was her cousin—they knew about her record, they
knew Clay hadn't set her up with Uncle Mike in more than a
month. And they knew one thing I hadn't known: She'd been seen
in the building last week, once with her boyfriend, Hardy
Cummings, once without him. They also said she was broke, that
she'd given up on her greeting card thing, and that she needed
money bad. The last part was probably something the two of
them had just made up, but probably something that was true as
well.

"And so who else did he ask about?" asked Sonia.

Before I answered, Flo came over to deliver the two coffees

107

and to take our order. *The Name Game* came on the radio. Aunt Pat introduced Sonia as "Sunny, my new baby sister," and Sonia blushed and sneaked a peek at me.

Sonia and my aunt ordered egg sandwiches. I ordered a corn muffin and lemonade. Aunt Pat and Flo made some small talk, just tone and gestures to me. I was more tuned in to Sonia, and Boy at the table behind her. Sonia sat with her shoulders hunched and hands in her lap. Her mouth was closed tight as she eyed the conversation, anxious about something, just waiting. Boy, in the background, finger-read the crime page of the newspaper. Knocking his knees, occasionally shivering in the air-conditioner's cold draft, he hunched over the *Jersey*, squinting, lips moving, intense and nutty-seeming, reacting to the articles like someone was secretly whispering them to him.

"Joey . . . Joey," said Aunt Pat, calling my attention after Flo had left. "So what else did he say? What more'd he want to know?"

I wasn't certain exactly what she was driving at, if she was asking for herself or was working for Brian or Clay, if there were pieces she had that I didn't, if her pieces were the same as Sonia's, whose eyes, wherever they landed, were less steady than usual.

"I don't know what you're talking about," I said, but I said it too much like an accusation, and they both took it like I saw them, not Resto, as the interrogators. They were annoyed with me, saw I was stalling.

"You know what we mean," demanded Sonia, pushing herself forward for the first time.

"Yeah, Joey. What'd he ask about Brian and Clay?"

Except for Boy's lifted eyes, we were drawing no attention from the restaurant, everyone's head down like a sleeping spell had been cast.

"He asked about them, too," I said.

They stared, nodded, waited me out.

While they were silent, "Joey, Joey, bo-boey, banana-fana fofoey, fee-fi-mo-moey. Jo-ey," wiggled from the radio.

"He asked how they worked it with the girls. He asked how well I knew Clay, what I knew about him. He asked about you, like how long I knew you, about you and Brian."

Sonia and my aunt glanced at each other, shaking their heads, thinking the same thoughts. It was Aunt Pat who spoke. "He thinks it was Brian and Clay," she said.

"No way," I said, waving my hand at her. "He thinks it's Natasha. That's definite."

"I don't believe that suspecting Natasha shit," said Sonia.

"Well, I do," I said.

"He's hoping you're stupid enough to say something about Brian and Clay," she said.

Aunt Pat was having some trouble breathing, wheezing. It sounded like there was a ghost trapped in her lungs. She pressed one hand to her chest, touched the other against her neck's pulse.

"Say something? Say what?" I asked Sonia.

"I don't know. Something. Looka, I know Brian had nothing to do with it."

"Yo, and neither did Clay," shot back my aunt, her wrinkled red hand still pressing her chest.

"I didn't mean that. I meant I can only speak for who I can speak for *directly*," said Sonia, reaching toward but not touching Aunt Pat's hand. "I mean, Joey, you don't even know what you're telling him. You might implicate your own ass. You was the last one up there, you know."

"Except for the killer, I was. What could I say? What that would get anybody in trouble?"

"How he'll take it, I mean. See. You don't know how he'll take what you say, what you might think is nothing."

"I'm not . . . I . . . oh, fuck it. I'm not stupid, Sonia." But what her and my aunt said had hit me. My head filled with heat. The heat cooled to fear, a knot of it in my throat, a near throw-up that came with tears. "I'm not a child," I wanted to say but didn't think I could get the words out.

"Looka, Joey," said Aunt Pat, her right hand off her chest, her left hand back to her neck, touching the pulse like she was reading her meter. "He's a bastard and he's putting your mom in a very bad situation. It looks very bad to people what she's doing." She formed the words slow and soft but by the time they got up her clenched throat they'd hardened, and they came out of her mouth separated, one by one, whispery but scratched. "You got to help her see the situation. Her judgement, man. Think, Joey. You don't see it. Think about what's happening here."

"She knows what she's doing," I said, trying to hide behind the words.

"Omph, right. Right," said my aunt, throwing her head back. Forgetting about her pulse. Fucking her pulse. "She thinks what? She's going to be a police captain's wife, that she's moving up and whatnot. Fat fucking chance." Throbbing green-blue veins bulged from her neck like a special effect, and you could see the irrigation right into her jaw, nearly to her mouth.

"She's your moms, Joey. You got to help her," said Sonia.

"She don't need help," I said, angry, at what I wasn't sure. "Not yours."

"Joey," said Aunt Pat. "He's a scumbag and he's using your mother to get information on Brian and Clay, and maybe on you, too. Sonia's right." She was showing too much pep to have taken her methadone that morning. Triple doses of caffeine had buzzed her brain, lit it on fire. Her muscles, the ones that worked her jaw and throat and tongue, tried to keep up but they'd never ever work all the hard drugs out. Spit-slopped and slurred, the words squirted from her lips like half-chewed candy. "He's at your house every freaking day now, snooping," she said, the last word coming out "schneurpen."

"Think about what this is doing to Brian," said Sonia, placing her hand on mine. "He's your brother. You got to show *some* loyalty."

I tried to think what it was doing to him, but I had no clue. "Doing to *Brian?*" I said. It wasn't something I'd thought about before.

"Yes. Think about it, Joey. They're putting pressure on him."

"Resto's playing Susie, your mother, in a big fucking game, can't you see it, Joey? He's not interested in *her*," said Aunt Pat, her eyes popping like a Bulgie doll's. Like her neck's had, the veins along the back of her hands rose up. The old needle marks, spots where death had arrived, showed up a shiny, pale pink against the darker hills. "You think it's coincidence that all this love affair's happening now? Don't make me fucking laugh, man.

Huh," she laughed, a hard, loud cackle.

Boy looked up and looked back down, looked up and looked down, played his fingers over the back of his other hand. Nodded at me for no reason I understood. Flo whispered something to her father—he was upset, about what I wasn't sure, maybe my aunt and her history and her language—then she came to us carrying three plates.

A huge red-and-black Atlantic City bus pulled up outside and the old folks stirred, like fairy dust had been sprinkled, their souls strengthened enough to wake up their bodies.

"Two sandwiches for the ladies. A corn muffin for the young man. Anything else?" asked Flo. "Then, there you go. Take your time, folks."

"Thanks, Flo," said my aunt. She wiped the white saliva pasted to her dry lips with her knuckles.

Flo put her right hand on the table, leaned on it. Making sure her back was flush to Boy and the guy behind him, Flo nodded her head in the direction of the HouseRAD. "He ordered the eggs florentine—and tea black," she said, her lips pursed and eyebrows raised like she was so impressed.

A little laugh popped through Aunt Pat's lips. "You're an angel, Floey," she said.

Flo winked. "Ever together," she said and tossed an offering of Salem 100's onto the table. She moseyed back to her counter stool and lit one up from the pack there. Except for the HouseRAD, who waved lamely to get his tea refilled, the restaurant fell back to sleep, the four guys at the counter occasionally squirming on their stools but unable to lift.

"My Clay's got a heart of gold, Joey," said Aunt Pat. Sonia shut her eyes and shook her head, allowing me to watch her.

Spent, flushed, and out of breath, my aunt lit a long white-filtered cigarette. She whistled the smoke out her nose. "And Clay tells me how he's the only one Brian can talk to, how it's eating Brian alive but he won't confide in nobody but Clay."

Sonia smiled.

Something was wrong with the picture. Brian confiding in Clay, that big asshole? No. I looked at Sonia, whose eyes, hard and clear as she sipped her beige coffee, sealed me from speaking. She stared and stared at me. Even when I looked back at my aunt, waiting for her to finish, Sonia stared.

Sonia let a silent moment pass, let our eyes turn to her. "I'm telling you, Joey, I know Brian had nothing to do with it. I can't speak for Clay *directly*," she said, knocking elbows with my aunt, "but I can for Brian. I'm telling you Brian did not—"

Halfway to her mouth, the coffee cup in my aunt's hand began to shake. "Oh shit," she said, like she felt the beginnings of an earthquake. She set the cup down hard, onto the table not its saucer. She pressed her hand to her chest. Mouth opened wide, she sucked in clumps of air without an exhale and only grew shorter on breath.

"What? You okay?" asked Sonia.

"My friggin' thyroid's acting up," she gasped.

"It's oversecreting again, right?" said Sonia.

"Yup, I'm fucked. I'm fucked good. Definitely. Sony, please. Do that accupressure like Clay showed us. You know the spot."

Sonia began pinching my aunt's shoulder blades. "He ain't good for you, Patty. I'm telling you, really, he ain't. He got you in the middle of this now, too. It's too much stress."

"You're wrong. It ain't Clay's fault," she said, and drowned the half-a-Salem in what remained of her coffee. She looked at me. Sonia looked at me. I looked at Sonia. Sonia looked at my aunt. Boy watched us all. Again, he nodded at me.

"It ain't his fault," said my aunt. "I know what my problem is. It's physical, it ain't mental. It's this freaking damn hyperthyroidism." I looked at her, my eyes opened wide. She laughed at the word herself. "What are *you* laughing at?" she asked, giggling. "It's a word. It's a real word, Mr. High School Honors. Don't you know it?"

EIGHT

AT THE ACME I WAS CHECKED OUT BY A CASHIER I'd never seen there before, a middle-aged woman with stringy, unwashed grey and brown hair. She may have been the mother of a kid from school because she smiled at me like she knew me, but I didn't recognize her. She cried and sniffled and smiled through the whole checkout, going very slow, having to repack the bag, paper in plastic, three times to get everything in one, though the only things I'd bought were a pound of coffee, a quart of milk, a can of Draino, a roll-on antiperspirant, Sure, a two-liter Coke, and a container of frozen eggs. She was slow, too, in counting out my change, the dollars slipping between her fingertips, and she had to keep interrupting herself to wipe her nose against her shoulder, shaking her head and smiling and glancing at me with embarrassment at each delay.

As I carried the groceries along the avenue then down Hutton to the house, I thought more about the woman than I did about my conversation with Aunt Pat and Sonia, and in a timeless blink, I was at our front gate. There was my mom, coming out the door. She was on her way to Uncle Vic's to put in a new lock, a loaded Limited Express bag at her feet. I went inside and up to our apartment, put the things that needed to go there in the refrigerator, and came back down to join her.

My mom handed me the black and white plastic bag. It was so loaded down with the new lock, which must have weighed five pounds by itself, and with the variety-store hammer and screwdriver and tapes and nails and screws my mom had placed in there I was afraid the handle would snap off and I wound up carrying it against my chest—very unmanly.

Once upon a time, twice upon, three times upon a time, there had been tools in our house, but the tools always left with the man who owned them, and whatever tools had been owned by Brian's dad, or even by mine, Seth, the Unknown Father, never made it to this address when we moved here eight years ago.

Three men had lived with us at 208 Ogden. The first one was Guy, a name I hated. He was a man who lived with his sneakers untied and tattoos up and down his skinny arms. He was Aunt Pat's boyfriend, and he overlapped a little with Brian's father, or at least the rumor of his father. Actually, I'm not sure they were ever in the house together. Being the neighborhood handyman—very good when he could see straight was the reputation—Guy had the best tool collection of them all. He was on drugs, though, usually, and in the first week he was here he started three projects—tiling the bathroom, dropping the living room ceiling, and putting a vent in the kitchen. Unfortunately, after the landlord discovered him and Aunt Pat living in the first-floor apartment, they were shoved up here into one room, the living room. That didn't last long. The day after Valentine's Day that year, Aunt Pat attacked Guy with his metal snippers. My mom breathed a long sigh of relief at the results—he lived and left. None of the jobs he'd started were completed, but the good part was that he was in such a hurry to get out, when he split he took his canvas and leather toolbag but not all the tools and for months afterwards we'd find them around the house. By the middle of the spring, he'd moved to Atlantic City and never came back for the tools. Somebody said he was doing real good down there, owned a dog and everything.

The second man was really a neurotic overgrown kid named Boo, another boyfriend of my aunt's. He was six-three and weighed about two-eighty. He had a square strawish beard that hid his neck like a hula skirt and wore bib overalls that made him look more like a gigantic toddler than a he-man. He brought in a few tools of his own, but those were mostly of the inherited kind—hammers loose in their wooden handles, pliers locked open, wrenches rusted shut—and they were more useful for doorstops or for keeping slipping windows propped open than for work. He got depressed, shrunk back into himself, any time my aunt used the term "man's work," which seemed like it was pretty often.

As different as he was from Guy, their stories were alike. Both started out in the empty downstairs apartment, both got booted upstairs, and neither lasted a month. With Boo, though, my mom and my aunt had agreed that my mom would take the couch and the bedroom would be their little apartment, my aunt and Boo's, and that they'd pay rent, thirty dollars per week. But after ten days upstairs, most of it spent locked away in my mom's bedroom, Boo split, taking most of Guy's remaining tools with him. That's when my mom instituted the rule that Aunt Pat was welcome but her boyfriends weren't, a more than generous rule that she's stuck with for the four years since.

The last man to live here was a boyfriend of my mother's who appeared not long after Boo had split, when I'd just turned eleven. Not knowing if the guy would turn out to be my stepdad, he was the only one that was hard for me emotionally. His name was K'nallu Ollanai, or something like that, and he'd moved into the neighborhood just a month before him and my mom met. He was in his mid-twenties, which was nearly ten years younger than my mom. He was an African, darker than any black man I'd ever seen, a built-like-a-marathoner Kenyan who was taking classes at Jersey City State College. He had no tools, but he had some money, more than us anyway, and when Aunt Pat asked him to put in a new sink and toilet in the bathroom if he had some spare time, he went to Sears and came back with all kinds of stuff. It was like a party when we opened the packages.

The hard part was that he was sleeping with my mom, fucking her right next door. To make it worse, not only did K'nallu have an apostrophe in his name, he had the habit of walking about the apartment in just his leather slippers and a turquoise terry-cloth robe. Half the time he was carrying a plastic cup with his toothpaste and toothbrush in it. If he hadn't been my mom's boyfriend, or if he wasn't *so* black, if he had been even a Denzel Washington kind of color, maybe I could have took it, even liked him, but he was sleeping next door with my mom. And he was real black, snake black, and no matter how nice he was, I couldn't quite look at him straight. Maybe my mom couldn't either, because he barely beat Guy's and Boo's one-month stays before she asked him to leave, which he did pretty willingly, like he hadn't understood he'd been free to until asked. K'nallu took his tools, too.

Since then, we haven't owned a toolbox or even very much in the way of tools. What we did have was from Drug Fair, the 99¢ bin—two underweight hammers, two screwdrivers (a long, skinny flathead and a Phillips too big for any screw we ever needed to turn), a pair of pliers, and nails and screws and washers spilled out of their clear plastic boxes. We kept them in the bottom drawer of the kitchen cabinet, company with other things we had nowhere else to put—a hole puncher, half a pair of scissors, gift ribbon, a doorknob, a protractor, rubber-banded card decks short of fifty-two.

There was no handle on the outside door of Uncle Vic's. You just pushed it open. Inside, in the tiled foyer, the doorbells had the names of the residents adhesive-taped to the mailbox part. From the names there and from the comings and goings I'd been noticing, the new owner of the building seemed to be going out of his way to attract a lot of foreigners—two South American families, one Korean, an apartment on the first floor crawling with Arabs—all moved in in the past year. Either that, that he was going out of his way, or he couldn't find any more white families looking to live here.

You didn't need to get buzzed into Uncle Vic's building, not because the second door didn't lock, but because it only locked. Stuck in its out position, the bolt hit against the door frame, keeping it from closing. Even with your arms full, like mine were, if you could slip your toe between the door and the frame, you could pull it open toward you.

Some genius of a decorator had just fixed up the inside of the building so that the ground-floor and the second-floor landings—the owner must have run out of material before he got to the third floor—were all covered in the same blurry tan and blue linoleum, but where he had his real inspiration was in covering the stairs, both the steps and the risers, and even the lower sidewall of the staircases in the same linoleum, so seamless you could fill it like a tub. Above the linoleum, the walls were the same as they were on the third floor, Uncle Mike's old floor, mustard colored, shiny where they bulged and shadowed where they buckled.

Uncle Vic's apartment door was open. I could hear his

kitchen TV. His ears plugged with hair and wax, *The Price Is Right* was turned up way too loud, drowning out the Mariah Carey humming from the apartment at the opposite end, where another new tenant was moving in. From halfway up the flight, we could see into Uncle Vic's. He was at the kitchen table, the air-conditioner turned off, a breeze blowing through the opened window next to the AC. At the landing, my mom took the bag from me and laid it down. We didn't even enter the apartment.

"We're gonna start now," she told him.

He didn't turn. "Not necessary, not necessary. I told you that, but go ahead, have it your way," he said and turned the TV up even louder.

I couldn't help but think how easy it would have been for the killer, despite the three doors, all meaningless, to walk up the one flight, to strangle Uncle Vic, or to blow him away, to lift and toss him from the window.

"We'll do it for my peace of mind," said my mom, eyes rolling and head shaking.

We didn't own a toolbox, not only because we didn't own hardly any tools, but also because we weren't big on transporting what we did have all around the neighborhood. The exception was the one or two times a year when we had to do some work at Uncle Vic's. We may have had next to none, but, unless you consider a stapler and a toilet plunger to be tools, Uncle Vic had no tools at all. He had figured out how to fill and use his stapler, but remembering how to open it so he could staple things into the wall was a sometimes deal. The plunger he knew how to use but didn't, afraid of what it might bring up.

My mom pulled open the cords at the neck of the Limited Express bag. She took out the new lock in its cardboard and plastic, and a flopsy pair of steel scissors that wouldn't stay shut. She dipped back into the bag and pulled out a roll of scotch tape and a CD case with a folded yellow paper inside. She unfolded the paper and taped it to the hallway wall, nice and straight. On the yellow paper, in three colored pens, she'd laid out her whole day. On first go, she'd given herself more time for this task, the new lock, but that time was whited out, reduced to fifty minutes, and now from twelve o'clock to two it said, "Pioneer—fill in for

Benjamin." Then there was another work shift from six o'clock until ten. Between the afternoon and evening work hours she'd written, "Haircut, Supper, Study," and on the outside of ten o'clock, "Study, Study, Study!"

"Hey, Susie, look at this Nordic Trac. How much do you think?" asked Uncle Vic as a Price Is Right girl in an exercise leotard pumped her arms and faked exertion.

"I'm too busy," yelled my mom as she studied the back of the cardboard instructions, ready with her scissors.

"Susie, it'll only take a second. Come on, look."

She stepped into the apartment, listened to the bids, sneered at the bad ones, waited for a final look at the machine. "Four eighty-nine," she said and came back.

The doorknob already had a lock in it, but the lock took a cylinder key that I don't think anyone had seen in half a century, and the chain lock that Brian had put in a couple of years ago looked okay but the doorjamb was rotted and the screw could have been knocked out with the nudge of a shoulder.

"Yes! Yes!" cheered Uncle Vic, bouncing up in his chair. "We win, we win. Honey, you could clean up on this show. Oh, you are the It Girl!"

My mom cut then tore open the lock's packaging. She smiled and gave me a thumbs-up.

Using just a fingernail, she was able to unscrew the chain's plate from the splintered frame. "I been so afraid for Uncle Vic," she whispered. "I'm having nightmares that the killer's coming back. He's all alone, Joey."

"Wo-wo-wah-wah. Hey, Joey," called Uncle Vic. "Looka that skirt on Jennine. Madonne. It's a mini-mini. What's that made out of, that material? It's like rubbers on a boot or something. Wowie, baby!" He blindly patted the table for a cigar but his eyes stuck to the TV.

The part of the chain lock that had been screwed into the door instead of the frame, the square plate part, was much tougher to get out with our thin screwdriver. The door was hardwood and the screw heads thick with paint. My mom scratched at it with the tool's tip, then, with all her weight, pushed the screwdriver to the door. "If the person did it once, he or she'll do

118

it again, I believe. Look at him." She nodded Uncle Vic's way as her shoulder stayed pressed.

"Why you whispering, Susie?" he called. "You know how I'm against whispering."

"You're against everything," she joked, then went right back to whispering. "Anybody could just knock him over the head and take his savings."

"Susie, I asked a question. Why you whispering?"

On the table next to the TV was my uncle's Pep Boys ashtray, a coffee cup, half a glass of tomato juice, and the keys and change and crumpled bills—singles, fives, and a twenty—that would make their way into his pants pockets.

"Be careful what you're doing, would you?" I said. My mom's braced-to-the-door thumb was smack in the lane of the hard-pressing screwdriver if it slipped, and I could see it tearing open the skin. "Let me do it."

She handed me the screwdriver and stepped back.

"Oh, Joey, look at Shonette. Put that chisel down," Uncle Vic called, referring to the screwdriver. "Booties and mittens, like one of Santa's elves, and a bikini. What a pair of legs. Look at Barker smiling. Sure, you bastard, I'd be smiling, too. Susie, what's a pedophile?"

She shook her head, then held her hands in prayer under her chin.

"Christ," she said. "It's quarter to twelve. I got to wash up." She headed for the bathroom, her blouse all bunched in the back of her black Wranglers.

I decided I was going to get that plate off the door before my mom came out.

"Good grief, you believe this garbage, Joey? This guy's dressed like a hobo and he wins a Chrysler. You could take a shower if you're gonna be on TV."

I shut the door and leaned into it, as my mom had, put the screwdriver in the groove, set it straight, fiddled my fingers, watching my little forearm muscles flex, then "uuh-hoonk," I lunged in. Too hard. I snapped the blade of the screwdriver from the handle. "Stupid. You're a stupid fucking jerk," I fumed. I jabbed the splintered handle into the door, pulled it out, and flung it onto the floor.

There was a hard knock, then a hesitation before the door slowly opened. It was Brian, leery, standing two feet back, off from the center of the doorway, his eyes on the broken tool. "What the fuck's going on? What are you doing, Joey? Idiot!"

"Brian," said my mom as she popped out of the bathroom, face shining, shirt neatly tucked. "Where have you been, honey? I haven't seen you in two nights."

"So I'm sorry. I was at Clay's."

"What were you doing at Clay's?"

"I wasn't doing nothing," he said with a little twist to his wrist that meant to end the questions.

"Idiot. Don't call me idiot. What are you doing here?" I asked.

Even more angry, his eyes bright but sinking into his face, harder to find, "What's your problem?" he asked. "I see you at Uncle Mike's, I see you now, and that's all you say, 'What are you doing here?' It's not your business. I came to see Uncle Vic."

"Cut it out, you guys," scolded Uncle Vic, still watching television. "You need something, Brian?"

"I'll talk to you later," he said. He walked away from me, toward the table and my uncle.

"Looka this guy, Brian," said Uncle Vic, pulling out a chair. Brian sat.

"Brian, why do you hang out with Clay?" my mom asked.

He shrugged. "I'm gonna get a place of my own. Very soon."

"You're old enough if you want to," said my mom. She looked at me, noticed the stab hole in the door, the screwdriver blade and broken handle on the floor. "Now what are you going to do?" she asked.

"I'll get it off with a butter knife."

"Yeah, right," said Brian. "You got a Coke, Uncle Vic?"

"Go ahead, get one. Watch the show with me a little bit. It's the jackpot finale."

"You should stay away from Clay," my mom warned, staring at me, her ally, as Brian pushed the chair toward the refrigerator, grabbed a Coke, and pushed back.

"Why? Is he in trouble? Ma, you're not giving away police secrets. Why should I keep away from Clay?"

"Mom, Brian needs someone he can talk to," I said, and I went to the drawer for a butter knife. Brian didn't turn around, didn't say a word. "Right, Brian? You can confide in Clay."

No reaction.

"I do not have any secrets from you, Brian, police or otherwise" said my mom, shaking her head, making like she was going to fight back.

"I don't care about Clay," said Brian, disgusted with the line of questioning. "You want to know why I don't come home, this is why. It's bullshit."

"Watch your language, Brian. This is my house," said Uncle Vic, holding up a single finger like someone he'd seen orating in a play.

Using our small hammer, I tried to tap the butter knife between the plate and the door, to pry it.

Uncle Vic looked at me then at Brian. "Totally unnecessary, totally unnecessary. A waste of manpower," he said. "Brian, they think I need help, protection."

"Yeah. It is a good idea," said Brian.

"Oh, it can't hurt. I'll grant you. But it ain't necessary," said my uncle.

"Will you help Joey with the lock?" my mom asked Brian.

"Not now, I'm too tired. Besides, there's too many people here," he said, rubbing his eyes with the balls of his thumbs. "I'll come back later. Leave it, Joey. I'll do it tomorrow."

"I'm not gonna leave it. It'll take five minutes."

"Promise me next time you'll call from Clay's."

"Yeah, I swear. I swear on a million Bibles. May Almighty God strike me with lightning," he said, now and then snapping his head to emphasize a word. "I'll promise if you'll promise to shut up about Clay."

"Brian, that's your mother. Careful. Respect, now, respect," said Uncle Vic, putting a cigar in his mouth, puffing to light. The cloud half-filled the room. "You ever gonna shave that awful beard?" he asked. "You look like a beggar."

"Maybe. I'm thinking about it." Brian pushed back the

chair and stood up. "You sit here all day. How can you watch this junk?"

"I'm here all alone," pleaded Uncle Vic. "What am I gonna do, Brian?"

"Sit in the park," he said, back-shuffling until he nearly bumped me in the doorway. "Do anything. Go up the avenue. Get out."

"I'm gonna finish this myself," I said, giving Brian a final notice.

"I don't care. Go ahead, finish it. I'm going home to sleep," he said. "Uncle Vic, I'll come back later."

"Good, good. You're welcome here."

The old screws came loose with a pull of the butter knife and took chunks of door wood with them.

"Excuse me," said Brian, and he left as swiftly as he had appeared, before my mom had a chance to attach herself to him.

"You sure you can finish that, Joey?" she asked.

"Yeah, one way or another," I said, knowing I'd get the job done but knowing, too, that somehow it'd be half-assed, that I'd never get the lock's big bolt to slide properly into the socket, that it'd probably need to be done again.

"You, too, Uncle Vic. Do what Brian said. Get out, be with people."

"Oh stop, would you please? You turn a sane man crazy. Now you got me worrying about them damn screws. Don't you know me? Joey, make sure they're in good. You gotta turn clockwise, you know."

"Everybody likes you, Uncle Vic. Everybody. Just get out more," said my mom, one hand on the door frame, about to swing herself out.

"Well, that's true," he said and turned away from the TV to observe my work. "I'm a very well-liked person."

"Go out sometimes, okay? Don't just sit there," she said. She stepped into the hall. "Let people know you're alive."

"Oh, your mother, Joey. She got a way of saying things," he said, holding his head in both hands. "She's a pip."

PART III

ONE

THREE MORNINGS LATER, THAT MONDAY, MY mom asked me to look for Brian. Our guess was we'd find him at Clay's.

A block up and two blocks over from our house, Clay lived on Palisade Avenue, one of the main streets in High Gate, a bus route and 40-mph zone. At one end of Clay's block was a laundromat, at the other end an abandoned Exxon station. All twelve of the houses near the Exxon end were identical three-story yellow flat-roofs separated by alleyways the width of double garbage barrels. The first floors of the buildings were storefronts. Some of them had been turned into apartments, bedsheets covering the big front windows. Two of the other fronts were soaped over and vacant, and there were four stores still open: Lucky's Newspaper and Lottery, Zina's Exotic Pets, Galaxy Travel and Insurance, and White Knight Liquors.

Clay lived in the house behind the house two down from the corner laundromat, a house with no storefront but with a ground-floor apartment and a hodgepodge flight of steps—wood, cement, metal—that came out into the concrete front yard. A house behind a house, like Clay's, was pretty rare in our neighborhood as far as I knew, but hidden like they were, there could have been plenty more I didn't know about.

I turned into the alleyway and a black woman in her twenties was coming toward me, away from Clay's. She was wearing mannish blue pants, sort of heavyweight for summer, and a royal blue knit shirt—a Hudson County Prosecutor's Office seal on the chest. She squished herself against one of the walls so I could squeeze by, said, "Hi." I grunted back and she just waited, waited till I was nearly out of the alley and I turned around for another peek. All happy, "You're Joey, right? Joey Scadutto." She pointed to the HCPO seal on her shirt. "I'm gonna be calling you, okay? I'm with the office. This is our investigation. You know that, right?"

"Yeah," I said.

"Cool," she said. She waved, smiled, white teeth and eyes in a chocolate face. "Hey, man, cute shorts, the whole look. Nice."

After I turned the corner, I looked down at myself—Knicks jersey, baggy beige Paco shorts, skinny legs like Wile E. Coyote, no socks, Converse high-tops, scissor-cut to low tops. Nice look? Right. Spoken like a true cop.

Clay's green vinyl-sided house looked like a two-car garage with a peaked roof plopped on. All four sides of the house had the same pair of small, centered windows, but between the littleness of the windows and the fact that the sun could rarely find a way through all the houses boxing Clay's in, the inside was always dark. Because it was so dark and messy and musty smelling—like it was set on top of a mosquito bog—Clay conducted all of what he called his business on the front patio, although I don't know if it really counted as a patio. There was a sidewalk, slippery and new but already cracked, four feet wide and running the length of the house. The two-by-fours used for framing it had somehow gotten permanently cemented in, and tacked across the top to two more standing two-by-fours and to the roof of the house was a rippled pale blue awning, a racket in the rain.

Sitting out there were Clay and my aunt.

Under the awning, at a round white wire table, four bare feet up on it, they looked like the center of the universe, in their own minds at least. It had been three days since I'd seen my aunt at the Al'n Mo and she looked a lot better. Her hair, a mix of blonde and brown, was pulled back into a ponytail. Her face was makeup free, pebbly in white and pink, but it was clean and clear-eyed, almost fresh, the way a face looks after a soaking in acne medicine.

"Hey, kiddo," she said. "Welcome to Loco Central."

Clay was barechested and full-body tanned, down to his toes. He barely looked real. He was wearing only white Dockers and was reading the *Village Voice*.

"Who was that cop?" I asked as I wandered closer.

"That," said Clay, "that was Officer Rhonda Wilkinson of the Hudson County Prosecutor's Office. *Not* the police department. Get that straight, okay? Doing guess what? Looking for information about guess who?"

"Who?" I asked, kind of panicked.

"Uncle Mike," said my aunt.

"Oh, good. I thought you meant somebody living."

"Well, that too," said my aunt, lighting up, sucking in the smoke till her cheeks collapsed.

"What did she want?" I asked. I stood just a few feet from the table but was careful not to take the last chair, afraid that would make it harder to leave. "I mean, what kind of information?"

"Oh, wait, wait now. She just wanted to talk," said Clay, holding his hands open in exaggerated innocence. "That little chocolate angel only wants to chitchat." He closed the paper and pushed it aside.

"She wants to talk to you, too," said my aunt. "She's a cutie, right, Clay? All jive and smiles while she's looking to twist in the knife."

"Yeah, that's what she said when I passed her, about talking to me. And Resto wants to talk to you again, Clay. My mom told me. He said he'd talked enough to me already," I said, figuring I needed to confess that I wasn't being called again before it came out another way.

"Hey, that's cool, Joey, no sweat. I could have told you I'd be called again soon as I walked out of there the first time. No sweat. I'm feeling like Public Enemy Number One, yo."

"You're my number one," said my aunt, petting his hair like he was a thing of beauty. He frowned sadly. "Oh, don't worry, baby, Sonia'll come around." I didn't ask, figured it was some problem they'd been talking about, probably Sonia was talking bad about him. "More coffee, honey?" she asked him.

"Please," he said and handed her his white and gold Forbes cup. Smiling, she lifted her feet off the table, swung her legs, stood, and wiggled inside. I noticed the TV was on in the empty house, a promo for Nick at Nite.

127

Clay kept his left hand behind his head as he tapped a Winston from the pack and lit it with his right. He spoke, letting the cigarette jiggle from his lips. "This getting to you, Joey, all this crime and interrogation and shit?"

"No, I don't give a fuck about it."

"Good boy," he said, blowing a cone of smoke from the side of his mouth. "Nothing to be scared of, little man."

"What about Brian? How's he?" I asked.

"Brian." He tossed his head back and laughed. "He's just pissed. Pissed about all the hypocrisy."

"What hypocrisy?"

"I don't know." He laughed again, tapping his ash onto the ground. "Whatever. Brian thinks the world's a rotten place." Clay took a drag that puffed up his cheeks. He shifted the smoke cheek to cheek, like he was rinsing his mouth in it. "And Sonia. She thinks I'm the bad influence. Of course, I'm not supposed to know about this." I didn't really care what Sonia thought about him. "She's pals with Patty. All of a sudden I'm no good for her either. I hope she ain't filling your brother's head."

"So who does what's-her-name, Wilkinson, want information about?"

"Among the living?"

"Yeah."

"I thought you didn't give a fuck about her, yo."

"No, I don't mean that. I don't have nothing to worry about."

"Relax, I'm just fucking with you. I don't know what she wants. She made it sound like mostly she wanted information about Natasha, but I don't believe. I believe *her* less than I believe most cops. Rhonda Wilkinson, man. She be slick," he said, hunkering his round shoulders. "She be a strong black sista', oh yeah."

"I don't know why she wants to talk to me. I hardly know Natasha. I met her like twice or something. I don't know any of her friends, Hardy Cummings, Buddah Hayes, nobody."

"So just tell her that. Tell that to Wilkinson. Who the fuck is that nigga? Look, Joey, don't be a pussy, man. You got nothing to worry about. Don't embarrass your race."

The sun, reflecting off a corner of the house one down, where the vinyl had been ripped off and the foil-covered insulation showed, threw a patch of pale light onto the concrete behind Clay. He leaned back and stretched into it. "Ah, what a day, man. This is beautiful."

"Did you see Brian today?" I asked.

"Yeah, you missed him ten minutes ago. He slept here. He left with Sonia."

"He slept here with Sonia?"

"No, Joey. Just Brian slept here," said my aunt, back with us and carrying a Meister Brau tray with two coffees, a slew of Sweet 'n Lows, little restaurant portions of creamer, and a large Burger King cup of Sprite, probably left in the refrigerator overnight. "Sonia came for him this morning," she said. She lit up another Carlton and put her feet up next to Clay's.

"No, my mom asked, that's all."

The soda was weak and flat, the cup paperish and soggy.

"Sit down," said Clay.

"Na," I said. "You know. I'm looking for Brian, for my mom."

"Joey, did you say that Prick Resto's going to be annoying Clay again?" my aunt asked. An all-knowing grin formed on Clay's mouth as he let go his cone of smoke. "Brian, too?"

"Yeah."

"At least you're out of it," she said. I shrugged. "No, Joey, don't be embarrassed."

"I'm not embarrassed."

"I mean, Christ, you should be glad."

I turned toward Clay. He nodded sleepily as I spoke, like whatever I said didn't matter. He nodded and nodded. "Resto said he wants to come up to the tutoring center to talk to the two of you there."

"So be it."

"What's he snooping up there for?" asked Aunt Pat. I shrugged again, practically shrugged out of my jersey.

"We'll welcome him with open arms."

"When do we have to see the other one? Wilkinson," I asked.

"Oh, shit, that's right," said Clay. "She wants to talk to me right before Brian. Me at noon. Brian one-thirty. You, I don't know. Three maybe. I hope Resto's not coming to the center this afternoon. I'd hate to miss him," he said sadly, and he wiggled his toes against my aunt's.

"You know where Brian and Sonia went?"

"She had to do something home, in Hoboken. Brian, I don't know. I think they're having money problems."

"What's your rush?" asked my aunt as I started to back away.

"No," I said. "My mom wants to know about Brian."

"Jesus, tell her to stop worrying already. Oh, and tell her I'm clean. Clean and happy, real happy," said my aunt. I didn't look at their toes.

"I hope Resto don't bust your balls too much."

"No way."

"We all have to deal with the other one," I said as I backed toward the alley.

"Whatever, little man."

"Wilkinson, I mean."

"Yeah, whatever. Got it—you mean Wilkinson."

"Remember what I told you, Joey," said my aunt. "Be careful what you tell to them. They'll twist it."

"She's nothing, Pat. She ain't shit," said Clay.

"Yeah, but he's so young," she said. "You'll be okay, Joey." I kept backing. "Should I put on some tunes?"

"Bye." I waved. They ignored me.

"Yeah, baby, good call. Tunes." Clay leaned forward, took his feet from the table, reopened the *Voice*. "Hendrix, yo. It's a Hendrix day and the sun be shining."

TWO

FROM THE CORNER OF CLAY'S BLOCK, I COULD SEE diagonally across the street into the park, all the way to the Cliff Walk. To my surprise, there was Uncle Vic at a middle-of-the-park table. Next to him, standing, his thighs pressed against the table's edge, was Brian. He was talking and Uncle Vic was nodding, eating what looked like a sandwich. Brian put one hand on Uncle Vic's shoulder and his other hand out to shake. He turned away, then spun back, said something more. He turned again and walked off toward Cobble Road.

I crossed Palisade to the edge of the park. But I walked slowly through, watching Brian while I kept myself out of view. If my mom's style was square, then Brian's was none at all. No turned-back baseball cap, no Doors or Everlast, no Tommy Hilfiger, nothing baggy, no No Fear, no Nike, no South Park. Any of that would have meant choosing, and, for Brian even choosing one t-shirt over another from the Wonder Store irregulars bin was humiliating.

That morning he had on a grey and red polo shirt, buttoned to the chin, a size too small, and made of a knit material that clung and made him look even more round and middle-aged than usual. But he also had on new, still-creased black chinos that, surprisingly, fit him good, not too tight, and not too long and under the heel in back. They may have cost more than the $9.99 he usually spent on jeans. I wondered if Sonia'd picked them out.

Instead of heading straight down Ogden toward our house, Brian veered up along the Cobble Road wall, back toward Palisade Avenue.

He barely lifted his feet from the ground when he walked. He shuffled and hesitated, slid a foot forward, barely off the ground. He hit down first with the balls of his feet, not the heels. When his body tipped forward, it seemed his toes clenched and tried to stop him, but it was too late and his weight too much. After a hesitation that allowed him to check out the territory in front, he rocked and lurched forward.

He'd walked all the way across the park, from the Cliff Walk to Palisade, while I continued to angle away from him, into the park's center and toward my uncle. I figured Brian was going to Clay's, but he surprised me again when he turned down Cobble Road. He disappeared for a minute until I could walk back the way I'd come and adjust my angle on him. He slowly shuffled under the overpass, past the spot where Prince had been killed, disappeared again.

Brian's dad, Richie Lorre, was the only man my mom had ever been married to. My own dad was a real short-term thing for my mom, out of her life before I was born. But that difference, having a dad who was in and out of his life, on and off, just made it harder for Brian. We used to talk about it a lot—nostalgically, of Richie and mom's dating and the old days—usually all three of us, sometimes just me and Brian, though mostly I was only a listener, then one day Brian said he didn't feel like talking about history anymore. Months passed and it's never come up again except bobbing in our thoughts.

Richie stayed with my mom for a year after Brian was born. Then he left for a year and a half, then he came back before Brian's third birthday. He left again six months later. That second time when he left, he stayed in High Gate and Brian would see a lot of him, mostly on the street. Those years, between Brian's turning six and turning eight, I was pretty much just a baby and to me Richie was just a man, my mother's ex-boyfriend, my brother's dad, but I had no way of understanding how different it must have been for Brian. The third and last time Richie came back was for longer and I was a little older.

I was sitting on the concrete in the front yard, in the shade of the porch, playing Legos, and Brian came trotting down the block, all happy and shit. I remember him calling Richie "Dad," not knowing if he was using the word for himself or for us both. Richie stayed almost two years that time. Brian even played soccer one fall—I think I was in second grade—and I remember seeing Richie at a game, cheering the orange-shirts like he'd never missed a day in his son's life. He left for good in early December, before Brian turned ten. Three days later, I found Brian crying on the couch under The Minuet.

Having his dad there and gone again and again wore Brian out. It made him old before his time. I practically cry myself when I picture Brian back then and imagine how it must have felt, his heart like Gak pulled by eight hands.

Now. I mean, now he doesn't care about anything and resents those who do. He doesn't care if he's wearing clean socks or dirty, if he catches the bus or misses it, if he's all alone or with someone. He doesn't prefer obeying over disobeying and doesn't prefer it the other way either. It seemed like that was the way he would always be.

I was at the fence overlooking Cobble Road when Brian reappeared from beneath the overpass. Instead of going into Uncle Vic's through the back basement door, or even following the road around and down to Hoboken, Brian crossed what there was of a smashed-up sidewalk along the edge of the road and stood at the entrance to the Hundred Steps.

The Hundred Steps are ninety-four stone steps that are probably less than a hundred years old but that I'd bet are in worse shape than a Mayan ruin. On their way to the Hoboken train tracks, the steps zig-zag down through the jungle that's the palisades. Because it's so creepy there, with missing steps, trash turned to mud, broken bottles, rusted cans, poison ivy, slugs and rats, snakes and possum, and dead cats with flies feasting on their guts, their eyes, their buttholes, I'd never had the nerve to go down more than eight steps, to the first landing and switch back, so whatever was beyond that point, I didn't really know.

Brian stood right at the edge of the top step. All of a sudden, the overhanging branches opened up and out stepped Sonia, tiptoeing like there was no safe place to rest an entire foot. They stood close, Sonia in tan cargo shorts and a violet vest over a black T-shirt, everything loose. She stood close and Brian leaned away. But that was Brian. Even the grungiest girls who'd ever hung up the park—the ones who braless and barefooted, their hands held high and fluttering, would run through the park's worn dirtways to leap into the arms of a guy they hadn't seen since homeroom, a whole two days before—would barely dare to lay a finger on Brian's shoulder, patting him gently but stiffly just to show they weren't afraid.

Sonia undid the top button of Brian's tight polo shirt, checked out the look. She put her hand on her hips, one foot forward, stared at his well-fitted pants and nodded her head, smiling. He lifted his head to meet her eye to eye and he smiled back. Then, with a backhanded wave, Brian brushed her away, indicating that she should turn and head back down the steps. She did. She started down and reached behind to grab on to his hand for balance.

THREE

UNCLE VIC HAD FOUND A PRETTY SPOT ON A beautiful morning. The trees surrounding the table kept out the late-morning sun and created a playground for mostly invisible chattering birds. The umbrella's low-hanging branches cut off the skyline halfway up the Chrysler Building, in the midsection of Manhattan, but downtown, at an angle through the trees where the low branches were bare, the World Trade Center was in full view and, under a pale blue sky, so were the ghosty bridges and grey-blue hills and homes of Brooklyn and another island.

At the table, hunched over the day's Monmouth Racetrack entries, horses' charts dirtied by the oil and lettuce of his Blimpie, was Uncle Vic, his back to me. "Hey, what do you know," I said.

I startled him. He jumped up and turned toward me, his eyes like a puppy ready to do battle with a wolf. "Christ, Joey, say something when you come up behind a person, would you? Learn, huh? You could get yourself shot that way."

"How'm I gonna get shot? You don't own a gun."

"I know I don't own no gun. I was talking off the cuff. I could have gotten one, though, couldn't I. You didn't think of that, smarty-pants, did you?"

"Uncle Vic, I was saying hello."

"Hello? I didn't hear no hello. Be careful, sonny boy. It's a dangerous environment," he said, his lips shiny from the sandwich's oil. He tapped his chest. "But that don't stop Vic Scadutto. I'm venturing out. Remember, I'm liked."

"*Well* liked."

"Ah, now you're thinking."

"What did Brian want?"

"The kid wanted a little money. I told him sure."

135

"What does he need money for?"

"He says he owes it to Sonia, the skinny little girlfriend. She reminds me of Charlie Chaplin, skinny and in them baggy clothes."

"Me too," I laughed. "But she's got less money than him. What does he owe her money for?"

"Oh, that's personal, Joey. You don't ask them kind of questions of people."

"How much?" I asked, picking up and eating some of the scraps of turkey and tomato that had fallen onto the paper.

"Two hundred. I said, 'Yeah, sure, okay, Brian. For you. You're my nephew. But once and once only is enough. I'm no soft touch,' I said. I bluffed him a little." Uncle Vic snickered. "I don't think he'll ask again. Eh, I'll throw him an extra twenty anyways."

"You'll throw him an extra twenty?" I asked, squinting at him and sucking the vinegar from a slice of tomato.

Uncle Vic might be careless with where and how he kept his few thousand dollars, but that didn't mean he was overly generous with it either. To him, every item in every store was overpriced. Whatever you bought or were buying, "How much?" he wanted to know, always more of an accusation than a question. By his counting, that twenty bucks was enough to buy a weekend in Asbury Park.

"I know what I'm doing, you wait and see. I'm getting in good. Vic Scadutto's everybody's friend. Everybody likes Uncle Vic, and it's gonna be even more so from after today, wait and see."

"Yeah, Uncle Vic. Everybody likes you is right," I said. "My mom wanted to know where Brian's been. I got to go tell her. She's at that restaurant in HouseRAD where she started working."

"Yeah, okay," he said, sort of grumpy, like he was doing me a favor. "I'll come with you. I need the walk."

"Okay. Let's get going."

He jumped up and wiped his hands on the seat of his pants, rubbed the glisten off his lips. He lifted his tissuey yellow sports shirt, a flat-bottomed, two-pocket job like he liked. Under the shirt was a fanny pack, black with a yellow plastic logo I couldn't make out. I laughed at it. "What's the matter? You never seen one of these before? My God, they been around for years. I seen plenty of these. Where you been, sonny boy?"

He unzipped the fanny pack, pulled out a White Owl, unwrapped it, tossed the cellophane in the direction of a trash can. Struck a match. Puff-puff, puff-puff. "Stick with me. You'll be liked, too."

We walked through the park like father-son images. Although I was already two inches taller than him, and I had a minimum of two more to grow and would probably top out at five-seven, maybe five-eight, Uncle Vic was my grandmother's brother, and we had the same wavy hair, mine a shade lighter, and the same dimpled chin and bowed legs and monkey hands with broad fingernails.

"Looka these," he said. He balanced himself with a hand on my shoulder and put a foot forward and I looked. He hiked up his pants leg. At the bottom of his brown slacks, the hem stitching showed up a shade darker. On his size-six feet were white sweat socks and a pair of black Air Walks. "These sneakers your mother bought me are like walking on air. I should let her pick out all my shoes from now on," he said.

Into a breeze coming up from right over the Statue of Liberty, so strong today that you could smell the salt of the Atlantic Ocean, we walked to the end of the park, past Freddie and Ty McGuire playing two-on-two with a couple of older Korean girls in yellow Lakers uniforms. Freddie and Ty hadn't gotten any better. In fact, it looked like they'd surrendered, picking up the ball and running with it more than trying to dribble the thing. The Korean girls, who seemed to see the littler boys as props more than opponents, didn't seem to care whether they followed the rules or broke them. The outcome would be the same. The girls just scooped up the rebounds and slowly dribbled down-court.

Me and my uncle went on into HouseRAD.

Until the early fifties, a trolley trestle rose up from Hoboken to this section of Jersey City, providing a connection between our neighborhood and what old people and those who honor the old days and ways still call the Tubes, what's now the

Hoboken and Exchange Place Path Stations to Manhattan. The trolley station, a church, a hall, a pair of diners, and a handful of stores—a florist, a drug store, a magazine and news shop—grew around the tracks, but except for those things, the section that was now HouseRAD was mostly small- and medium-sized factories and warehouses—brick walls and loading docks, caged elevators, green fire escapes, and round yellow chimneys. Hidden among the big buildings were clusters of cabin-sized homes.

It's been almost half a century since the trolley and everything around it shut down, and longer than I can remember since any of the factories operated. For years, Warehouse Row, or House Row, was a mess, a place of rats and rust and arson. The warehouses were as crumbled as bad teeth and swallowed up by weeds and vines that not only crowded the buildings, but, from the foundation to the bombed-out roofs, were overtaking them, climbing the fences and walls, mingling with the wiring, creeping through the ducts.

It all came out of the blue to us when in 1996 the city got a NJ State Urban Arts District Grant. We only found out about it when the billboards advertising for tenants popped up at the fringe of High Gate—two by the Holland Tunnel, two where the out-of-town trains and busses converged on Journal Square, three along Kennedy Boulevard. If they advertised about it in any newspapers, the *Jersey Journal* wasn't one of them. Then, at the end of the summer of '96, like a "Private Property—Do Not Enter" warning at the edge of the park, a sign appeared. On a black metal post, it was a swinging wood sign, big as a large-screen TV, with all the writing—the name House Row Arts Development District, the name of the governor, of the county freeholder and the county planner, of the mayor—burned black into the reddish wood.

We laughed. We figured, Who in their right mind would want to live *there*? According to what I'd heard, the people who moved in, even though the rents were subsidized by the Arts District Grant, were paying as much to live in a one-room apartment in a dilapidated warehouse as they would for five rooms in a much nicer two- or three-family in our neighborhood, just across the park.

Uncle Vic said, "Oooh, hmmm. I always loved the way that coffee smell comes up with the salt water. Reminds me of your grandma's bungalow at Chadwick Beach." He was referring to the same breeze that brought the smell from the ocean and harbor also bringing the smell from the Maxwell House factory in Hoboken. But that wasn't so. He was hallucinating. Maxwell House had been shut for five years.

"It's like walking on air," he said, bopping in his Air Walks. "Get it? Cute one, huh?"

The first two blocks of HouseRAD were deserted, cleaner than they used to be but not much cleaner. All I knew about the building my mom worked in was the address, 101 Ogden, so I checked numbers as we approached. We crossed onto the third, the next-to-last block of HouseRAD. This strip was more fixed up, but very old. Between the warehouses, on the cliff side of the street, the side we walked along, were pioneer-looking, one-family homes. The houses' bodies were mostly natural colors, greys and light browns, and the woodworked frames were either painted in funky purples and yellows and blues that matched the wildflowers lighting the front gardens or were stripped of whatever paint had been there and were awaiting a new coat.

"It's nice here," I said to my uncle, but he was bopping, he was walking on air.

FOUR

FTER THE ROW OF ONE FAMILY HOUSES THERE came two still-deserted factories and a vacant lot, then a stretch of four two-story brick houses. The Pioneer Cafe was in the next to the last one of these.

The weirdest thing about the Pioneer was that it wasn't really a restaurant or a cafe at all. It was the first-floor apartment of a house. And the funniest thing about that weirdest thing was that, weird as it was, I thought it was pretty cool, even though for me something being called weird had always meant fucked up, the opposite of being cool.

The building had six stone steps, real stone, I think, not slick stone facing, and a long stone porch that was roofed by white canvas and rope and reminded me, like it probably was supposed to, of a Conestoga wagon. On the porch were three big old water barrels turned upside down that served as tables. Some folks were standing at these as they sipped their coffees and ate their muffins. The same like with the restaurant being in a house, it struck me as odd but kind of pleasant to watch the people. Instead of seeming restless and bitter about having no place to go, they looked like they were enjoying it.

Also on the porch was a wicker and pillow rocker. Sitting in it was a dummy of Uncle Sam without the hat. The dummy was covered in white denim. Over the denim he wore a dusty black suit jacket. He had white hair, a white beard, an American flag in his jacket pocket, and a white-bowled pipe sewn into his hand. On his lap was a blackboard with blue and white words painted on: "*Pioneer*: one who goes before, preparing the way for others; one of a species that starts a new cycle of life in a barren area. *Cafe*: derived from French, originally along the Seine River, a coffeehouse and meeting place."

Instead of just strutting in, me and Uncle Vic paused a few feet inside the door as if we were waiting for an invitation. I was. I knew that in some restaurants you couldn't just walk in. We checked the place out, at least I did.

The cafe had four rooms. In the back, to the left, was the kitchen, right where you'd expect the kitchen of the original house would have been. There were two dining rooms in the front and one in the back. It all smelled of the freshly shellacked hardwood floors and of the coffee and biscuits and eggs being served.

After the emptiness of the blocks leading there, I was surprised at how crowded the place was. You could barely hear the hillbilly yodelling that was coming from the radio over all the talking and clatter. The most crowded room of all was the back room, the one with the view out to Manhattan. There were a few people in each of the sunlit front rooms, a pair of men and a pair of women, all in their twenties or thirties, and there was another couple, a kid named Morton Somebody who had just graduated high school, there with his girlfriend. I was always embarrassed around Morton because of the way my family was and the way his family was—his dad wore a suit to NY every day and they had a second house in the mountains. What mountains, I had no idea. Morton always acted better, I thought. But he gave me a real friendly hello, reached way across the aisle to shake my hand. His girlfriend, who I didn't know, seemed to recognize me, too.

My mom had the back room to work. Given the tip thing and all, that was probably the prime spot, and though this was only her fourth or fifth shift, she seemed to be friendly with a lot of the customers. Unlike us, they called her Sue. To go along with the new name, my mom had a new hairdo, too. The wave was gone. Now the hair hung straight and loose as a skirt. A shade lighter, her hair was cut flat and a little rough at the bottom, like it had been pulled and sliced instead of brushed and clipped. She looked a lot more professional than the other waiter and waitress. One in each of the front rooms, they were younger and sloppier and a lot slower, like they hardly knew they were working.

Little by little me and Uncle Vic inched forward. We stood in the archway between the front rooms and the back, blocking things as we tried to get my mom's attention.

"Sit over there," she said. With a platinum credit card between her fingers, she directed us toward two pushed-together tables where a woman was already seated. "Go ahead," she said, waving the card, but we didn't move. "There's someone there," I mouthed, figuring my mom could read my lips. She came toward us, shaking her head and smiling, already at home in the surroundings. "Go ahead," she said, turning and guiding me, one hand on my shoulder. "That's the way they do it here. Just say, 'Excuse me, do you mind if I sit here?' It's not a big deal to them."

"No way," I said, gently turning from her hold. But already Uncle Vic had hitched his pants and started on over.

The woman was reading a Boston newspaper. Uncle Vic stood a foot from the edge of her table, still unnoticed, waiting, legs spread. He moved his hands to his belt buckle and I rushed over.

"Excuse me," I said to the woman, "do you mind if we sit here?"

"Be my guest," she said, friendly enough but quickly back to her newspaper. We sat, me next to the lady, Uncle Vic across from her. He stared at the woman like she had some nerve for intruding on us.

"Uncle Vic, look at the menu. We got to order something. I got to be somewhere. The menu, Uncle Vic."

The fiddle-music show was over. "Goodbye from Lake Wobegone," said a twirled-around-itself voice I immediately hated. The show coming on next was about birdcalls or birdsongs, bird somethings. Part of a series, no less.

The woman held the edge of the newspaper in one hand, sipped the coffee she held in the other. Uncle Vic tapped her paper. "What was today's number?" he asked.

"You mean the lottery?" the woman asked, surprised and confused but ready to be helpful. Like a pair of kittens, one asleep and one awake, her left eye moved and her right eye didn't.

It was hard to tell the lady's age. Her short, thick hair was mostly greys with a few blacks mixed in. Much of her face was crinkly as used wax paper, with a million tiny creases around the eyes and mouth and a few longer ones carving her forehead. Everything else about her, though, her gauzy, scoop-neck blouse, her sparkling jewelry, her twinkly eyes—blue-green inside black liner—and her marionette's build, thin and loose and lanky, all made her seem like a college kid.

"No, miss. Not the lottery. The track number. Belmont, you know?"

"Oh," she said, downhearted. "Hmm. I don't think I know what you mean. Is it the sports section?"

"Yeah, the track section. Horse racing. Ponies."

"Like giddyup?" she asked.

"Yeah, like giddy*ap*," Uncle Vic replied, shaking his head. "It's not giddy*up*."

My mom came over to take our order. "It's on me," she said. Uncle Vic ordered coffee and a tuna sandwich. "You know how I like it," he said. I ordered from the breakfast side of the menu, orange juice and an English muffin. "I'm busy as hell," said my mother and she jangled the heavy change in her apron pouch. "An acquaintance of yours was here just before."

I figured Marcy—maybe it was wishful thinking—her probably wanting to know if I'd gotten back to Mr. Rodriguez, if I was going.

"That Officer Wilkinson," my mom said.

"She called herself an acquaintance?"

"No, she didn't. Joey! She said she'd just met you."

"She wants to interrogate me, right?"

"Not at all. She wants to talk to you, for you to call her. It's nothing to worry about, honey."

"I'm not worried," I insisted.

"Shoot, I'll be right back," said my mom, and she started off toward the kitchen.

"Don't trust her," I called to my mom, not caring who looked around. "Don't be so stupid."

"Hey, Joey, careful. Cut it out!" scolded Uncle Vic, taking a slo-mo swing at me, missing by a clear foot. "Here, come over this side, switch seats." He wanted to show the woman how to find the track number. We reversed seats and, once settled, my uncle held his stumpy hand out to her. "I'm Vic Scadutto."

"Nice to meet you. I'm Day Glow."

"I knew the DiAgllos from Marion Section, Fourth Street. Sam, Maria, Little Frankie."

"No, it's more a first name."

"That's a weird first name, miss."

"Yeah, I know. I know it is," she said. She nodded and smiled. I was surprised her teeth were so messed up—gappy after the front four and grey and yellow. "What's your friend's name?" she asked in my direction.

"Joey."

"Joey Scadutto. Great. *Parle Italian?*"

"No," I said and turned away.

"Do you bet the numbers?"

"Huh!" said Uncle Vic, like the question was insulting. "Huh!"

"Huh!" went Day Glow, not to make fun, just as a reflex, like an animal instinct, one chicken returning another's squawk.

"Numbers? What a question," said Uncle Vic, and he took out his cigars and began looking around for an ashtray. "I can tell you every candy store, every bar, even a dry cleaners within a mile that books numbers," he bragged. "Maybe two miles."

"Here," she said, opening up the paper all the way. "Now show me where's the Belmont number."

"The Handle," said Uncle Vic.

"Uh-huh," said Day Glow.

"Oh, never mind. Look," he said, but he was stumped by the paper's layout. "In this friggin' paper, I don't even know. It's an out-of-towner."

A laugh popped from the woman's lips, and, like old saloon buddies, she smacked him on the arm.

My mom came back with the coffee and OJ. "Joey, what do you mean, 'Don't be so stupid.' You know how rude that is?"

"I know. I'm sorry," I said. She had to take the college test that afternoon, in just another hour, and this was a bad time to mess her up. "I just mean don't trust her, Mom. Wilkinson."

"And why?"

"Christ, Mom. See what I mean? Because she'll use you."

"Joey, she said the same thing like Buddy told me last night—they want to make an arrest soon," whispered my mom. "I think she meant Natasha Matthews. Did you know her and her boyfriend were in the building the day of the murder? She said just what Buddy did. Don't get all jumpy and paranoid."

"Mom, you don't know what she thinks. Why does she want to talk to me then?"

"Oh, how do I know? I don't know why the cops do everything they do. I guess they're being thorough, right? Ain't they supposed to?"

"She's lying," I said. "I just have a feeling, that's all."

"Joey, she wants you to call her this afternoon, as soon as possible. You gonna do it? I gave her my permission."

"Yes, I'm gonna do it. I don't want to be arrested."

"Joey! Why do you talk like that?"

"Because it's true."

A call for my mother came from the kitchen. "Sue, help, help. We got to move these."

My mom reached under the newspaper, grabbed Day Glow's chicken platter, and took it with her as she hustled between tables to the kitchen.

"The trolley used to come right up the hill from Hoboken, right over that last corner, Fleet Street, named after Freeholder Fleet, right up here," explained Uncle Vic. "This was a hot property. When I was in eighth grade and they had the factories going they had an NRA parade on this block where we sit today. I got the day off. I was just a kid. But that was Roosevelt for you."

My mom came out of the kitchen loaded with plates on plates up and down one arm and two juices in a three-fingered grip in the other hand. I could tell right away she was upset.

She stopped at the first table in the room and dropped off three of the plates. That left her with just our two. The man, a kid really, at the table before ours asked for his check, and my mom, having already anticipated the request, cut him off midsentence by dangling the check in his face. She spun toward the table against the wall where she owed the juices, but she pulled away from the check guy before he'd taken hold of the bill, and as she tried to halt herself so he could reach again and grab hold, the juice splashed onto the wall table. He pulled the check from her fingers, and her hand moved to her back pocket where it pulled out a rag that she used to wipe the table before putting down the two juices. "Sorry about the spill" and "Here we go, two juices," she said, all in one breath, then spun toward our table.

I think it was my meanness and suggestions about Wilkinson, whether she could be trusted, what she really was after, that had upset my mother, pushed her inside her head. Like it was her way to, all my mom's movements became mechanical, a second ahead or behind.

"Mom, your hair's cool."

"Thanks." She looked at me, drawn back to the world. "That's so sweet of you."

It had gotten to a point where anything anybody said about me made me squirm.

"I got to decide if I want bangs or not," my mom said. She placed down my muffin with her left hand. With her right, she reached across to set down Uncle Vic's tuna sandwich. He stared at the sandwich like he expected it to morph. My mom asked me, "Did you find Brian? Wilkinson wants to talk to him, too."

"Brian's with Sonia. They went down Hoboken."

"Did you know that the zip code changes two blocks up from here?" Uncle Vic, still staring at his plate, asked Day Glow. "We got six zips in Jersey City. We're a big town."

"Sonia's very good for him," said my mom. "Can you see the change?" she asked.

"Not really," I said.

"Wait now, Susie," said my uncle, poking the food next to his sandwich with one finger. "What the hell is this?"

"Tuna fish, lettuce and no tomato, melon chunks, and potato chips."

"That's what I thought," he said. He raised his eyebrows and turned to Day Glow. She wanted to give him the right reaction but needed a clue.

"Potato chips? For lunch? Now that is odd. Is that crazy, Joey?"

"I don't know, Uncle Vic. Just eat the food, please."

Day Glow laughed, showing off those bad teeth again. Her mouth was in a little *O*, like she was hooting, but no sound came out.

"You got some sense of humor, sister," my uncle said, and she laughed even harder, a stiff, huffy inhaling laugh that made it seem like she was choking on a bone.

I was anxious to get my phone call with Wilkinson over with, so I rose to leave, letting my uncle stay there with his new friend. I tried to get away while my mom was back at the kitchen, but she waved and called me to her.

"Here, Officer Wilkinson gave me this," my mom said. She handed me a prosecutor's office card and turned it over so I could see another number written on the back. "Look. She even gave me her home phone number. Call her either way, she said. She doesn't mind if you call her at home. She said call her right away if you can. If not, call her tonight at home."

"All right, Mom, Christ! Don't worry. I'm gonna call right now."

"That's good," said my mom as I excused my way between tables. "That's good, Joseph. See you later."

Come on, I thought. What's this *Joseph* shit?

FIVE

I LEFT THE PIONEER AND HURRIED BACK TO THE PARK. There, at a pay phone between the basketball court and the Park House, I dialed the number on Wilkinson's gold-lettered card. No one answered and, after four rings, the call transferred, then I heard a second click as it transferred again, probably to our precinct. I told the guy who picked up, a sergeant whose words bubbled through his coffee-slurping mouth, why I called. He put me on hold for a long minute. "Shhhhp. Detective Wilk'son wans you to be here in a owa."

"Yeah. Tell her I'll be there, in an hour."

"Gotcha."

It was only a ten-minute walk to the police station, so I had time to kill. I walked through the park, toward our end. Following the route Brian had taken earlier in the morning, I headed down Cobble Road and stood at the entrance to the Hundred Steps. I cupped my hands in a semi-salute to block the sun from my eyes.

The top part of the Hundred Steps was so surrounded by weeds and overhanging tree branches that it was more like the entrance to a tunnel than a clearing. Bobbing like a boxer, I tried to find an angle where my rods and cones could agree, and I'd be able to see through the shadow and light to the first landing, eight steps below. But from my first move forward, I couldn't make out anything at my feet, each slab of crumbled concrete and each root and each rusted support blending into a dark green and silver murk. I felt my way through, touching onto smooth green branches and cat's-tongue leaves, and made it to the landing. By then my eyes had adjusted to the dark, and I was shocked blind all over again by the sunlight burning in from my right.

From the landing, the path switched back left. Where the ground was flat, it stunk from a permanent pool of feather-floating black water and moss and rainbowy scuzz that had settled in a basin against the stone wall. The switchback had a few steps of its own, but these were only three inches high, more like platforms than steps, three or four feet across. At its end, the steps made another switch to the right, and this led to a tunnel that was three times longer than the top set of steps, and much darker and denser, real jungle growth. Unlike the first set, which were more or less whole—whole enough that you could count them—these steps were so smashed and sunken that the entire section was a slope of mud, some of it fudgy, some hardened to a shine, the mud partially hiding glass and rubble and iron underpinnings. The only way for me to get down was to switch to even slower side-footed steps and to skitter as much as walk. Where the low wall alongside the steps had been busted through and a pool of sunlight brightened the rising hill, there was a smashed TV set, a smashed air-conditioner, the half-eaten back seat of a car, the remains of a campfire oozing green foam, and two twigs tied together into a cross as if a grave marker. Above them, dangling like giant Christmas ornaments from the branches near the tops of the trees—mutated palms with flopsy cigar-shaped leaves—were a pair of shopping carts, a lounge chair like the kind my mom and aunt used, a baby stroller, and a faded Captain America paper kite.

At the bottom of these steps, I followed a flat section of the path to the right. I came to a dry, rolling stretch above the side wall that must have gone on for thirty feet. If, instead of following the turn to the left, you hopped the wall, you'd be up on that plateau, nothing there but humping dry rocks glittering in the sun, tall yellow grass, a park bench, and, behind the bench, a slope-climbing patch of trees whose shadows, as the sun was at that minute, came close to the bench, waved at it, but never touched.

It was a Bowers Street Park bench that must have been dragged to this spot twenty years ago. You could still make out the chipped gold-lettered J.C. Recreation Dept. stencil on the back. Cinder blocks sandwiched each of the curlicue legs to keep the bench from wobbling and sliding right out of the grips.

I climbed the hill and sat on the bench and I took off my shirt. I hunched forward, elbows pressed into my thighs, head tipped down. My ankles were skinny and dirty, and the sun gave a dirty yellow sheen to the skin stretched over my shin bone. Since the last time I'd checked, my pale leg hair had turned brown.

I leaned back, stretched out my arms across the back of the bench. My shorts waist was way loose and where the bunching went out I could see clear down to my underpants. My belly was flat and scrawny, not totally bald like it had been, and unlike my browned arms and legs, my stomach was fish white. My chest was hairless and without a trace of pecs, more deflated than pumped. I caught a whiff of my armpits, and the smell was okay, mannish even. I sort of liked it.

And I liked how everything around me was dry and warm—the dust on the bench, my legs in the sun, the grass against my ankles, the air on my chest, the back of my hand touching my lips. I shut my eyes.

It was just two more days until Mr. Rodriguez would be back and only six until the next Wagon Train would leave. I could go, my brain was saying. Why not? Why couldn't I? I could go.

I forced the words into my throat and, as I painted a blue and yellow and green prairie picture, I tried to lift them to my mouth. I could go.

A breeze came from the harbor and my nipples hardened. I dropped my chin to check out the nipples and noticed I had a hard-on, too. Maybe it was the adventure and the great outdoors. Maybe it was just Marcy. It would have been nice if she was on the bench here, soft and understanding and smiling, big and open. I could have let her touch me if she was on the bench here. I might even have put my arms around her.

Mr. Rodriguez would have asked, "Why, Joey? Tell me, why does the idea of anyone, with the possible exception of Marcy Harrigan, the idea of anyone touching you make your skin crawl?"

"Mr. Rodriguez, I do not know," I'd say. For some silly reason I talked that way to him, without contractions. Maybe it was to make fun of being white. "But I do know that even being asked about someone touching me makes my skin crawl."

He'd sit back and ponder, a finger to his lips, his brow crinkled. "Maybe, Joey—well, did you ever consider that it might be something about your skin?"

Right on the bench, I cracked up laughing and opened my eyes to the bright sky.

"Shit," I whispered. Shit, I better get going. I wasn't sure how long I'd been there—not real long—but it couldn't be more than half an hour until I had to be at the police station. Fuck.

I turned my head right, eyes into the blinding sun, and I quickly shut them, squeezing out the burn. I felt like a sun-soaked sponge. When I moved my arms up from the backrest, they were heavy, and instead of the muscle and bone carrying the flesh and blood, it seemed like my will had to lift all four. When the harbor breeze blew, the leaves' shadow, grown a foot or two since I'd first sat, waved over me, cooling the air. Half asleep and as dull-witted as I was, I mistook the fanning of shadow for the breeze itself, and when I realized my mistake, got a kick out of my own stupidity.

When finally I rubbed my eyes clear, I stood up. I took a few steps back to bury myself in the shade. I turned and reached out for a tree limb to steady myself, but I lost balance when I bumped toe-first into a grass-hidden, bow-shaped root. To stay standing, I pulled at the rubbery tree limb in front of me, but it gave too much and I slipped, twisting my ankle. My foot came halfway out of the sneaker and I felt the rip of muscle tearing.

I was just at the beginning of the back section of trees, and to lift myself, I reached in toward another fanning limb, heavy with silky leaves. I grabbed on to what felt like an interior branch. But when I pulled, it came loose and I nearly slipped again. It wasn't a branch. It was a black cable, three or four feet long, and copper and silver wire showed through the white insulation at its ends. It was the same cable as the kind stacked at the tutoring center. I shook the limb but no more cables dropped down. I swiped my hand through, felt nothing loose. I pushed the limb aside, bent, and, favoring my swelling ankle, stepped under the tree's umbrella.

Sunlight slipped through the leaves and came in over my shoulder. At first, the waving metallic tips of so many cables hanging from so many branches looked like still raindrops. But as I squinted and approached, I saw what they were. And I knew whose they were and what they were for.

There were eight at least, maybe ten, maybe even a dozen, some hanging straight, some in a *C* shape, three more on the ground curled like fetuses.

I wrapped the cable tight around my hands, closed my fists on it, yanked, quivering the line and digging it into the sides of my hands.

This was the spot where Brian had planned it. This was where he'd measured the length, where he'd measured his strength. This was where he'd decided to test himself on Prince, where he'd decided when and how to kill Uncle Mike.

Over and over I repeated the pulling action, full force, until the pain spread through my wrists and deep into my arms.

SIX

I N HIGH GATE, WE HAVE CERTAIN BELIEFS. WE
believe that God speaks through the weather pattern,
Instant Lottery, and traffic light sequences. We believe in
loyalty and in Custer's Seventh Cavalry. We believe you gotta
ride the whole ride and we believe in going down with the ship.

We believe there are certain things better left unsaid and
we believe in the things we do say for how they make us feel and
not for what they mean.

We believe that for every drop of rain that falls a flower
grows and that tomorrow's the first day of the rest of your life
and we believe in the king of kitchen plaques—the one about
courage, serenity, and wisdom.

We believe that we are normal and that people who don't
think we are are weird, and, of course, we believe that weird is
bad.

We believe that blacks are just dying to get into our neighborhood. And we believe that as the blacks see all the foreigners—the Arabs, the Koreans, and the Filipinos, the Russians, the
Pakistanis, the Central Americans—seeping in more and more,
ruling some blocks of their own, it drives them crazy that they're
still kept out. We believe that as the last neighborhood in Jersey
City where white people are the majority we may not be able to
keep everyone out, but at least we can them.

We believe that compared to theirs, the blacks', our neighborhood is safer, cleaner, richer, healthier, and holier. We believe
they'd give their gold teeth to sit in our parks, shoot at our hoops,
shop in our stores, go to our schools, and live in our homes.

And that was the point. We weren't going to let them, and
we didn't try to keep how we felt a secret from anyone, black or
white. Let the drops of rain shower upon all of God's creation, but

the flowers growing here, whatever their health and beauty, were ours, all ours.

And I wondered what Detective Wilkinson knew about our beliefs.

I'd only been in the North District Station three times in my life, the last time being three days before when I was interviewed by Resto, but the place sounded and smelled so familiar it made my stomach ache. That wasn't all, though. My ankle had swelled and was turning purple. I thought a bone might be broken, but as I entered the building, I didn't want to limp, afraid the cops would notice and I'd have to come up with a lie I hadn't yet settled on.

The four cops who stood around the intake desk, its contact paper peeling off the right corner, ignored me as I inched forward from underneath the lobby's chandelier. One cop was taking sandwich orders for the other three, a sergeant who must have been past retirement age and two younger patrolmen, one white, one Hispanic. A fifth cop, the one behind the desk, in the seat Sergeant Paluka'd been in a few days earlier, was an unwashed little vulture. He couldn't have legitimately passed the police fitness test unless "faint pulse" was the bottom-line qualifier. I assumed he was the one who'd taken my phone call and made the appointment with Wilkinson, but after he'd ordered a ham and mozzarella on an Italian roll, he went back to his coffee and *Weird Tales* paperback, pretending like I wasn't there.

It wasn't until the sandwich runner had left that one of the other cops, the old sergeant, pulled me over by the arm without as much as a "Can I help you?"

"I think this boy's here to see the detective," he said and pointed to the down staircase in the back hall.

"Would that be the T.N. detective?" asked the little vulture, swarming half hidden behind folded arms.

"Knock that T.N. shit off, okay, Carl? It's not funny anymore," said the sergeant.

"Yes, sir," he said, hiding his mouth with a brush of the hand and wrist. "Is that who you want to see?" he asked me. "Sergeant Wilkinson?"

"I have a one-thirty appointment with her."

The other two cops—the pink-faced blonde and the Hispanic filing his nails—looked at each other like I'd said something stupid. I couldn't figure out what.

"Just go downstairs, kid," said the Hispanic one, wanting to get rid of me. Maybe it was because the word appointment was too respectful. "Knock on the last door to the right."

The vulture behind the desk pulled me over and leaned my way. He kept waving me closer and closer. When he could reach, he pulled me by the thumb. "Be careful. She hates white people."

I nodded, said, "Thanks," walked down the hall stiffly, careful not to limp.

Past the paint cans, brushes, drop cloth, and ladder that still clogged the hall, I turned left onto two short flights to the lower level. The hallway in the basement was narrow and windowless. The recently painted cement walls were black from floor to shoulder, pale green from there to the ceiling, the pencil line that had been used to separate the two colors still visible. The basement's only light came from a pair of fluorescent bulbs stationed at each end, and the only decoration was a yellow and black Fallout Shelter sign, its screws and bent edges crusted with rust.

The room I'd been directed to wasn't just the last room in the basement, it was the only room. The one other door down there was a metal double door that led outside, to the back. At the opposite end of the hall, on the floor, was a cash register, a wheelchair, a blood-pressure gauge, and a white leather couch standing on end. The hallway there, at that end, turned left into a section that had no light but that leaked a damp cat-litter draft.

Detective Wilkinson's door had a knob coated in electrical tape and a latch bolt held in by the same black tape. In the center of the door was a manilla folder stuck through with a push-pin, Detective Rhonda Wilkinson, Prosecutor's Office written in script letters double-drawn in green and red marker. Before I knocked, a woman's voice called, "Come on in."

The knob didn't turn. You just had to push hard.

"Hi, Joey. Thanks for coming. Make yourself at home,"

Wilkinson said with a backhanded sweep across the room, just as dingy and even more dim than the hallway. Her desk was in the center of the floor, her swivel chair behind it, a leather bookbag to the side. Across from her, I sat in a smaller round-seated rolling chair. It seemed like we were talking in a prison cell.

"I been coming here for almost three years. You can thank Lieutenant Resto for the accommodations. Anyway, hi," she said, and we shook hands. She had a dark chocolate complexion and rosy black-edged lips. Her eyes were set far apart and rose at the corners like Asian eyes. "I'm Detective Sharhonda Wilkinson. Just call me Rhonda."

On the desk was a glass bowl burning a cinnamon-scented candle. It kept the smell of the cat litter out of the room but was itself pretty hard to take. Also on the desk, opened to a middle page, was an Arco Police Sergeant's Exam Book. Next to that book was another one, *You Too Can Make It Happen*, by Oprah's boyfriend, Stedman. "Good book," said Wilkinson, nodding. Her hair hung in braids from a part down the center. Each braid was tipped in a gold or red foil cap. " 'You are not your circumstances, you are your possibilities.' Exactly. Good book, good advice." She winked and gave me a thumbs-up then slid both hands into her briefcase, an old-fashioned, snap-and-clasp, plastic-handled bookbag. She took out a batch of files.

"Where'd you get those shorts, man? I told you, I love them," she said as she flipped through her folders. It was bullshit and I didn't bother to answer. She didn't seem to mind.

Pen in hand, ready to write, "Okay, so tell me what you know about everyone's chief suspect, the notorious Natasha Matthews," she asked, though it was a folder with my name on the label, not Natasha's, that she opened.

"Hardly nothing," I said. "I'm positive I don't know anything more than what you already know."

"You're *positive*? Well, I don't know too much," Wilkinson said and smiled. She had high cheekbones and a small, puckered mouth pressed by two bucked teeth. When she smiled, and the teeth peeked from her lips, she looked like the Easter Bunny. "I know she's an ugly girl. I swear, I put her picture in my head and I think of her and I think of a goddamned baboon, you know.

Don't you?"

"No, I don't think of no baboon," I said, already annoyed with Wilkinson and her dumbass jokes or games or tricks.

"Hey, but don't you think she did it?" she asked, scratching the tiny ear she found through the ropes of her hair.

"I don't know who did it and I don't hardly know anything about Natasha Matthews. No, well, I know one thing. I know she wanted to start a card business."

"Yeah, she still into that. That I do know. Some of them brothers you see on the street up around the college, selling incense and shirts and tapes and whatnot, she made some of the cards they sell. I like them cards myself, though. I'm a sucker for corny, too," she said and she laughed and her teeth peeked out.

I said, "I know Natasha was related to somebody just arrested for murder, a second cousin, I think, maybe."

That sentence wiped the smile from her face. She stared at me, disappointed, like she knew I'd gotten my information straight from Resto's mouth and considered it worse than useless. "Oh, is that so," she said. I was sorry I'd said it that way, blurting it like I was trying to pin something to Natasha. I was afraid it made Wilkinson trust me less and dislike me more. As she wrote in my folder, she said, "We all related to boys been arrested for something." She stared at me, her eyes white and red around copper brown centers. They could have been sad or angry, calculating or drifting, all those things at once. "Hey, Joey, you know what? You don't even need to go to no second cousins. The people right around her, her boys, they're all criminals of one sort or another. How about her boyfriend? Hardy Cummings, the big dope. This young man's a fool. In the Youth House for joyriding with an uncle when he was eleven. Drugs, weapons charges, assault, drugs again since then. He ain't even turned twenty yet. And you know what? Listen to this. Every teacher we've talked to from seventh grade to when he finished high school, a B student, every one says what a doll he is. And most of them are white, these teachers. That's Hardy Cummings." Her heavy-tipped braids swished as she shook her head in exasperation, like a cartoon momma hen with too many little ones to track.

"It's probably her and her crew done in Mr. Mayflower. Shit, it just makes me sick to think of all these black children committing crimes. Imagine how I feel, in this job," she said, and she stared at me again. All I could manage was a shrug. "But, hey, you know. Before we arrest anybody we got to check everything or we look bad. I don't know who else it could be, except it could be anybody, though, right?"

"Yeah. Of course it could be anybody."

She tapped her penpoint, rubbed it in circles across the back of the page until the ink ran, but instead of writing, she put the pen down and launched into this chatty story about her boyfriend, and though I knew more about him in twenty seconds than I'd want to know in a lifetime, her lecture went on for half of forever. The whole time she stared at me with that gaze, a momma again, a loving momma even, but this time one who might have to whup her kid.

Demetrius, the boyfriend, was twenty-nine years old and he was six-two and he was half Jamaican/half Carolina homeboy, whatever a Carolina homeboy was. Demetrius, like I could give a fuck, had come up the so-called hard way and had graduated from Rutgers Law School exactly one year earlier. He had just started a job interning at the African-American Legal Defense Fund in Elizabeth.

Staring back at her, I tried to seem bored but patient, mixing my message like she did, trying to gain the upper hand.

She picked up the pen and began doodling in my file. "Demetrius is a man strong in mind, body, and spirit. I tell him about this case. He's real interested, all ears. He gets crazy about this racial stuff. Sometimes too much, too intense and angry, even for me."

I laughed. She laughed back.

"What?" she asked.

"What's this case got to do with race?"

"Oh, come on, man, you smarter than that. There's two sides to a case," she said like a law student herself, and I figured this was Demetrius talking. "There's everything that happens before a crime, and there's everything that happens after it, to solve it. Everything that's happened *since* Mike Mayflower—I love that damn name—*since* he was strangled, it's all been about race. You must see that, I mean."

I did, I saw what she meant, that we didn't give a fuck what happened to the nigga girl. "I don't want her arrested if she's not guilty," I said. I wanted my words to come out as an accusation, not an apology. I think they did, but she kept on.

"Demetrius thinks the murder was an 'inner circle' job," she said, still writing in my file, her hand moving in such relaxed, flowing loops I couldn't tell if she was doing words or doodles. "I'm not writing anything," she said, watching her own hand. "It just helps me think."

"Uncle Mike had no inner circle," I said.

I heard water gurgling, being sucked down a drain. Along the wall behind the book boxes I noticed a green-painted pipe that dumped into a grate in the room's back corner.

"Well, in other words, anybody who'd call him Uncle Mike—to Demetrius, that's the inner circle. That's the way he thinks," she said, playing with her braids. "So let's forget about Demtrius and everybody. My question to you, Joseph Scadutto, is how can *you* be of help to *me*?"

I looked around. There wasn't nearly enough light in the room. I squinted at the ceiling. Nothing there.

"I can't be of any help," I said. "Don't you know all of what I already told Resto?"

"I think I do. I know what he wrote down."

"Well, then that's it."

"And how would you know that, Mr. Scadutto? Did you see what he wrote?" she asked in a jokey way that reminded me of Mr. Rodriguez in class when he wanted to make a point without pissing us all off. I shrugged. "All right, don't get antsy and mad at me," she said. I appreciated that she used "antsy and mad" and not "antsy and scared," even though I knew she knew better. But a second later she was pushing me around, making up for being too sweet. Maybe she was listening to Demetrius. "Yeah, yeah. All right, now listen. I'm very much by-the-book, Joey, with my interviews, so if I ask you anything that makes you uncomfortable or you'd rather not answer, you let me know. Got it?"

"Go ahead," I said. Straightening up, I knocked my sore ankle against one of the chair's rollers. It throbbed.

"Let me write down that I made you aware of that. Okay, now. I tell you, man, I am a by-the-book detective. I got to be," she said. Then, like Resto had, she asked about Clay. "Tell me, what's his story?"

I tried the same thing I'd tried with him, with Resto—where Clay was from, what his job was at the college, where he lived—and got the same response: "No, I mean what's he like. His personality, you know . . . he seems a little . . . ," she said and, holding the pen between her fingers, she made an Italian gesture with her hands, rocking them back and forth, medza-medz. "I mean, what's the word?"

"He thinks he's sort of special, sort of an intellectual—he thinks of himself as that."

"Yeah, yeah. Like better, above it all."

"Mmm-hmm."

"Like the rules don't apply to him. He should be able to do whatever he wants."

"Yeah, that's him. But there's lots and lots of people like that, not only Clay. The world's full of them."

"Oh yeah? It is? And are you Mr. Nanuet's defense counsel?"

I clammed up.

She sucked, the black bitch.

I'd hardly said anything but already felt like I'd said too much. Don't say nothing to cops, her or Resto. I should have known better.

"Is he somebody you'd trust? Joey?" She closed my file, tilting her head in her first feminine move, like she was the cute girl interviewing me for MTV. Fat chance. "Really, would you trust him?"

"I don't know. I might."

"Well, you either would or you wouldn't. Trust is trust. Imagine you're Brian. How would he answer the question?"

Brian didn't trust Clay for shit. Clay may have thought he did, my aunt may have thought so, but he couldn't have.

Slowly, I said, "I have no . . . idea," pausing to let her hear the word "fucking" that I thought before the word "idea." "Why don't you ask him?" I asked. She smiled, showed her bucked teeth. "Maybe you have already."

"As a matter of fact, yeah. Brian mumbles a lot, but he knows what he's saying."

"And what did he say?"

"Oh, Brian wouldn't trust Clay, not at all. That came through clear." She put her gaze on me. "How could I put it? He knows Clay's got his own, I don't know," she said, nodding, shifting her eyes left and right, up and down, as she bounced words around in her head. "His own . . . rules."

"That's Brian's opinion."

"I know, and you and Brian are two different people, right?" she said. "You're fifteen, he's almost nineteen."

"He is. He turned nineteen."

"And how old's your mom?"

"She'll be thirty-eight," I said. Wilkinson wrote it down.

"Damn, nineteen and fifteen. It blows my mind," she said. "It depresses me." A fizz and puff of smoke came from the cinnamon candle's wick, surprised us both. She smiled, I didn't. "I bought this card from that guy I was telling you about," she said. She opened the folder with Natasha's name and took a greeting card from it.

"What guy?"

"One of them guys by the college who sells Natasha's cards," she said. The card was on off-white paper, the kind that's got little fibers in it. There was a drawing on the cover, a skinny black woman with a long neck and a Martian-sized head, her arms stretched out like Christ's, shackled heavy chains hanging from the wrists, a tropical, maybe African, shore in the background, inked in gold. "Damn, I like these cards," she said, pretending she was about to frisbee it across the room in frustration. "You know that boy Hardy Cummings, the one been with Natasha a lot, the assault charge I mentioned, that was assault *and* robbery. Took down a man for fifty dollars. That man lost his eye. Now, how much more would Natasha's pal, the one the white teachers like so much, do for twenty thousand dollars? According to Resto's report, Hardy was *seen* around Uncle Mike's, too, with Natasha. That is incriminating, now, ain't it? This boy's gonna have pity on a nasty, old, sick white man? Come on. That's the way some of these people think. I tell Demetrius, comes in all colors, man. When Hardy assaulted that other man, he was fourteen years old, younger than you are now. Much bigger, six foot already, not as fat as he is now, but imagine, fourteen. He was a baby when he committed that crime. By the time he was your age, he was incarcerated for a year. His life was determined right there. You know what I mean? Squashed, squelched out, whatever. They talk about being too soft on juvenile crime. Yo, man. Way yo. Kids do time, too. Do time all the time," she said. She folded her arms like she was finished and I was supposed to pick up the conversation. It pissed her off when I said nothing.

"Okay, then give me a second to get my stuff together here." She shuffled through the folders on the desk, shoving some in, pulling others out of the bookbag beside the desk. "I hate coming to this precinct. I can take a lot, but, I mean, they treat me the worst here of all the places in Hudson County. Ah, awright, I'm ready—hell with it. Let me ask you questions about yourself on the night Mike was murdered, strangled. Ooops, wrong file." She smiled.

"Could you put out that candle?" I asked.

She didn't say anything, just blew it out in a tight jet without looking at me. She found the right file. It was a second one with my name on it, "Joseph P. Scadutto" typed across a red label. "I want to tell you again, Joey, you're a witness aiding in an investigation," she said and rested her hands atop the opened folder. "But if I ask you a question which you don't want to answer, you can refuse it and get your lawyer here—actually, not here, at my home office—and we'll go through the whole bullshit procedure. Don't just nod, Joey, you have to say okay."

"Go ahead, yes. Okay."

"I hate to be so formal with you, man, but I have to be by-the-book. I really believe in that, for my sake and yours, people in your position. Joey, there's so many people arrested falsely because of coercive, biased, and unethical police practices. You know what I mean. It drives me crazy, it really drives me nuts," she said, lifting her hands, cupping them around her ears. "That's Demetrius's field, where he's interning. He gets those kinds of cases all the time. That's why he's like he is. He sees children, kids your age. Man, but the one big difference. Those ones are always children of color, never white ones. My God, you seen the numbers of African-American boys and girls in correctional facilities? Makes you want to cry. Well, makes me want to cry. Joey, these are boys and girls, just like you, children, not men and women. You're a kid, right?" She gave me that look again, soft-hearted but just. Like this is gonna hurt me more than it does you. She unfolded her hands, puffed them in the air like she was letting the truth fly free. She was trying to get me to like her, but I was tired of the show. "That's why we got to be so careful with Natasha. You know what I'm saying? That's why we got to make sure the lieutenant goes slow and that he understands his role. He ain't the boss. You know, in our society we just rushing to build prisons to fill them with black folks. Hey, you think anybody in this building truly cares if Natasha Matthews or Hardy Cummings truly killed that man as long as they can put somebody in jail? Naw, no way," she said. She looked up at the ceiling, through it maybe to the first floor, shook her head and smirked. Shut up, please, just shut up and let me leave. "Eh, don't get me started." She smiled. "You, you're in a much better situation. No, no, Joey, I just mean you're at least in a *fair* situation. That's all anybody can ask for. But your poor lieutenant, he must really want that Natasha Baboon arrested. The whole damn county knows he wants that director's chair come next year. That's why that boy and girl better have themselves some damn good lawyers. I don't know. They just better. I pray to Jesus for them, guilty or innocent. Oh, there I go, see—getting into my social-work mode. Where we at?" She pulled apart her folded hands and, as she thought, karate-chopped her left hand with her right. "Where were we, where were we, where were we? We was talking about you, Joey. You were—where were you on the night Mike was strangled? Say where you were."

"You know where I was. I was downstairs in the building with my family," I said angrily, staring past her at the blank cement wall.

She put her hands up, like Joey, stop with the anger bit. "Joey, who's your lawyer?"

"I don't have a lawyer."

"No? Does your family have a lawyer?"

"No. I don't think so."

Sometimes it was real little things, like Do you speak Italian? or Does your family have a lawyer? that I had to answer no to that humiliated me.

"Jesus," she said. She smacked her hands together and brought them to her chin in prayer. "Then your family must at least know someone who's a lawyer, or know someone who knows someone who's a lawyer," she said, her smile spreading into a grin.

"Why do you care?" I asked with a big attitude, probably too big—letting it out, maybe, that I was really asking her to please leave me alone.

"Joey, remember, any time you don't want to answer questions, no problem. Just speak up, hear? Now, you were downstairs, but you were also upstairs."

The pipe water gurgled again, and the dingy room went even darker.

"Yeah. So? You already know all this."

"I just want to make sure I got your story straight."

"It's not a story." My jaw unlocked and the words screamed out.

"All right, okay, Joey," she said, my shout still ringing. "I'm sorry. I really am." Something came up her throat and she had to seal her lips to push it back. "I want to help you, and I want to get the facts straight, okay?"

"My Uncle Vic lives on the second floor. Mike was on the third."

"Right. You go upstairs to invite Mike down for dinner. Then what?"

"Then nothing. Uncle Mike's door was locked."

"But didn't you already know someone was in there?" she asked, squinting at the doodles she had made in my folder.

"No, not for sure. Only maybe. I didn't know it for sure."

"The door's locked, though. Right?"

"Uh-huh."

"Which lock is locked?" she asked. She stopped squinting,

stopped doodling, just froze like a statue.

My chest squeezed and my head went warm and dizzy. "The chain lock," I said, afraid to lie.

"That must have meant someone was inside. So what'd you do?"

"You know what I did. That's when the Korean saw me."

"Mm-hmm. Mr. Woo."

"I left. I didn't know what Mike was doing."

"He might have been in the apartment but just not answering."

"Yeah, why not?"

"You didn't know what was going on in there so you just said the hell with it."

"There's nothing wrong with that. What was I supposed to do?"

"Hey, nothing," she said, her eyes wide and face open. "I'm saying—I'm just asking the questions so I know what went on. Now, where was Brian at that minute?"

The question came from the blue. I was about to say he was at Clay's, but a picture of him inside Uncle Mike's, pressed to a wall, came to my mind and I could only stare back at her.

"Never mind that question. You can't account for someone else anyway, can you?"

"No. Uh-uh," I said, still thrown.

"You didn't know what was going on so you left. You were just inviting him to a damn dinner. It wasn't the end of the world if he didn't come. Joey? Joey, you want to stop?"

"No," I said. My face had gone from hot to cold and I put my hand up to massage my throat loose.

"But now, hey, now we do know what was going on. That as you stood there, right, as you stood there Uncle Mike was being strangled to death. Could have been Natasha and Hardy, or just Natasha," she said, counting the possibilities on her fingers. "Or could have been just Hardy, killing him that minute, strangling him. Or it could have been an inside job—one, or a group, of the people we know. Or could have been someone altogether different, some maniac we got no clue about. Right?"

165

"Right."

"See, that's the whole reason, the only reason, I brought up the lawyer thing. You really should do it just to protect yourself. And see, I mean, it's a good thing that you got this relationship with the lieutenant. It's not bad. But this is not the lieutenant's case, Joey. And you know me now. I'm not in any rush to lock up two more niggas. If they're guilty, well, that's different. That's a different story. But first we're gonna check everything out, thoroughly, the right way. We take the case as it comes—a day, a month, a year. This is too serious. Everybody gets treated equal in our society. That's America."

SEVEN

I STEPPED OUTSIDE THE STATION HOUSE FRONT door and glanced across the street into the window of the Al 'n Mo, my eyes squinting through the sunlight that angled in over Pershing Field. Talking to Boy Evans, but looking toward the precinct steps, like maybe he'd been waiting for me to come out, was Brian.

It seemed as though Brian was doing the talking, though his lips moved so little when he spoke it would have been impossible to tell, except for the way Boy, his hands cupped around his coffee, eagerly nodded his agreement like a horse trained to count. I jumped the precinct steps and hop-skipped away, past the Polish Deli, past the awning of Bettinger's Funeral Home, past the Carvel (Under New Ownership), and, on the corner, past Health and Beauty, where the clock read 2:46, meaning, as we all knew, that the time was 2:40.

I turned off Central, onto Hutton, and walked along the side where the sun shone in my face. Before coming to the block Saint Paul of the Cross was on, I'd have to pass by the stink of the electrical fire that had taken down the Jet Age Laundromat on the corner of Cambridge and the worse stink of the dog lots on the next block, Hutton between Hancock and Cambridge. Because it was so much simpler to concentrate on the pain pulsing from my swollen ankle than to think about the conversation I'd just had with Wilkinson, I struck my foot hard and with every step tracked the rays of pain up my leg. It seemed good this way, maybe not really good at all, maybe just not so bad, with my ankle aching, the sun in my eyes, the stink up my nostrils— though maybe not too many people would understand it. But I picked feeling the pains that I shared with everybody else, that I could talk to other people about—"Goddamned sun," "Fucking stink," "You believe this bitch of an ankle won't heal?" I'd pick feeling these pains, things you could speak, pick 'em any day over the private ones you could barely talk to yourself about.

"Joey, Joey," I heard Brian yell. He had turned the corner and was jogging toward me, out of breath from the thirty-yard hustle, more exercise than he was used to in a week. "Hey, how ya doing?"

He'd shaved his beard, except for the stringy sideburns, and this made his face brighter and less round and revealed him as though the gates of a stockade fort had been opened. His hair, usually flat and unwashed in a single oily blanket, was a mess of short swirls and tufts and spokes, the left side more squished and matted than the right, overall a mixture of clusters pressed and clusters standing, as though an army had marched through brush. It may have been a punky mess that replaced the old lifeless layer, but Brian's hair was clipped and shampooed and one shade lighter than usual, and he looked an awful lot cooler this way than with the Frank Sinatra style he usually wore.

I pictured Sonia doing it—sitting him in a chair, snapping scissors above his head, playing beautician.

Side by side, me and Brian reached the corner, and I caught the first whiff of the Jet Age Laundromat's wet ruins.

"I got to talk to you," Brian said. "It's real important."

We continued down Hutton.

Unlike Brian's dad, mine (my father—he was never a dad) was a real short-term thing for my mom, in and out of her life before I was born. My father was a cheat on her real boyfriend of the time, someone named Charley who was going nights to Seton Hall for a master's degree in business. My mom was twenty-two when I was born, this guy Charley was twenty-three. They'd gone to Saint Paul of the Cross together where he was a year ahead of her. He wasn't any valedictorian like she was, but he was one of the smartest boys, and he went on to graduate college, and maybe he even completed that master's degree. Then my mom fucked up.

My father's name was Seth Hawkins, but not even my mom could remember what he looked like until we came upon a Polaroid of him in the drawer of a bureau we were throwing out a couple of years ago. Even then his image barely rang a bell with anyone who'd been around at the time. For my mom, it rang a bell less so than the nightgown she had on in the picture.

Seth was a little guy, but not that little, with a small girlish face—slitty eyes like mine, thin lips, a nose that barely rose off his face, more nostril than cartilage. He was sitting on our couch, holding a can of Silver Bullet in a salute to the camera. My mom was sitting on the sofa's arm, her right leg across his lap, her left leg raised. She was wearing only that thin nightgown she still remembered, probably pink though it came across orange in the photo, and a Yankees hat. Her right arm was across the back of the couch, around Seth's shoulders, and her left arm was in the air, her hand holding a beer can, too. She was tan and he was pale. Her eyes were wide and her face shiny, you could see the tingling tip of her tongue against one of her wolf teeth, and you knew it was only a few minutes after the snapshot that Seth would be on top of her, seeking her hole. I was pretty upset about it, and I dated the picture June 16, 1984, exactly nine months before my birthday.

Me and my mom and Brian, Aunt Pat and my mom's best girlfriend of that year, Dolly, and that girl Allina, the one who'd just moved in downstairs, were the only ones I knew of who saw it. They all laughed at how much I looked like Seth, thought it was cute, but looking like him only made me feel like a failure, empty and ashamed.

The smell switched once we got past the burnt laundromat and to the dog lots. It got worse. And the sidewalk switched, too, from smooth to cracked, each rectangle of concrete lifted at a different angle, as though an earthquake was erupting in super-slow motion.

Brian was eager to talk. He was energetic, and kind of nervous about it, too. He was never any of those things—eager or energetic or nervous—and I had a feeling about what was coming. "Look," he said and stepped closer, nearly in front of me, showing off his new clean face. "This is crazy, man. Let's duck in somewhere. Let's go behind the church. Come on. I got to tell you something."

His clothes, tight-fitting brown jeans and a darker brown T-shirt, were as styleless as ever, but the smell they'd carried, that all his clothes had carried for over a year, since he'd started spending less and less time at home, was gone. It had been a smell like they'd

169

been soaked in soapless water but never *washed* before they were dried, and the odor of sweat and spilled coffee and cigarette smoke and grease had been baked in instead of washed out. That was gone, replaced by a laundry detergent smell.

"What, does she wash your clothes, too?"

"No, no, she don't," he said, grinning. "That's me." Just that little bit, saying "That's me," grinning, even glancing at me as he grinned, was real different. With both hands, like a movie actor, he swooshed back his hair. He reached into his back pocket for a flannel baseball cap, a grey one with a maroon bill and an oval maroon patch, "John Doe" printed across. He put it on. "This, Sonia did give to me," he said. "I sort of like it. It's okay, right?"

I didn't answer.

The change that made Brian eager and nervous also made me trust him less. When he didn't care about or want anything, the truth was as good as a lie and silence better than either. Now there was something he wanted and he knew silence wouldn't get it done.

"Go ahead, into the schoolyard, you first," he said.

"No, you go ahead. You go ahead first."

"It doesn't matter who goes first, Joey," he said and started walking down the stone steps alongside the church. "Don't make it harder, okay?" he said over his shoulder.

Saint Paul of the Cross was the church where me and Brian had been baptized and taken Holy Communion. Brian had gone as far as receiving Confirmation when he was twelve and graduating there on the day of his fourteenth birthday, but me, being born on the down side of my mom's life, I'd already left the school, and the faith, before either Confirmation or graduation. In my fifth-grade year, all the Catholic schools doubled tuition, and that was the reason my mom gave for the pull out and the transfer to Number 8. But it seemed to me that since I'd started, we'd been the poorest and most messed-up family in Saint Paul's, the one with the most decay, poorer and more messed and more decayed than most of the public school families, too. Maybe it wasn't so blatant there, at Number 8, but still it was obvious to me, carried around in our walks, our smiles, our words, our smells, I thought, the trash in us visible from a block away.

The transfer out probably didn't just explode on us

overnight, when the tuition went up. It was something, I think, that had been in the making for a couple of generations.

In 1973, my mom had graduated from Saint Paul's first in the class and won a scholarship to the Academy of the Sacred Heart. She started at Sacred Heart just before my grandma was institutionalized at Secaucus Meadowview, for what I was never sure, though I'd made up the details of a complicated story that included crime, addiction, and illness. My mom lasted at Sacred Heart until the second month of sophomore year, when my grandma died.

The church grounds and four buildings—the church, the school, the rectory, and the convent—took up the small square block, Hancock to Sherman and Hutton to Griffith. Set on Hutton, right in the middle of the block, was the church, with the ten-year-old Loaves and Fishes Counselling and Rehabilitation Center bulging off one side. It was a quilt-and-daisy sort of place. Over its door, a yellow, white, and green banner hung from a brass rod. In '93, Aunt Pat had been the organization's treasurer for a few summer months, but after seventy-two dollars was missing she was asked to leave and never again show her drug-sucking face on the property. Across from the Loaves and Fishes side of the church was the rectory. Across from the other side was the convent. Behind the church, separated from it by a school-yard the shape of a righted Z, was the school. With all the three- and four-story buildings going this way and that, the grounds, except for blots and slices of sunshine in shapes like geometry-book drawings, were cast in shadow.

We approached the church's black-painted metal fire escape in one of the Z's short legs, the passageway between the church and convent.

Brian stuffed the baseball cap into his back pocket. "I'm gonna tell you the whole thing," he said as he looked over the steps, climbed all ten of them to the top platform. Around us, the beige and brown buildings blocked any view of the street except for the narrow opening next to a Sacred Heart shrine. Overhead was a deep blue, cloudless sky, the sun hidden by the church roof.

We faced the convent's yard and clothesline. Out there, past the church shadow, the sun beat onto and through the blue and white nun garments.

"All right, Joey," Brian said, looking down at his hands. "What do you know about Uncle Mike's killing? Tell me all you know."

"I thought you were going to tell me."

"I want to know where to start, okay?"

"I know everything," I said, though that was half bluff. "I found the cables down over the hill."

"Shit," he said, his fingers drumming his thighs as though he'd have to adjust what he'd prepared. "Shit, I wanted to tell you before you found out somewhere else." He turned to face me. "All right, Joey, look, I killed a man," he said. His eyes were direct, focusing my attention. His jawline, where his face was newly shaved, was raw with razor burn. "All right, why did I kill him?" he asked. He asked my question, and I had the feeling that the me he was talking and listening to moved freely in and out of his head. I wasn't sure if Brian could tell the difference, if I had an existence my own. "Let me tell it then. Did I kill him for money, for the twenty thousand dollars? Partly, yes I did. I knew about the money. For chrissakes, the way he was, everybody knew. Twenty thousand dollars, Joey. That's a lot of money, man."

Listening was harder than I'd expected. I could feel everything tightening in the base of my skull and the muscles of my shoulders and neck, even my brain muscling up and tightening. "Why did you want the money so bad?"

"I didn't want it *so bad*," he said, holding out his hands palms up.

"What were you going to do with it?"

"I don't know," he said and smiled, playing a goofy big brother caught in a dumbass stunt. "Nothing right away. I don't know. Hold on to it. Invest it, maybe. I just wanted it. Fuck it. But anyway, now I'm stuck with most of it, just holding these bonds, most of them. Joey, there were about four hundred fifty-dollar bonds. They got his name on them. Would you know what to do with them? I don't know anything more about money than you." I turned away from him and his head turned with mine. Facing the clothesline, our gazes travelled parallel. The nun garments rose and fell in the breeze. I could smell the chlorine.

Brian huffed, then went on speaking more softly, less

intently, like the worst was over. "All right, would I kill a man for money? You know I wouldn't, Joey. I don't want to say the money wasn't nothing, but I wouldn't kill a man for money. Money's bullshit, too," he said. I glanced at him. He soothed his shave-reddened chin and neck with his fingertips. "Joey, you know me. Am I a money person?"

I wouldn't give the satisfaction of agreeing. I rested my elbows on my knees, hung my head, and rocked.

"Ah, you know I'm not. I'd have to hate the person to do that. To take a life. I'd have to hate the person. And, all right, I did hate him. I did hate Mike Mayflower, and you know why, Joey?"

He stared at me, I could feel it without seeing it. Then I stared back as he measured what he was about to say. I watched the words bob up and down in his throat till they were assembled how he wanted them. The tiny muscles along his chin and jaw-bone twitched like ants were playing under the skin.

I knew what he was going to say before he spoke.

"When I was little, he abused me. Uncle Mike. When I was nine, ten, eleven years old, he sexually abused me. Must have been twenty times altogether, always in his apartment." I knew what he was going to say, but still it made me nearly vomit. I had to swallow down the puke that leaked up. "You don't trust me, do you?" he asked, trying to make me back down, angry that I dared not believe him. He shook his head. "Look, I never told anybody, not even Mom, but it happened, I swear. Like I'm telling it is how it happened. All right, listen. You tell me if I'm lying. I'm nine years old." The words came out angrily, a shouted whisper, neither fast nor slow, his lips barely moving. "I walk up to his apartment to watch a Jets game. It's in October. I get up there and he's in that fucking bedroom, watching the game from bed, a white spread, all frilly, all neat. He's got a TV on the dresser and he says, 'Let's watch from here.' I laughed. I was scared, I thought it was weird, but what did I know what I was supposed to do? 'Come on, little Brian, next to me,' he says." My skin went goose-bumpy then crawly and I shivered. My brain knotted more and more. "Uncle Mike starts laughing and he lifts up the covers and he shows me this big hard-on. Biggest thing I ever saw in my life. 'Oo-ooh,' he starts going, pretending like it's hurting him. 'Brian, please, you crawl under the tent.' You know the

173

way he talked. 'You can make it soft for me again.' He took me by the shoulders—"

"Shut up! Shut the fuck up, Brian," I screamed. I screamed it as loud as I could from as far down in my belly as I could reach. I couldn't remember the last time I'd screamed.

"It fucked me up, Joey. It fucked me up so bad. I don't trust nobody. I don't trust nobody because of him. I don't love nobody. Joey, I hated him with every ounce. Imagine what he did. Imagine it. Imagine it, Joey."

"Shut up," I screamed and a cold bloom, like a stain, creeped up my neck and climbed my skull.

"Quiet, Joey. Quiet," he said, nodding toward the convent and pressing down the air with his hands. "Come on, Jesus!"

But I liked screaming. I liked screaming as loud and as hard as I could, right in his face. "Shut up! Shut the fuck up!" And I didn't even remember what I wanted him to shut up about or whose face I was screaming into, barely what "shut up" meant. I just wanted to yell, to go deep down and yell hard and loud, to push *nothing* back down. "Shut up, shut up, shut up," I yelled. "Shut up, shut the fuck up." I smashed my open hand against the stairway rail.

Furious, Brian pursed his lips like he wanted to spit out the taste of me. He grabbed me by the shirt and lifted me, hustled me, practically threw me, down the stairs and back behind the church.

"Joey! I can be arrested if you're an asshole about this. So *you* shut up. It's time for *you* to shut up. You got it? You know what I did now, okay. All right? Now you know what can happen to me."

"You're a scumbag, Brian," I said and I spit. "It just happened that this child molester had twenty thousand dollars lying in his apartment."

The whole of the center court we'd moved into, between the church and the school, was in shadow, cool and dark. A green damp climbed the base of the church wall. High up, the flap windows of the stained glass were pushed open.

"Fuck, Joey. You're not listening, man." His hand, between us, got straight and the fingers spread, like he was about to count them out. He jerked his hand at me, almost to strike, as he spit out his words. "Number one, of course I wanted the money. I said the money was a thing in it. But I also hated the fuck. I hated Uncle Mike. Didn't you hear any of that? And what else? Nobody liked him," he said, ripping his hand through the air. "Nobody liked him. Why should that prick have all that money, have so much money lying around? He was going to die soon anyway and take it all to the grave. The man was a scumbag."

Metal rope hooks clanged against the schoolyard's flagpole. Somewhere, maybe the other side of the school, girls counted jump rope.

"Nobody liked him. Nobody liked him, Joey," he pleaded. "And what was going to happen to the money? Who was going to get it?"

"You weren't."

"Oh, Christ. The money was just my excuse. It wasn't the real thing."

I shrugged my shoulders, shook my head. I'd heard as much as I could, as much as I was going to understand.

"I wanted to kill him, that's all. Fuck the money. Shit, Joey, why the fuck shouldn't I have killed him? That was the real thing of it. Once the idea got in my head, I couldn't find one good reason not to kill him. If I could have come up with one reason, *one* reason not to, I wouldn't have. That's what I'm asking you now, all right? Not why did I kill him, but why the fuck shouldn't I have killed him?"

"Because he was alive and now he's dead."

He smiled like he was victorious. "That's not a reason," he said. "Joey, that's not a reason. My answer to that is, Yeah, so?" He stepped away from me, his hands in front of his chest, half in conclusion, half in jesting defense, more confident. "Joey, I confessed to you. I trusted you."

"You strangled him, Brian. You wrapped that cord around his neck and you strangled him."

"Yeah," he said and nodded, matter of fact. "That's what I did. I wrapped the cable around his neck and I strangled him. And a minute later you were knocking at the door, calling, 'Uncle Mike, Uncle Mike. It's Joey.' I was five feet away from you. He was dead and my arms were hugging him to keep him up." He wiped the spit from the corners of his mouth then pointed his finger at me. His anger lifted him taller. "I don't want to go to jail,

Joey. I have no intention of going to jail. Understand that I have no remorse, no guilty conscience. There was nothing wrong with what I did. I mean, no reason I shouldn't have. So I don't have any nightmares, Joey."

No remorse, no nightmares, nothing wrong. I started walking away, up the sunlit passage between the rectory and the Loaves and Fishes, under its yellow and white banner, toward the street. I was sad, a little bit, but not angry. And I was too worn out to be scared. My legs had gone numb and the hot and cold patches had stopped circulating around my body. It was only my trembling hands that tipped off I felt anything at all.

"You killed Prince, too, you know," I said.

"I know. That was harder. I thought it would be easier, but it wasn't," he said. As we approached the steps to the street, I looked down at the ground and Brian looked at me. "I thought if I couldn't kill a dog, how could I kill a man. But Uncle Mike should have been the test, not Prince. Prince was good."

Once we hit the sidewalk and sunlight and were back in the world, Brian's voice changed. He was just one brother telling another about a chemistry exam or a tough football practice, or telling any secret brothers would share. I listened and nodded, but the whole thing was too casual all of a sudden, on his part and mine. I'd gone somewhere. I'd gone west, on the Vision Quest, left here and gone toward the next week.

Where Prince was inside me, I could still feel, but where the rest of this was, Brian and Clay and Uncle Mike, it was dark and numb and wordless. I was relieved not to care about them. I breathed, my brain eased. I just wanted to survive one more week. I could leave then.

Brian was still talking about Prince. "It was much, much harder it turned out. I'm sorry I did it," he said, scraping the soles of his shoes over the ground, fitting the John Doe cap on his head, bending the brim. "I know you were close to him. I liked him, too. I'm sorry I did it. That was wrong."

"That was fucked up."

"I admit it."

We crossed Sherman—two more blocks toward Palisade, another half block to the park. It would be ten minutes until I got away from Brian. That would be about four o'clock. I'd get some rest and take a shower. I'd call Marcy after supper, talk about the trip, ask her if she wanted to do something. It would be only a day or two until Mr. Rodriguez was back. Four days until the orientation meeting. Seven days until Wagon Train Two.

EIGHT

T HE "HOUSE FOR SALE" SIGN HAD BEEN PASTED over again, this time with a "Sold" sticker. At the bottom of the sign, someone had written in marker, in foreign curlicue script, "For Apartment Information Contact Sam." Inside the foyer, the door to the downstairs apartment was open, and I could hear loud voices echoing and a radio playing the Princess Di version of "Candle in the Wind."

The key to our apartment was still in the door. I figured that my mom, her mind overloaded with work, love, worry, and that afternoon's college placement test had hurried off, forgetting it there.

She was out of the house, so maybe the test was still going on, maybe it was over, maybe she was working now or studying for Resto, whose captain's test was the next morning. Brian was off to look for Sonia. And there was no sign of Aunt Pat. I poured a glass of milk and made a ham sandwich, more out of emptiness than hunger. I went into the living room, laid my plate on the couch. I stared out the middle window. The street was deserted. I counted the sidewalk patches where trees had been taken down and new cement poured.

My eyes got heavy. My mind got heavy, too, like a beat muscle. A gloom came over me and I got scared, panicked, more scared and panicked than I'd been through all of it. Over and over I told myself, just like I had fifteen minutes earlier, I can get out, I can get out, but the words already seemed old. They'd lost their strength, and a frightened howl had grown up all around and swallowed them. I needed a rest. I needed to sleep, that was all.

I switched windows. The afternoon was still bright over New York, the sky blue and rose, but near in to us it had turned a hard nickel color. Over the Hoboken cliffs, heavy, darker clouds blew fast under the grey ceiling, and the damp harbor breeze, much cooler than the air around me, blew back the curtains and fluttered the blinds. I shut the window before I left.

In the bathroom, wanting for time to pass and things to change, I opened a new foil pack of Sominex and took two capsules before heading to bed. The bedroom was a lot darker than either the dusk outside or the apartment's other rooms, not nighttime dark, but grey and cool like a burial vault.

A few months before, in April, I'd gotten disgusted that my room had no personality—disgusted that, cracked and dingy, it was as pathetic as me and my whole family—and I'd tried to decorate it. That was a Saturday, the day after I got really interested in Marcy.

The Friday had been hot, near ninety though we were barely a month deep in spring, and, after spending the whole school day together doing nothing but sharing LifeSavers and chatting, a lot of the time about summer and Mr. Rodriguez and the Wagon Train, me and Marcy were walking down the giant school steps. Both our jackets were off. She was carrying mine as well as her own. She was trying to reset her pocket watch—a huge green plastic bubble thing that usually hung around her neck—when she dropped it. I picked it up for her and when I stood she blinded me with a kiss on the lips, her strawberry-flavored tongue wetting mine. What a taste! I sucked at it just as it was leaving. But I didn't say anything. I blushed and laughed like a jackass, didn't even take hold of her hand, just walked on, talking like nothing had happened. But I felt like our hearts belonged a little bit to each other and debated whether or not I was in love.

By myself that next morning, I took the Path Train to Greenwich Village, thinking about Marcy the whole way, not only about the kiss, but about the way her chest had felt against mine. And I thought about the way she looked when she answered a question in class, and about the hat she'd bought herself for Christmas but was too embarrassed to wear after one day back at school. I thought about the way her great legs—great calves, great thighs, even greater knees—soccer and basketball legs, looked on roller blades. She'd taken the sport up last summer and sucked at it. That she sucked at it was a relief for such a girl jock looking to go grungy, and she loved to play up what a spastic she was.

In Greenwich Village, I avoided the really weird stores, but I did go into this very funky C.H. Martins. I spent over an hour there and bought a whole bunch of stuff. After that, there were things on my room's walls—shiny black comedy and tragedy masks drooping from thumbtacks and rubber bands, a poster of a face by Picasso with the nose and eyes messed up, another poster of a lipsticked Mona Lisa, paler than I'd remembered her. At first, I liked the way it all looked, and just a few days later, that Monday or Tuesday, when this South American street vendor was selling cactuses up the avenue, I bought a real tall one from him because I thought it was cool. If I could have thought of some reason to invite Marcy over except the obvious one, I would have.

But soon after that cactus-buying day things started to go downhill and calling her became harder. The "For Sale" sign first went up, I quit the spring soccer tryouts after one practice, Marcy's dad landed a job with CompUSA the week my mom's unemployment ran out, and Marcy started to act cool toward me because I was being so weird toward her. After that, I pulled back, further back.

I stopped noticing the posters and the faces. I even managed to kill the cactus from neglect. I tossed the whole thing off— the almost-relationship, the almost-girlfriend—with a just-as-well until Mr. Rodriguez started sending me those letters.

I lay on my bed, waiting for the Sominex to kick in, and I picked up the Wagon Train information from my night table. Again, *bing*, it started seeming possible. Why wasn't it?

The Wagon Train was part of a bigger program called Vision Quest, which got its name from "the plains Indian youth's rite of passage from adolescence to adulthood." The "For Whom" section of the pamphlet said, "For at-risk youths, the Wagon Train provides safe, secure boundaries within which students can begin to safely discover and, in some cases, re-create themselves." Under the "Daily Routine" part it said, "A typical day in this 250-mile, ten-day journey begins at 6:00 A.M. and ends at sundown. Following early morning chores and a hearty break-fast, the wagons begin their daily twenty- to thirty-mile trek. Staff and youths live together in tepee families, two counselors and six youths per tepee. Each family is responsible for a wagon, its mules, and equipment." On the front fold of the pamphlet was a blurry color picture of the Wagon Train parading through Central Park, and on the back was an admissions application.

From an envelope on the floor, I took the letter I'd received from Mr. Rodriguez a week earlier, the one he'd sent the first day of Wagon Train One. The letter was postmarked Charleston, West Virginia, where the Wagon Train started. Wagon Train One was travelling to Cincinnati, Ohio. Mine would be covering the same ground. Mine.

I imagined hills mostly, yellow hills and tall grass, woods along a river under a pale blue sky, no buildings in sight.

I reread the names of the other five kids, one tepee's worth, who Mr. Rodriguez had sent the same letter to. According to the phone message he'd left, Marcy, Felix, Kerri, and Lanniqua had all signed on. That left just two for him to hear from—me and the only other wholly white kid in the group, Fran O'Connor, whose family had gone from owning O'Connor's Tavern to selling it and now to mopping its floor and taping up the beer specials signs. Even without Marcy, this group would have been pretty cool, from families more like mine. I liked that we were a less outgoing group than the other one, not so used to fun. We were the true "at risk," and Mr. Rodriguez must have had to drag in each one like he was doing with me.

The Sommies had nearly put me out. A cool breeze blew open the curtains and I rolled my face into it. Rain was on the way.

Staring at the shadowy far wall, my eyes rolled and my lids fell shut. I turned on my side, moved my pillow and hugged it. As I drifted, day changed to night and my thinking changed from words to sounds and pictures—animals calling from a for-est; steam-snorting ponies by a stream; a full-moon sky, blue not black, crowded with stars, with the whole speckled Milky Way. Six kids sitting around a fire, boy-girl-boy-girl. Bedtime and Marcy unzipping my tight bag, slipping in naked and silky, her hands on me, mine on her shoulders, riding down her back to her

181

waist, settling on her hips.

The phone rang. I opened my eyes and jumped up in one motion. It was night-dark outside, but, there being no working clock in my room, I didn't know the time exactly, guessed at it being late, near midnight. I made it to half-seated but fell back onto the bed and let the phone ring until the machine picked up. After that, I just lay there, worried, waiting for the phone to ring again, and it did five minutes later. A train of all the urgent, terrible things the call could be about chugged through my brain and this time, by the second ring, I hurried in the apartment's semi-dark to the kitchen but got there too late and the caller had hung up without leaving a message.

Shit, it was only eight-thirty. I went back to the bed, sat on the edge, tired, my head hanging. The phone rang again and I jumped right up, got it before the third ring. I was wanted. Clay wanted me. Brian was there, at his place. A "summit" Clay called it.

I walked the short park-skirting block from Ogden to Palisade, heading toward Clay's through an on-and-off drizzle. It was just a few minutes past nine and I was groggy from my mom's pills. I must have slept through a thunderstorm because everything around me was soaked and beat up. The sidewalks were puddled, with soot- and cellophane-running streams connecting one to the next. The streets were slick and scattered over with fallen branches and leaves, and the cars, though the air temperature must have been seventy, were wet and cold to the touch. Under the yellow streetlights, bright enough to throw shadows from the high wires, my neighborhood, which I thought could still look fairly okay when everything broke in its favor, was nothing but a wasteland of the filthy, the busted, and the boarded up. Even a lot of the apartments along Palisade that for the past three years had been packed with garrisons of foreigners were, I noticed, curtainless and vacant.

I approached the house that was in front of Clay's. It was 316 Palisade, Clay's 316A. The roof water dripping onto the three-story building's green and white aluminum porch awning splashed upwards like sweat popping from the head of a panicked cartoon character, its tapping as loud as a parade drum's rat-a-tat-tat. The streetlight across the road and the bare yellow mosquito bulb below the awning gave off just enough light that I could see the water trickling from the downspout. I watched it follow a rusty path across the pavement, toward the gate, and, at least until I turned into the alley, I could see well enough in front of me to know that even though I smelled dog shit, there was none under my next step. Through the alley, it was nearly black and I was on my own.

Across the patchwork backyard—lumpy asphalt over concrete—Clay's window shades glowed with an inside light, and the shack's warmth in the dampness attracted me regardless of who I knew I'd find inside. There was a water-tapping sound on Clay's porch roof, softer than the other, a tick-tock, and I could hear also a stream trickling into a ground sewer, an uncovered round hole, nearly clogged with Reese's and Snickers wrappers, in a cement gully between the front house and Clay's.

Clay's front door was wide open and from a dozen paces I could smell the marihuana. When I got closer to the door, other smells—coffee, potato chips, coconut tanning oil—mixed in with the pot.

Clay and Brian were sitting on an overstuffed purple sofa and loveseat set in an *L*, a coffee table in front of them, a white leather chair on the other side of the table. Behind Clay was a standing steel sunlamp.

"Yo, Brian," said Clay after sucking the joint, holding in the hit. "Near Man's here."

He blew out the smoke. Through a grin, with a whistling sound it streamed downward out of his mouth from between his front teeth, toward his chest. He clicked off *Happy Days*. Brian kept his nose and shaved face in a handheld video game, disinterested, not the person I'd been with a few hours earlier.

The living room had a low ceiling, wall-to-wall carpeting, and wood panelling, one wall's color slightly lighter, yellower than the other two. Off to my right was the kitchen and its fluorescent light and its window, real glass, not Plexi like the others with their scratches and smears, but only a rat-tail's length from the garage backing it.

Clay squeezed the joint between his fingers, snuffing it out. He lifted a can of Tropical Vacation air freshener from the coffee table. "Have a seat, my friend, we got to conference here," he said and gestured for me to sit in the leather chair, spraying at it as he waved. I sat, sank deep in the soft, cool cushions, and had to squiggle forward not to be swallowed.

"The girls are out shopping," said Clay as he cleaned off the coffee table, pushed to one side a checkered NASCAR ashtray, a pack of Benson 'n Hedges, a plastic bowl of crusted onion dip, an opened bag of barbecue chips, and a copy of the *New Yorker*, still partially rolled for swatting. He brushed off the crumbs and seemed pleased with the empty table. He put up his bare feet. "They should be back soon. They been gone how long? An hour?"

Brian shrugged. He tossed the handheld onto the cushion beside him, blew into his palm where the soft skin was peeling, turning calloused. That was odd. It made me think maybe he'd been doing manual work, and that made me think of the new apartment. Brian stretched, rubbed his eyes like he'd just woken up. "Aw, shit," he moaned.

"Okay, boys, here it is. Me and Pat have been talking," said Clay, an elegant cigarette between his fingers, waving it as if he wasn't aware it was there. "Me and her have been talking about the three of us, us three here, us not talking enough. We do not know what's going on with one another in terms of this here investigation. Am I right or not? Have you guys been talking?" We shook our heads, nope. "See, I thought not," he said and flopped over his wrist. He put the Benson 'n Hedges to work, letting it do his pointing for him. "Now, so far I've had two interviews with Resto and one with Wilkinson. You guys?"

"One with each," I said.

Brian didn't answer, wouldn't look at Clay. "Are you worried, man?" Brian asked, studying his puffed palm like he was talking to it.

"No," said Clay, insulted. "But I ain't stupid either. I been around, yo."

Clay was such an asshole. What reason could Brian come up with for not killing *him*?

"As far as I'm concerned," Brian said, "the investigation's over, and Natasha's gonna get arrested."

Brian was lying. He knew better.

"Resto wants to, but what evidence do they have?" Clay asked, finally lighting his cigarette with an old flip-top steel lighter. "That's what we don't know."

The fluorescent kitchen light flickered behind me, but in the living room, the only light came from a table lamp set at my feet, on the carpet. The bulb must have been 150 watts, but the light shot straight down to the floor and up in a cone to the ceiling, leaving the rest of the room troubled and whispery and stoned.

I joined the lie.

I told what I knew about Natasha's cousin, Buddah, about her record and his, about her being broke from the greeting card thing, about her boyfriend Hardy, what a hood he was, how he hated white people, about Natasha being seen in the building the day Uncle Mike was killed, about Hardy hanging around.

"Sounds pretty good to me," said Brian.

"Nah, no way. That's nothing, man," said Clay. "They better have way more than that, especially if she got a nigger jury."

"That's what we know they got, Clay. Who's to say they don't have a lot more? They probably do." Unlike the afternoon conversation where Brian's eyes were alive, here, with Clay, although he was trying to persuade him, the aliveness and the intention were hidden, his tone and his low-voltage gaze back to normal—worn, but not quite indifferent, too agitated for that.

"That's what I'm asking," said Clay, pointing his cigarette first at Brian, then at me. "Do we know all they got? Do we know, I'm saying, who did it? Do we know who killed the man? We don't know, do we?"

"I don't know," said Brian. "I don't know, but I have an opinion. I told you. I think Natasha's guilty, and I think she's gonna be arrested soon and this'll all be over."

"Joey?" asked Clay, surprising me. "What do you say?"

"I don't know who did it," I said. I leaned deep into the cushions. I reassured myself that there was no way I could tell Clay the truth.

"But you think they're going to arrest her?"

"That's what my mom thinks," I said. "My mom's saying just another day or two."

"There you go," said Brian. "I mean, she knows what Resto's thinking."

"True," Clay said, head nodding, the tan-lines of his neck opening and closing like accordion bellows. "But what about the other one?"

"Clay, this ain't like you, man. If the evidence comes in, the evidence comes in. What's Wilkinson gonna do?" said Brian, more forcefully, his irritation pushing the words, making his voice higher. "And if we know as much as we do evidence-wise, about what they got on Natasha, you can be damn sure there's a lot more we don't know about. Hey, Clay, I don't think they're even considering us anymore."

Clay shook his head. "Why not?" he asked, directing the question to me. "Why not? Why aren't they considering us?" He leaned back and folded his arms across his chest, sulky and stubborn. "Tell me that."

Without hesitating, I teamed with Brian again. "Because all the evidence has come in against *her*. We didn't do anything, so they got nothing against us," I said. "Why you getting so scared? Suspicion ain't evidence, Clay."

"They know I introduced Mike to her, her and a lot of others."

"Yeah, and have they already questioned you on that?" asked Brian, slumped in the loveseat, legs spread.

"Twice."

"Well. Nothing came of it then," insisted Brian, shaking his head, pulling live skin from a popped hand blister. He didn't look up, said dryly, "I know it's hard to accept that you're not a murder suspect anymore, Clay, but facts is facts. You'll get over it." He looked up at Clay. "Don't feel left out."

"Waaa," cried Clay, relieved, ready to grab on to the joke. "I wanted to do mind games with the coppies," he said, boastful again, a second after being bullied from his doubt. "You're right. You're right, guys. But listen, man," he said. He raised himself up on the couch, knees against the table, took aim with four rocking horns, the pointers and pinkies of both hands. "One thing I learned, sometimes talking is better than silence. It clarifies."

Half a joint and a minute later, footsteps splashed through the puddles, and we could hear whispering, Sonia and Aunt Pat conspiring about something, Aunt Pat seeming to have picked up some of Sonia's accent.

"Uh-oh," said Clay. "I'm telling you boys, uh-oh. I know your aunt."

Sonia entered first and walked toward us without a hello, avoiding contact by making as if something was in her eye. When Aunt Pat came through the door seconds later, her posture was like a palsy victim's. She waved with her left hand, but she was turned from us at the waist, twisted even more so at the neck so her face was hidden on the far shoulder. She hustled into the bathroom. Sonia watched sadly, shoulders slumped, lips red. She sat next to Brian. He patted her knee as he watched Clay.

"Pat. Oh, Pat. Come out here, please," called Clay, ready to play Brady Bunch dad.

It wasn't going to work.

"I'm peeing," she shrieked and flushed the toilet. "Do you fucking mind?"

Clay laughed and gave her the finger. "What a fucking world," he said. "Pat, please come out. Please come out. I want to talk to you."

"Cut it out, Clay, or you're gonna make me have a fit," she warned, and she punched the bathroom wall.

On the loveseat, next to Brian, Sonia's elbows were on her thighs. Her chin hung just inches above the coffee table. Her eyes and Brian's never met.

"How much did she have?" Clay asked Sonia.

"Two beers and two shots of schnapps," she said.

"God, man. That's fucked," he said, pointing the blame at Sonia. "Don't you know she can't drink?"

"I can't stop her either, yo," said Sonia, drawing up enough strength to fight back.

Everybody knew what happened when Aunt Pat drank. You had to, because even if you'd never seen her in action, within the first five minutes of meeting her she'd tell you how booze affected her, as though that would explain whatever followed.

"She was doing so good, too," said Clay. Aunt Pat hadn't

had a drink in four days, for her a long ride on the wagon. "And now this."

Sonia started to cry. She hid her face in her hands, little and delicate—the hands and face both.

"Did she have anything else?" Clay asked her.

"I don't think so. I don't know. She was alone in the ladies' room."

"Shit. That's Aunt Pat," said Brian, wagging his head. Ready to stand, he rubbed his hand down his thighs to his knees. "We should leave them alone."

"No, wait, wait. You don't gotta go," said Clay before he called again to my aunt. "It's okay, sweetie, really. Nobody's mad at you. You can come out. You can do it, come on."

In the silence that followed Clay's words, I shut my eyes and took a deep breath. I pictured the Wagon Train, slow clomping horses through a field. It was a meditation, an oasis in a throbbing brain.

"Fuck no," yelled my aunt. "I cannot do it."

"Yes, you can. Yes you can, hon." Clay reached into the ashtray, pulled out the marihuana crisp. Lit it and squinted as he drew on it.

"I can't, I can't, Clay. Don't you fucking get it?" she sobbed, raking up phlegm. "I'm sorry, everybody. I know I'm fucking up your fun."

"Come on, we got to go," said Brian.

Sonia stared at the bathroom door, then walked to it. "Patty, do you need me?" she asked tenderly, stroking the frame like she was stroking my aunt's shoulder. "Patty, let me come in. Peppermint Patty, Peppermint Patty. Did I let you down, Patty?"

"Come on, Sonia, would you?" called Brian. She ignored him.

We could hear my aunt crying inside, a sort of wheeze she'd gone into, but she made no attempt to answer Sonia.

"This is what happens," said Clay. "She pretends and pretends and pretends. Then it's all not a joke anymore."

"Exactly," said Brian.

"Then it hits her, like this is my fucked-up life. This is my fucked-up self."

"Come on, Sonia," said Brian gently, reaching out his hand. "Let's book. Clay and my aunt have to deal with this."

Clay nodded.

"Patty," whispered Sonia, still at the bathroom door. "You'll be okay. Patty, you want me to stay?"

"She said no. Let's go," said Brian.

Sonia turned her head, tired of Brian's pushing, as she backstepped away from the bathroom. "She didn't say anything."

"I don't know how long I can take this," Clay said. He ambled barefooted, all aches and pains, over to take Sonia's place at the bathroom door. He knocked gently, whispered mockingly, "Oh, Patty, it's Clayboy. Come out, come out. Oh, Peppermint One."

"Aaaaahaan," she wailed, sad and angry as wounded prey. "You ass, you big ass, fat ass."

"Come out, come out," called Clayboy.

"Fuck you!"

"Come out, come out, little darling."

"I'm not a child, you jerk. You're an ass, Clay," she said, and a laugh broke out at the end of her sentence, like a second person was in there with her. "Clay's an a-ass, Clay's an a-ass," came the words in singsong. She smashed and kept smashing the toilet flusher in rhythm. "Clay is an a-ass, Clay is an a-ass."

"You're gonna break the toilet, you know. That costs."

"Good. Great. Fuck you and your toilet," she said laughing and smashing. "This feels great, man. Clay is an a-ass, a great big fat one."

Clay was pissed. He waved a backhand at the door, frustrated that she wouldn't play fair. "See? It's all make-believe to her." He plopped back onto the couch and clicked on the TV. "I don't know. I don't know how long I can take this stress. I got a life to live, too, you know. I don't want to be in this shit all my life."

"I'm ready," said Sonia.

"Yeah," said Brian. "We got a lot of fixing to do tomorrow."

They'd made it to the door. I found myself standing at the edge of the kitchen. My choices were to leave with them or stay with Clay and my aunt. I crossed the floor to the door.

"What am I supposed to do with her?" asked Clay, staring at the World Wrestling Federation. Apollo was running to his dressing room, his hair on fire. His slobby manager chased after him with a bucket of water.

It had started raining hard again and the sound picked up from the metal awning. Sonia and Brian made a run for it, toward the alley. I waited in the doorway.

Pat called to Clay, "Where the fuck's the Herbal Essence?"

"There's none left. Don't you remember you finished it? Use whatever's in there."

The wind whipped the rain and as it fell from the roof, waves splashed me.

"It's fucking Rogaine shampoo," she screeched.

"So? Use it. I like it." He looked beat and bloated. With his chin on his chest, it was a struggle to lift his voice loud enough for her to hear.

"I hate Rogaine. It sucks. It gives me nausea."

Clay stared at the television. A guy, one of the Village People, was jumping spread-eagle from the top ropes, but the mat was empty. He had something to prove.

"You don't drink the shit, for chrissakes, you put it in your hair."

"I know that. I know that, you fat ass. The smell, I mean. I wouldn't drink it. I'm not stupid," she laughed.

PART IV

ONE

I TOOK TWO MORE SOMINEX WHEN I GOT HOME FROM
Clay's, and the next morning, Tuesday, the first of July, when
I dragged myself out of bed and to the bathroom, barechest-
ed, in my underpants, again not knowing the time but figuring
I'd slept late, voices filled the kitchen. I felt like I was ninety
years old.

I turned on the bathroom light, a single white globe above the
mirror. I glanced at my face. My eyes looked sunken but felt achy
and swollen. There was grease in the fold where my nostrils met my
cheek. A few dark hairs were coming in between my lip and nose.

I turned on the faucet full power and leaned my elbows on
the sink, my head hanging above the pooling water. I listened to
the kitchen conversation through the water's hiss and splash.

I picked out Resto's voice, and I knew it had to be late.
He'd been scheduled to take the captain's test at eight and was
already back from that.

I washed my face, dried it, burying it in the stiff white
towel's chlorine. I brushed my teeth, threw on some powder, wet
my hair and ran my fingers through.

Resto and my mom were planning the rest of their day. He
wanted to take her to Hoboken, to the Barnes and Noble Cafe for
brunch, or maybe it was lunch.

I leaned toward the mirror. Complexion gone from yellow
to pink, I looked better, much younger. Low on my chin, reddish
blonde hair was twinkling in the white light.

After brunch, my mom and Resto were going to celebrate
their tests being over and pick up some audio books my mom
wanted, some stuff she had heard about on the radio at work.
She had the rest of the day off and they were talking about some
sort of work they had to do at a place in HouseRAD. I crossed the

hall back to my bedroom without looking into the kitchen. My ankle was swollen badly and had turned a darker blue and purple. I guessed some little bone must be broken.

I dressed—black cargo shorts and a black, white, and red basketball jersey—then walked quietly toward the kitchen, hoping I'd get a look at them before they did me. By the kitchen clock it was quarter to eleven, and Sonia was sitting at the table along with my mom and Resto. Her hair was pulled back and held in a short ponytail. Clean and clear-eyed, she had a little bit of make-up on—the something coating her skin, making it dull instead of glossy, the something black around her eyes making the inners seem shiny and moist.

I took two steps closer, up to the aluminum floor stop where the hall's linoleum met the kitchen's. My mom was writing a check that Sonia was waiting to take.

Handing it to her, my mom asked, "You're sure fifty's enough?"

Resto was the first to notice me. He smiled and winked. He was dressed like usual in a T-shirt and jeans, but what was not usual was that they were wrinkled like he'd picked them up from the floor instead of peeled them from an ironing board.

My mom's new haircut, short split bangs in front, buzzed in back, looked real good. It showed more of her face. She looked cute in a sleeveless zipper-front white shirt.

"Hi," I said.

My mom turned. "Jesus, Joey, you look like a train wreck," she joked.

"I just woke up." I thought I looked pretty good. "Is there any coffee left?"

"Just that," said my mom, pointing to the stove.

It looked like molasses burned to the bottom of the glass pot. "Maybe I should just suck the grinds," I said.

My mom, knowing that I didn't drink coffee, that I didn't know nothing about caffeine, laughing, said, "Suck the grinds, Joey? Huh? 'Maybe I should suck the grinds'? Say what?" Still smiling and shaking her head like we were a family on the mend, maybe even on the rise, she turned to Sonia. "Have you told Joey?" she asked.

"I don't think so."

I sat at the table, drank the cold dregs from my mom's cup. The bitter grinds found hiding places between my gums and teeth and my mouth went into secreting fits that had me licking and swallowing the rest of the conversation.

"Me and Brian just got an apartment," said Sonia, cheery-eyed for my mom's sake, though she knew I wouldn't care.

"Say congratulations," said my mom.

"Congratulations. I think I already knew you had. At least I had an idea," I said.

"Joey," said Resto, "why don't you come with me and your mom out for brunch. You didn't have any breakfast. We're gonna celebrate our tests being over."

"Maybe we should be going to Novena instead of brunch," joked my mom, running her fingers up the back of her neck, under her hair, still unfamiliar with the feel of the air over the razor-cut.

"Oh, don't even think like that. I know you did great," said Resto, one finger grooming an eyebrow. "Come on, Joey, why don't you come."

"Yeah, sweetie," said my mom. "The three of us can talk."

Another summit.

"No, no, I don't think so," I said and sipped some more coffee-bottom. I couldn't snap out of this hungover role-playing, even though I realized how ridiculous I must have seemed.

"They sold the house," said my mom. "Did you see the sign?"

"Yeah, yesterday. 'Contact Sam,'" I said. "For a good time, contact Sam."

My mom laughed at my weary little joke. "You sound like Brian now," she said. "You know, we're gonna have to move this time."

I was surprised but wouldn't show it. This wasn't the first time the house had been sold since we'd been living in it. I'd assumed, or had stayed thoughtless enough to assume, that nothing would change.

"Is that for me to do?" I asked and nodded to the box of Uncle Vic's provisions—in one half, clean sheets, clean pajamas, clean socks and undies, a clean pair of pants; this week's *People*, Sunday's *Parade*, a brown bag of deli supplies, a quart of Listerine, a quart of Lestoil in the other. My mom always packed the box that way, heavy on one side, light on the other, so you could hold it in your right arm if you needed your left to search for keys or open a door.

My mom said, "Uh-huh. Come with us, though."

"Naw, I don't feel like. The box is for me?"

"Yeah, but any time, though, Joey. You don't got to do it now," said my mom gently, bobbing her head this way and that, searching for a soft spot in my eyes. "Come on, you don't have to do that now."

"Come on," said Resto.

"No, no thanks I said. No is no." My mom seemed disappointed, maybe concerned. Even to myself, when my words echoed back, they sounded like Brian's. "I'll just do the box, okay? Maybe we'll do something later."

"Yeah, I may as well go, too," said Sonia, rising as I did. "Thanks again, thanks so much, Susie. I'm gonna go to the place. I'll probably see you later," she said to my mom. "I'll walk you past Uncle Vic's," she said to me.

Sonia was trying to get to something. I didn't know what, but she was trying to move toward some way that she wanted things to be in her life. She wanted to work things out, to move stuff into position. My mom, too. She may not have been good at it, but she had a way she wanted things to be. This here and that there. Resto had it, and Clay had it, and now Brian had it, too. I had none. I had no way that I truly wanted things.

That's why the Wagon Train trip would do me good. Time. Time to think.

I carried the box and Sonia shut the door behind us. At the top of the staircase, in the stuffy, sagging hallway, I felt sad relief, like we could stop pretending and enter the world where we'd be who we were the night before, bad people, our real selves.

I needed to get away.

Down the stairs and out the building, out the gate and past the first two houses toward the park, there was no talking between us. Another house down, box in arms, I bounced onto my bad ankle to let Sonia pass a spot where the sidewalk was crumbled and prickly grass grew up around the fire hydrant. I winced. Sonia took a swiping glance at me and I stared back.

"You know he thinks that what he did is all right," I said.

"Yeah, I know. I'm trying to change that, Joey." Though I couldn't believe her all the way, she said it sort of humbly, like my opinion counted. But fuck her.

"Yeah, and how are you trying to do that?" I asked.

The ground was still wet in spots from what must have been a second overnight storm. The sky was now blue, the air bright but cool enough that I should have worn long sleeves.

Sonia scrunched her bony shoulders. I could see them slide inside her loose Inca-style sweater-shirt.

She didn't answer for a dozen steps, until we stepped off the curb, about to cross to my uncle's side of the street. That little change in style—the bit of makeup, her hair back—made her look like she was ready for a teen magazine portrait shot. "By loving him and letting him feel love," she said. Her nose reddened, her eyes filled, her lips softened and swelled, like they were tearful, too. "Then his heart'll open and he'll know what he did is wrong. He'll feel sorry."

Fuck her. Fuck her.

"And then what's he going to do, once he feels sorry?" I asked, staring cold at her hurting face.

"And then what's he going to do?" she repeated. "This is your brother, Joey." She wiped her nose, came up different, angry. "Try to be a better person. Try to lead a better life, to do something good for people. Why you fucking snickering?" she asked, reaching both hands halfway to my chest like she wanted to shake me. Street life jumped up in her, lit her eyes. She wasn't gonna let me push her around. "What the fuck *you* want him to do, asshole?"

What I wanted him to do was say he was sorry, that what he'd done was sick, that he'd never do it again. Just what she'd said. I shook my head, spit out a brown coffee spit, but didn't answer. I stared at her as hard as I could, trying to match her toughness.

"What do you want, huh?" she asked, her anger still rising into my face. "You want him to do twenty years? That'll be good?"

"No," I said, staring so hard it felt like the word came out of my eyes more than my mouth.

"You want his whole life fucked up?"

"No, I want him to know what he did was wrong."

"So! Me, too, man."

"I want him to promise to never do something like that again."

"Oh, he won't do nothing stupid like that. I know your brother, Joey. But you. You don't care if his whole life gets fucked up."

She didn't see what I was getting at, but she might have been right anyway. I wasn't sure what I wanted.

"And you want somebody else's life fucked up for what Brian did?" I asked.

"Joey, man, that ain't my problem. Your brother's the one I care about. He's who you should, too. He's family, man, and I want him to be rehabeeleetated," she said with a suddenly heavy accent, like it was right out of a kitchen argument between her mom and her mom's live-in. "You want to make him do punishment. That's your thing. You think he should be punished. Fuck that, Joey."

She won. She knew what she wanted and I didn't know what I did.

By the time we reached Uncle Vic's the box was sagging in my arms. I rested it on the fence and rested my chin on the soft towels until I realized I looked like a puppy. I lifted my head and raised my eyes up to Uncle Vic's window. It was the only window in the house with nice curtains.

Sonia started in again.

"That's what has you so fucked up. He made a big, big mistake. Uncle Mike this, Uncle Mike that, Uncle Mike was dying. Like he told me, there was no reason he shouldn't kill him. To him. To him, I mean. He took it almost like a challenge, though. Like fuck the world, fuck the world. This is how fucked up I think everything is. Like he was spitting in everybody's face, you know."

"I don't blame him for hating Uncle Mike."

198

"Whatever," she said, bouncing my words around in her head. "No, that wasn't it, Joey. Not so much hated him, didn't like him, didn't care about him. He didn't matter. Nothing mattered. He wanted to prove he could kill him and that it wouldn't matter. Just like, why not?"

"That's what Brian says, but there's got to be some really deep stuff there, after everything. You know what I mean—feelings," I said. I lifted the box and put a foot on the first porch step. "Some anger, big anger."

"No, now you lost me. Anger what?"

"He must have told you, too. He had to, right? I think what had happened mattered to what he did a lot. A lot, man. Brian just don't know it. He's repressed all how he feels."

"What are you talking about?" she asked, alarmed, jaw clenched, faint blue infant's veins showing at her temples. "What happened? What he tell you?"

I could see up into Uncle Vic's window, but Sonia's back was to it. The box was heavy as lead and my muscles were shot. I boosted the box with my knee to keep it from slipping.

"He told me all about what Uncle Mike did to him when he was little."

"Uh," Sonia said. She put on a smartass, Puerto Rican puss. "The sexual abuse, right? He said Uncle Mike did this sex shit with him."

"Yeah," I said. She'd confused me.

"Oh, Christ, man," she said and stared at the ground, kicked at a black pebble, trying to suck back her anger. "He told you that? That's what he told you? Yeah, then he's an asshole. Then he ain't learning. He ain't," she said softly, still staring at her kicking foot. "That story about Uncle Mike's bullshit. That shit never happened. Uncle Mike, man. I was the one he had sex with, not Brian. Me and Brian made up that story just in case. But he wasn't supposed to tell it to you, Joey."

Something began to come up my windpipe, something soft and real and gagging as a water balloon. I stopped it at the back of my throat, and it almost stopped my heart as I swallowed and pushed it back down.

In Uncle Vic's window the thin curtain peeled back from

one side, and without the white backing to reflect the sun, that portion of the window blackened, and I could see the outline of a man, a greyish blue shadow swaying into then backing off the black.

"Me and him talked about this whole thing, using the alibi, but he wasn't supposed to lie to you about it. I told him, 'Joey's your brother, yo.' This was like our backup story in case he was found out, you know. To mitigate, man. We went over what we'd say." She talked with disappointment—a junkie's girlfriend who'd caught her man stabbing after he promised—but the anger was gone. I took it as a sign she loved him. "What we'd say happened in childhood, all this terrible shit, would be part of the explanation, just if he did get all hung up, you know. But he shouldn't have told it to you. I thought he was doing better than that."

I glanced up again. It was Brian in the window, sideways, his profile half hidden by his shoulder. The curtain fell back into position. Behind it I could see him backing away.

She came up with an explanation for Brian's lie. "You was a test for him, I bet. I know how he thinks. If he could lie to you, he could lie to anybody, because that's the way he feels for you."

I lifted the box and pushed my butt against the door.

"Your brother is so smart, Joey, but emotionally he's so stupid. That's what he needs me for."

"Right," I said. I was into the mail foyer, still holding the door open with my backside.

"Yo, Joey, don't hate him. Don't do nothing stupid. We got to help him."

"I got to take this upstairs," I said. I knew that Brian had seen us. To me that meant Uncle Vic was safe.

She jumped up the steps, angry that I didn't seem to be paying attention to her. She grabbed on to the edge of the box, bending it out. "Don't do nothing stupid, man. I'm telling you."

"Telling me what?"

"Just don't do nothing stupid, I'm saying."

"All right, all right. Let go."

"Okay," she said but held on until she finished her piece.

"Please, Joey, you can see how he's changing. He's happier

and that's the start of everything. His heart's gonna open again. But, Joey, you can't expect it all at once. I can help him," she said and patted her chest with her free hand. I tried to pull away. "Don't send him to jail, Joey. It could be years, yo. He ain't gonna hurt nobody else. I know him, man. I know he won't hurt nobody else if that's what's bothering you. Is that's what's bothering you? What's done is done, forget it, okay?"

TWO

I KICKED OPEN THE BOLT-OUT FOYER DOOR. ONCE inside, I put the box down and push-kicked it to the base of the stairs. The hallway smelled of air freshener and the floor was still wet in spots from mopping, the first mopping it had had since God knew when. I stared up at Uncle Vic's door, imagining my uncle and Brian at the table, watching TV, Brian waiting for me to knock, to either take his beating for lying or to throw it back in my face.

But when I climbed the staircase and knocked, the door cracked open and I walked into an empty kitchen. Even the TV's green-black screen was silent. I didn't say anything, didn't call out, just looked up and down, into the living room where I'd seen Brian, and in the other direction, through the hallway and into Uncle Vic's bare-floored bedroom. I put the box down on the table and walked toward the living room, half expecting Brian to jump from some shadowed corner, but no one was there, and the curtains hung still. I passed back through the kitchen. As I approached the back hall, I smelled cigar smoke.

The bathroom door was locked. The smoke smell seeped from its edges.

"Uncle Vic, you in there?"

"Joey, that you?" he called, the voice squeezing up his throat as if he was being choked.

"Yeah, are you okay, Uncle Vic? You okay? What's the matter?"

"Your mother keeps giving me beans. I'm all bound up."

"Where's Brian?" I yelled into the pale green door.

"He just left. Didn't you see him?"

"No. Where was he going?"

"Oooph. I don't know where he was going!" The words came out like bleeps through a trumpet. "Give me some zips, Joey, to relax me."

202

I went into the kitchen to unpack the box and began calling out names. "Kalamazoo, Michigan."

"Main Post Office, 49008."

"Greensboro, North Carolina."

"Main Post Office, 27410. Oooph. Keep asking. Something's coming."

"Anchorage, Alaska."

"Huh. They always ask Alaska," he said. It sounded like he hadn't taken a breath in a minute. "Alaska's the easiest one. Main Post Office, 99508. One more."

"Charleston, West Virginia."

"The Mountaineer State. Charleston MPO, 30140. Good, good. You can stop now."

When the bathroom door opened, out floated a cloud of smoke soon parted by my uncle.

"Everything's away already," I said, finally able to lower my voice. I placed the empty box in the box corner between the door and the refrigerator. "What did Brian want?"

"He wanted pitchers," said Uncle Vic. He walked to the table, fluffing his shirt from his back and belly, and he flicked on the TV.

"Pictures. Pictures of what?"

"Pitchers of his grandparents."

"What for?"

"What for? They're his grandparents, your mom's mom and dad. My brother Louie and his wife Netty. And he wanted a picture of our parents, too, mine and Louie's, his great-grandparents. What? So what, Joey? What's a matter with that?"

"All of a sudden Brian wants you to show him pictures? What for?"

"Christ. I just told you." He spun in the chair and held his hands out in front of his crotch like he was taking a collection. "What do I know why he wanted the pictures? He's got a new apartment, don't he? Joey, don't keep this up now."

"Where do you keep the pictures?"

"Don't be like me, Joey, a loner and a worrier. It ain't healthy."

"Uncle Vic."

"They're in the box, in the bedroom closet."

That was the box where he kept his money, the two thousand bucks. I didn't have to say it.

"Yeah, with my money. Brian's my nephew, for chrissakes. Joey, I known him since he was sucking your mother's tit. Sit down, relax, would you? Don't stand in my company."

He turned back to the television, snapped the dial from channel to channel, too quickly even to know what he was snapping past, like he was trying to snap it off. "You're making me agitate."

"Did he ask you for money?"

"The one time, like I told you. The two hundred dollars. He didn't want nothing today. He wanted pictures of his grannies. Oh, you're a pisser, Joey."

"All right," I said. I squeezed my head at the temples as my brain muscled up. "All right, I better leave. Forget me, I'm a jerk. I'm too nervous about everything."

"Uh-huh. Like me."

"There's nice cold cuts and milk in the refrigerator. Two cans of hearty vegetable in the cabinet." I pointed to a chair near the kitchen window as I stepped back toward the door. "There's all your linens."

"See? That's better," he said and reached to light a cigar. A flame puffed from its tip. "Joey, answer me a question. You don't think your brother had anything to do with this whole thing, do you? They're arresting the nigga girl, ain't they?"

"You have to use that word?" I asked, turning part of the way back toward him.

"What word? That's what she is, ain't she?" he asked. I could see he was about to agitate again. "Don't you turn on me, now. I'm all alone. I live alone. You're a worrier like me," he said. Half-turned in the doorway, I could feel his eyes seeking mine. "Don't make me a worrier like you. She is the guilty party, ain't she?"

"I guess. I don't know," I said and looked square at him. "Yeah, you gotta be right. My head's just all messed up."

"Sure. Think a positive thought each and every day," he said. He steadied his red pointer finger, shiny as a blister, and poked off the TV. He began tying his Air Walks. At seventy-five, he could bend like a chimpanzee. "You think it was the girl, or you think it was Clay? Tell the truth. You figure like Sonia, don't you. Your brother says that's what she thinks. Clay you figure?"

"No, no. I don't figure Clay. I don't know," I said. "I got to go. Let me go, all right?"

"You think like Sonia and Brian, don't you?"

"I don't know. All right? I do not know."

"Go ahead, go ahead. Okay. And listen, be outside, around people, Joey. Don't coop yourself up."

I shut the door behind me and turned toward the stairs. There, her back to me, turning the key in the lock of the apartment at the other end, was Natasha Matthews.

"Hey, boy. I knew I was gonna run into you. You and your pals." She said "pals" like it was a joke.

Natasha'd had her teeth fixed since the last time I'd gotten a good look at her. They were straight and yellow-white when she smiled. The blackness in her gums had shrunk. "I knew I'd see you boys. Tell Brian me *and* Hardy movin' in," she said with a bit of a Southern accent, "movun eeyun."

She held up a yellow bucket for me to see—in it was a bag full of sponges, bottles of Top Job and Windex, a box of Brillos. She turned toward me a little funny, shuffling her feet more than I thought she needed. She stood a little funny, too, real erect. I thought maybe she was pregnant. "Yo, there goes the neighborhood, right? Tell him and Sonia to come by," she said. The bucket, which she held in one hand to wave so long, had a Variety Bin "PAID" sticker on the side. She nudged the door open with her hip. "Make sure you tell Brian me and Hardy moving in. We'll cook some soul food for him and her and you if you want. Peace, Joey. Busy, man."

Maybe just by chance, maybe not, outside was Wilkinson, beaming with a smile that sucked her bucked teeth dry.

"Did you see who I saw?" I hid my eyes from the sun, which had passed the first park tree and had found a cutout directly to the porch. "Did you see that girl up there?" she asked like she was Natasha's proud guardian angel.

"I saw her. I talked to her," I said. I brushed the hair from my forehead, tapped my nose with the back of my hand, craned my neck toward the park as though I was looking for someone. I stepped away and crossed my arms against the chill that came with the shade.

"That's big news," she said. "Big news. How stupid were all of us? Now we making some progress on this case, and that apartment ain't the only thing. This shit's busting open—today, man. Today, Joey. After more than a week, now we got some evidence." She was wearing a scarlet, grey, and white Rutgers Law School baseball cap, blue-grey shorts over heavy legs, and a grey Police Athletic League knit shirt that showed off her upper body, the breasts that made you think more of pecs than sex. "But Natasha. That girl is clear. Shit, she's moving in the place. Think about it. Think about our own prejudices," she said. I hung my head. I was tired, and beat. My headache kept returning. "We know why Natasha's fingerprints were in the apartment. That was never a question really. We got Clay and your brother to thank for that. I just write two words on that one, 'Lewd Acts.' Now then, why was she hanging around here so much—'frequenting the neighborhood,' my ass. Yo, what was Hardy Cummings doing circling the building, walking the streets? Shit, that's a hard one. Probably the boy was looking for KKK, Kill the Nigger graffiti before moving in his pregnant girlfriend." I wasn't listening, wouldn't. I let my eyes fall nearly shut, slitlike and empty. Half asleep, I looked past her, out into the park. I tapped my nose with the back of my hand again. "Joey, don't act arrogant. It ain't you, man. Come on, look at me when I'm talking."

A rush of sadness swept down me, weakened me, and frazzled my molecules. As the pressure in me changed, I had to choke off the water-balloon thing that bobbed up from my stomach into my throat again. But I leaked saliva into my airpipe when I swallowed down, and I nearly gagged in mid-breath.

I didn't want to fight her. I knew I would have broken down and lost. Our eyes met. She saw how I was, all fucked up, and her eyes went from happy to not so happy. She tried to apologize for her gloating, make me understand. "Look at me, Joey. We almost arrested that girl," she said. I looked into her eyes. There was something different, though I couldn't figure what. I thought maybe she'd taken off sunglasses, but she held nothing in her hand. She looked into mine, trying so hard to explain that it was nearly a plea. "We almost arrested that girl, that girl right up there. Arrested an innocent girl trying to hold her life together for something she had no part of. Natasha nineteen years old. She got a record. She's black. She could have been in jail for the rest of her life. 'Frequenting the neighborhood.' 'Circling the building.' I read your lieutenant's report. *Fuck* that shit, Joey."

Don't do it to me, I wanted to say. He ain't my lieutenant. I can't help it, I wanted to say. But I didn't, I couldn't say anything. The balloon dammed up my throat.

"The lieutenant believes Natasha's guilty. He truly believes it. I'm sure of that. But why, why does he believe it? Simple, man. He wants to. You judge it. He believes what's easy for him to believe. So, is he a liar? Me, I can't accept that way. I can't accept it. Life's hard, but Resto got to be better. You know what I'm saying, he got to learn to do better." She shrugged then pointed a stern finger up at the window, tipped back the Rutgers Law cap, revealing her hair. "I'm so happy that girl is innocent. I want to jump up and down and let the tears roll out my eyes. You know what I'm saying?" I folded my arms across my chest, hands inside the arm loops of the jersey. Like she was trying to shake some sense into me except she was holding steady, not shaking, Wilkinson grabbed and turned me, startling me. She held my shoulders with her hands, my head with her eyes. "Imagine if *you* was arrested for something you didn't do, if you was arrested for something you knew nothing about." I tried to turn out, not hard enough though to jerk free of her hold, just to let her know I was resisting. "I'd cry for any child, black, white, yellow, brown. I tell Demetrius it don't matter to me. He don't understand neither. I'd cry for you, Joey, if you got mixed up in this shit. I'd cry for anybody, but I'd cry more for you, Joey. 'Cause you a good kid, you a real good person. You're my buddy, Joey Scadutto."

THREE

THOUGH IT WAS ALMOST NOON BY THE TIME I LEFT Wilkinson, the morning was still cool as I stood atop the Cobble Road overpass eyeing Manhattan. Urban blight had been washed clean by the overnight hard rain, and a breeze that followed the Hudson River all the way from the upstate mountains sweetened the day. Though clouds from the bay had come in to mix with the blue, they were silver and white clouds, huge big-bellied clouds as beautiful as a death song.

I turned and backtracked toward the Palisade Avenue entrance to Cobble Road. The streets were dry but the park was muddy and half of Cobble Road, where the mud had dripped and run, was caked over, shiny on top but squishy.

Needing another look at Brian's spot, I hurried toward the Hundred Steps. The breeze blew stiffer and my feet went blood-less cold where the water'd squeezed in through my sneakers. "It's cool, really chilly," I whispered to myself, as though it was this, the cold, that was making me frantic, making me step too quickly over the sliding mud and wet leaves at the top of the steps. "It's way, way too chilly for July," I whispered, shaking my head. "This is ridiculous for July."

Bad ankle or not, I practically leaped down the first eight steps to a gravelly, flat landing, then began the next, longer stretch of platformy steps followed by three sets of eight. Turning onto the last eight, deep and dark, I allowed my eyes to stare ahead, toward the Parks Department bench, and the clearing behind it, and the thick hill-climbing trees behind that where the cables had been. More and more strongly, like I was losing a tug-of-war, I had to see the cables. I stared ahead too long—as I was clomping down the steps, staring, I knew it was too long. I should have looked down at where I was going, not stared ahead into the

208

trees, trying to spot the twinkle of the cable wires' tips. Two steps from the bottom, I finally did glance down, a second late, just as my foot was about to crush the head of a glistening pale snake, its forked tongue licking up. I shrieked like a girl and lost my breath. I tried to leap over the snake but my weight had already shifted and my back foot slipped out. Instead of leaping over the snake, I just threw my body forward, my legs lagging behind. My shoulder smacked a tree limb that gave only enough to let my head scrape past. I tumbled into a mud-soaked nest of slush, leaves, red beetles, and an underlayer of half-decomposed plastic garbage bags. The bags clattered with the bottles and cans inside and, from the pressure of my fall, oozed juice that pooled when I thought it would run.

As I jumped up, the gook clung to me, slowly slithering down my shoulder, my arms, my legs. For a second, I mistook the creeping grey-brown water for more snakes. I shrieked again and I trembled and I cried. The crying only scared me more and the shock of my sobbing stopped the tears. I realized it was only mud on my arm, and that no blood was pouring from my forehead, that soon I'd dry off. The trembling lessened but wouldn't quit, and I took my next steps toward the bench with my arms and legs tingling. Under my good ankle, my left foot was nearly numb, squishing the water with each step. The right side might as well have been wooden. I felt nothing from the ankle down.

Higher up, I stood on that hump of yellow-green grass where the ground was dry and the air pure. In the sunlight, I took slow, deep breaths. I was careful with my steps. Except for sudden give-outs when I overreacted to the weight pressing down on my ankle—the picture I had was of two thin bones, one pressing atop the other, holding my 120 pounds—I came back to myself.

The dry land and open air pushed me into the future, one week forward, onto the Wagon Train. My breathing settled. The tightness gripping me drained and my muscles loosened. As I walked toward the bench, I touched the forehead bruise. It was stingy under my fingertips and damp with blood, but only a little blood, like a scrape would have made, blood that wouldn't come back once wiped away. I was calmed, things were okay.

Even my hand stopped tingling when I realized that under whatever interrogation was coming I wouldn't have to explain away a deep gash as well as a broken ankle.

The sun disappeared behind a fast-blowing silver-fringed buffalo cloud but quickly it was back. Then just as quickly, another cloud blew in front. Down on the Hoboken rooftops you could see the rolling play of the clouds and clear sky. In cloud- shadow, I approached the bench. "Damn, it's too chilly for July," I repeated, sneering at my no-name basketball jersey.

There was something I couldn't identify at first. There was a yellow stripe zigzagging through the trees. I took a step to the far side of the bench, nearer the woods, squinting my eyes. I dipped my head and leaned forward while holding my legs back. There was another yellow stripe, plastic, a few feet higher than the first but not quite parallel to it, and there was more twirled plastic tape connecting the lower with the upper. The closer I got, the brighter the yellow became and I could see the black print across it. I knew what it was. All of the cables were gone from the ground and from the trees. Many of the trees were marked with white-painted numbers. The "POLICE INVESTIGATION: DO NOT CROSS" tape circled that section of twenty or so trees and, in back, looped around stakes driven into the dirt behind the base rock of the hill.

I wanted to be out of there as quickly as I could, but I was cautious, too, trying to think clearly—quick but cautious, I said—fearful of a third bruise and a need for an explanation. So as I stepped away, I made sure I set my feet before I turned back for each peek at the site, and I walked carefully, even over the safer ground near the bench.

I jumped from the dry hump down to the steps. After the shift out of sunlight, I was blinded in the dark growth and I touched my way up the steps. I whispered to myself, "Joey, be careful, take your time. It'll be fine, it'll be fine. Quick but cautious." More crawling on all fours than walking, panting but safe, relieved like I'd escaped hell for purgatory, I made my way to the clearing before the final eight steps, and I looked up the hill. I could see Uncle Vic's kitchen and bedroom windows in the apartment house at the edge of the park.

It was cool and breezy here on earth, but the way those big clouds were blowing across the sky, reflected in the apartment house windows like a blue and grey wave, there must have been real gales blowing a thousand feet up. Behind the waves that crossed my uncle's kitchen windows stood Wilkinson straight on to it, looking down at me.

FOUR

HOME, I WALKED THROUGH THE QUIET APARTMENT to Brian's room. His door was locked. I listened through, from one silence to another. I knocked softly before taking hold of the knob.

It was loose. You could pull it toward you, the stem sliding an inch from the plate. *Boom!* I kicked the door with my heel. One kick busted the door through, knocking the lock's catch right from the frame, but the door's bottom corner ripped into the wood floor, and I had to kick again to knock it open.

I hadn't been in Brian's room for a long time, for what seemed like years, since childhood, and I was surprised and gloomed by the dark of that windowless half of the apartment, attached on Brian's side to the other half of the double.

Brian's mattress was bare, not so much as a sheet or pillow on it. Everything else had been taken out, gone to the HouseRAD apartment. The floor was smudged or scarred where furniture had been. I searched the walls for the ghosts of hanging pictures or mirrors but could find none.

I tried turning on the small shadeless lamp that was on the floor—a lamp that years ago had been in the living room, blue-bulbed under *The Minuet*—but the switch spun in its post. Slowly and deliberately, I walked around the room, aware of each step, listening for its slide across the bare wood's dust. I talked to myself some more, messing with make-believe voices, letting them do the soothing, envisioning a brain-line from the play voice to the real me—I felt foolish, even crazy, but it relieved me—a whispered momma's voice, then a booming voice, then a squeaky one, then a grandpa's. "Nothing here, nothing here, Joey. Nothing here to be scared of, young man."

I examined each inch of the rest of the room super carefully to be sure that when I left there'd be no chance to self-doubt, no need to come scurrying back, afraid I'd missed something.

Eventually, I turned to the closet door. I pulled it open. Not trusting my eyes in the dark hole, I got down on my knees and searched with my hands. "Where's the cables, boy? Where is ya?" I whispered, tapping my hand on the floor like a blind old man. "I know you gots to be somewhere. Where is ya?"

"Nothing there, nothing on the floor, Grandpa."

I stepped back and heard the voice telling me how to feel. "Just take it easy. All's well, son." Then I heard all of the play-voices in quick succession, but from a different spot, a corner of my brain, neither me speaking nor me listening, a third point that webbed a straight line into a triangle. I swooned as the stretch happened under my scalp, a rubber band of thought being yanked. Then, for being so dazed and stupid and weak, for letting my will fall flat, I whacked my head with the butt of my hand. I needed a tough brain for this, not mush, not a brain that would play tricks.

"Check carefully," I whispered, pissed at myself. "Careful what you're doing, fool."

I wasn't tall enough to see to the back of the top shelf. I stood on my tiptoes and patted it with my hands. Nothing there.

Then I checked the whole apartment nearly as carefully as I'd checked Brian's room. When I shut the kitchen door to leave and I marched down the stairs, on my way to finding and confronting Brian, a twilight feeling grabbed me, a feeling like I'd never return.

Down the stairs, in the foyer before the outside door, I reached for the knob but turned around, real jumpy, as if someone had tapped me on the shoulder. I stared at the door of the empty downstairs apartment.

I turned back to the outside door like I was about to go out it, then spun into the first-floor door's face. It had a personality— a guard from *The Arabian Knights*, somber and broad-shouldered, but vulnerable to an Open Sesame or a kick in the shins. Again, I turned away and quickly spun back. With the butt of my hand, hard as I could, I smacked it right at the lock and it flew open so easily and fast that probably a light breath would have done the job as well.

All the windows were shut, and the apartment smelled stale from being closed up since spring. As I walked through the front room, I could feel the dust and grime attaching to my skin. A mouse scurried across the living room floor, banged into a wall, bounced back and scurried and banged into another before disappearing under the radiator. But there wasn't a sound, not even my own breathing, and I felt like I was seeing incompletely, like through a video lens. I had to concentrate on keeping my balance. I searched for the grandpa voice, but couldn't find a trace.

The bathroom had been stripped. There was no shower curtain, only the pink plastic rings, and nothing in the cabinet or closet. There was no table in the kitchen, only circles of rust on the linoleum where the legs had been. There was a boombox on the sink counter, must have been left by the new owners. There was nothing in the closet, nothing in the cupboard but a Roach Motel with petrified guests lying on their backs.

The only difference between this apartment and ours was that there was a broom closet in the hallway down here where overhead the staircase rose to the second floor. I opened the closet door. At both ends, the closet was broader than its door, and in one corner there was what first looked like a trash can. I pulled the overhead's hanging chain. The bulb came on with a pop. I stopped breathing, and I put one hand on my belly. It wasn't a trash can. My throat wouldn't open and I couldn't get a breath in or out. It wasn't a trash can, it was a spool of cable, two feet high, maybe two-thirds full. "Property of HCCC" was printed in red marker across the aluminum top wheel. Finally, a breath burst from my throat, as though I'd just popped my head from underwater. I sucked for air and gulped, and a dust-stirring cough blew from my lips.

I kicked at the cable but it barely wobbled. As I backed toward the front door, the scratch marks where it had been dragged across the floor followed me out.

FIVE

THE ADDRESS OF BRIAN AND SONIA'S PLACE WAS 21 Ogden Avenue, a block and a half past the Pioneer, just two of HouseRAD's cabin-homes and a narrow vacant lot from the railroad cut that ended the street. No more than a half mile from our house, from 21's windows you could look out on half the world—Manhattan, Brooklyn, the Statue of Liberty, Ellis Island, Staten Island, the Verrazano Narrows.

As soon as I'd heard the address, I knew what building my mom was talking about. It was the end one of the three warehouses on the last block. That end of HouseRAD hadn't been fixed up yet, not even as much as the block around the Pioneer had. I didn't know what kind of shape the building would be in, if their doors had locks and the rats and possums were gone, if new trees had been planted and the hydrants fixed.

On that end block, some of the front doors did have locks, but most were boarded up. A couple had the doors swung wide open and rock music blasting through, like the hillbillies were at home. About the rats and possums, dead or alive, I couldn't tell. The fire hydrants hadn't been fixed: the two I saw were capless and dry. Trees hadn't been planted yet, but baby ones had been brought in. A dozen of them, six feet tall, stood like a sleeping army in burlap against the chain-link that dead-ended the street at the railroad cut.

Near 21 were five parked cars along a curb that was otherwise deserted. The "NO PARKING THIS SIDE, Tuesday and Friday, 10:00-12:00" signs hadn't gone up yet—I assumed theirs would be the same as ours, then said maybe not. But the Neighborhood Watch signs had, screwed a foot and a half from the top into the same metal poles that the NO PARKING ones were to be placed on. Two of the cars were BMWs, both needing paint jobs. The other three were jalopies—big cars, at least a dozen years old, bumpers hanging loose and rust-pimpled, antennas taped together, roof vinyl ripped. On their back windows were college stickers, some cars with three or four—NYU, Rutgers, Penn, Tufts, Cornell. I couldn't make heads or tails of who owned them, rich or poor.

The building's front entrance was two metal doors that you could only open by sticking your fingers into the rusted hole where the handle had once been and yanking. Above the doors, someone had carved and burned, black into raw wood, "Welcome to the Riviera." There was no lobby or doorbells inside, only a piece of lined yellow paper taped to the wall with the names of the tenants and their apartment numbers and a folding table strewn with the mail.

The belly of the building was still as much of a warehouse as it had ever been. It smelled of oil and caked dust, had a cracked cement floor, brown-painted metal columns to the high ceiling, and a grimy, peaked skylight the size of a two-car garage. Against the front wall were half a dozen stacked folding tables and several big cardboard boxes, partially ripped open but still holding their merchandise. The apartments themselves followed the building's shell, and since the staircase, just completed, was blocked by tar buckets and tape, the only way up was to use the freight elevator in back then walk the balconies that surrounded the center of the horseshoe. Each floor had four apartments, making for twelve altogether.

Sonia and Brian's door—not yet painted but whitewashed around the new brass knob and lock—wasn't all the way shut, and I entered the kitchen without knocking. The apartment, 2B, was one big room, the ceilings high enough to have allowed for the old warehouse's stacking and machinery. The only divider in the entire apartment was the wall of the kitchen, which came out halfway across the floor. A standing pink mattress, still partially in torn tissue paper, leaned against the windows opposite.

The back wall, the wall with the direct view of Manhattan, was all windows as far as I could see past the divider. There were windows, too, all along the side facing the sun, overlooking the railroad cutout and, further off, the whole of the harbor.

I heard Brian and Sonia back behind the partition. They were pushing something heavy that slid over the wood floor, sounded more like a cardboard box than a piece of furniture, and were talking sharp, echoey words that had a billiard-ball clatter and I couldn't at first make out. They had no idea I was in their apartment, and I couldn't remember why I was there. I could only trace back my steps as far as the elevator, the whole walk before that guesswork. I swung my foot from my bad ankle. The ankle was numb, the foot almost so. With my fingertips, like a braille reader, I touched along my forehead, but that triggered nothing either.

The kitchen table was a heavy wood door, painted purple and laid atop two sets of three-high cinder blocks. Four old wooden folding chairs were set around the table. Across their almond-yellow backs you could still make out the chipped gold stencilling, "Himmel's Funeral Home." On the tabletop was a loaf of unsliced dark bread, a carving knife with breadcrumbs stuck to the mustard along its blade, scraps of ham and Swiss on white deli paper, and, half in their bags, plastic spoons and forks, and napkins, and paper plates. Folded, pushed to one corner of the long table, was a Spanish-language church missal.

Three tall plants, the pots in red and silver foil, were on the floor, the only separation between the kitchen and the long empty space to my right side, away from where Brian and Sonia worked.

Jerking my attention back where it should have been, Brian walked to the corner window carrying a white stepstool and a new galvanized bucket. Barechested, with black smudges on his round shoulders, he looked both babyish and middle-aged, lost, sort of in between. He was unmuscled, still seemed flabby all around, but his pants slipped from his hips as though he'd lost some weight. His hair was brushed back, greasy looking, and tied into a ponytail no bigger than a peanut shell.

Brian climbed to the top step of the mini-ladder. Sonia came over and handed him a spray bottle of green liquid. I wondered if she'd confronted him with his lie, or if she was holding off. Even if she had already confronted him, all seemed sweet and normal, at least temporarily, any challenge to Brian put aside for a later date.

She stood below, holding on to both his calves from behind the ladder. Sonia said she was going to Sears to spend the fifty dollars my mom had loaned them, to buy paint. Brian said he'd work another hour or so then take a break. She said good idea, it's really nice out. Sit up the park or something.

I was there. I knew I was there for a reason. I was standing in the middle of their apartment because something had to be done. About the murder, about the investigation. Questions needed to be answered. Like what was going to happen next? And why had Brian been at Uncle Vic's?

Him and Sonia kept talking, back to what she'd get at Sears. Curtains, tablecloths, pillows. What colors would go good? Brian said, Hey, we only got fifty dollars.

I scratched my fingernails across my forehead bruise, making it sting, filling my eyes with non-crying tears, the ones that come when you're trying to blink something out of them.

What was he up to? He was trying to frame Clay, to isolate him, split him off from Aunt Pat. And if there wasn't enough evidence against Clay, no more than there'd been against Natasha, then it would be his ass next in line. Best for Brian if there was another crime, this one with a blood trail leading to Clay.

Brian had said he had no remorse, no guilty conscience, no nightmares, and Uncle Vic had said that Brian only wanted to look at pictures of his grannies, for chrissakes.

I wandered a few more steps past the partition, into their direct view.

"Like a dark blue around the windows and woodwork, more ocean blue for the walls," said Brian.

"Sounds cool."

"I love it," said Brian.

There were different types of glass in the different panels of the window Brian worked on: grey-tinted glass and clear, pebbled and smooth, one in the bottom corner taped over with box cardboard. Nothing could clean the grime from the pebbled panes of the middle section, so Brian put his muscle into cleaning the clear glass at the top, spraying, rubbing, rinsing, even doing it again, his back oozing a coating of sweat.

"It looks real great," called Sonia from a corner spot where I couldn't see her.

I wandered further forward, forgetting they could see me.

Brian kept working. He never turned around. He rested his weight on one hand against the frame and pushed the cloth-covered fingers of his right hand into a tough corner. Sonia strolled into view—while away she'd changed out of her paint-smudged jeans and into cutoff sweats. With a scraper, she pointed out something just above the window.

She was there right in the open, where I could see her and she could see me. I froze. I kept my eyes on them. Where my heart pounded there was a big ache, like you get when you gulp soda too fast.

When I touched the shiny doorknob it jiggled, just a bit, but I imagined they'd heard it. I spun and ran out, sure that any second they'd come hunting. I pressed the hard rubber elevator button, but when the door didn't open, I panicked and ran to where I could hide, in a short cutout on the far side of the elevator. The small dead end was crowded with recycling—stacks of newspapers, stacks of magazines; two barrels of milk cartons, Fab and Cheer and Clorox bleach; two more barrels of empty soda and beer and wine bottles. I stood in the middle of their sticky leaks.

The elevator door clanked open, but two guys came out, two paunchy older men in their forties, one of them carrying a guitar case. Balding, with grey hair and beards, they almost looked like twins. I had to wait for them to get into their apartment, the one past Brian's, and by then the elevator had shut and moved up or down. I was about to rush out and press the button again, but before I did, the building's front door swung open, toward the street, and my mom and Resto entered the building. My mom, in her sleeveless black and white zipper-shirt, was laughing, loud and high-pitched. They stood in a shrinking angle of light as the door swung shut. Half drunk on her brunch juice, my mom held on to Resto's arm. From his free hand, he was swinging a key ring around his finger. He had an embarrassed grin on his face, a likeable I-know-what-a-jerk-I-am grin. They were both nodding up and down, yup, yup. They walked toward the elevator, my mom still holding his arm. He kissed the top of her head, the center spot of her shiny new hair, and she seemed to hold stronger, her whistling laugh still ringing around the building's brick belly.

When they neared the elevator, they disappeared from my view. I heard the elevator door open and close.

I shut my eyes and rested my head against the wall. I didn't know if when they got off I'd hide or show myself, needed to see them close up to tell if I could. But they didn't get off on the second floor. The elevator went to the third. I heard them walking along the balcony though I couldn't see them until they passed directly over Brian and Sonia's on their way to the far end, diagonal from me, where the apartment's view would be of Ogden Avenue in front and of the harbor along the side.

The only light in the building fell in dusty silver from the skylight. Like I was looking through the wrong end of a telescope, they seemed a mile away.

Resto went to unlock the door. It must have been apartment 3D. Behind him, my mom licked her fingertips then used them to rub a smudge from their door frame, a door frame that was shinier than the others, like it had just been varnished. Resto opened the apartment, elbowed the door and held it with one hand. He stepped aside and made a sweeping ladies-first gesture and my mom entered.

I would escape.

SIX

I WAS ONLY A FEW STEPS INTO THE PARK, ON THE cement path that cut from the basketball court to the World War II Memorial, when a 99S, clattering and blowing black smoke, squeaked to a stop at Palisade and Bowers, on its return route from NY Port Authority. The bus pulled away and the black cloud dissolved. Standing there were Marcy and Lanniqua, holding hands like queer sisters as they tried to cross. They each had roller blades slung over their shoulders, and I smiled. They must have done what Marcy'd told me she always wanted to do since her uncle took her there when she was eleven—roller blade in Greenwich Village, it's so cool. As they ran into the park on tiptoes, my heart rose and sank twice. I knew this was no time to try to talk—limping and mentally all fucked up like I was, I felt like a freak—and when I reached the memorial, I turned onto a different cement spoke, one that switched back, out of the park and onto Palisade, but away from them at the Hutton Avenue end.

I climbed the Hutton Street hill to Central, thinking maybe I'd walk into the precinct, maybe talk. I stood in front of Health and Beauty staring across toward the Al 'n Mo. All of a sudden I was bumped from behind. I turned my head. It was Sonny Grammachi, Flo's dark-haired, waxy-eared eleven-year-old. He reached around from behind my butt while he stayed hidden, his idea of a joke, and waved a pink flier in my face. "Enjoy Jersey City's Newest and Finest Alfresco Dining Experience at the Al 'n Mo Cafe, 336 Central Avenue. We specialize in Original Gourmet!" Lower on the page was a partial menu: Meatloaf, Fish Sticks, Stuffed Cabbage, Chicken Chow Mein.

"Have one, Joey," said Sonny, already as tall as me. "I got to give out this whole stack. My mother said I had to bring some

221

down the RAD, but no way I'm going there. Prob'ly some queer'll grab me."

"Yeah, and you'll never be seen again," I said, half sarcastic, half distracted as I tried to make out the scene in front of the restaurant.

"I know," laughed Sonny.

I took a flier from him and crossed over. On the sidewalk in front of the restaurant were three round plastic tables, the kind that wobbled even on a level surface, with two white chairs at each, so weak a fat person would squish them flat.

Inside the store, sweating the innovation, was Al Grammachi. He peered bug-eyed over the store's sun-bleached pink curtain like a kid who'd spent his life in a box. Moving in and out of the doorway, badder than a bouncer at the worst bar in town, was Flo in pink spandex shorts and a grey off-the-shoulder Everlast sweatshirt. She looked up and down the avenue, tapping her waitress pad against the back of her hand, flapping it like a spanking tool. Her puffy sunburned face, frowning from the sun glare, was scary enough to keep away anyone but the most hardened regulars, like Boy Evans and Aunt Pat, who shared the first of the three outside tables.

From two doors away, above the do-waah-ditty falling from the restaurant's doorway, I could hear my aunt, her voice, a one-woman rat-a-tat-tat of information and opinion, cackle and insult, was fucked up, and I knew that the previous night's episode at Clay's was no one-time fall from the wagon. Aunt Pat was stoned again.

She wore a silver metallic sports bra and aqua bicycling shorts. She stood up and looked inside, over the curtain, to see the time. I looked as well. A little before two.

My aunt dropped her cigarette to the ground and squished it. She started backing away, shuffling as quick as her stiff legs and wobbling top would move, but when she spotted me, she came to a rocking stop before tiptoeing, Pink Panther style, hands set like claws, toward me.

Stepping within one concrete sidewalk square of me, my aunt put her arms out and closed her eyes. When I stepped into place, she embraced me, grunting and slow to let go. She was fucked up all right. Even when she hugged as hard as she could, her arms had no strength. Finally, she let go and we got face to face. She smelled of whiskey, not just her breath, but, on that cool afternoon, her sweaty neck and face as well, as though she'd soaked in the stuff. She tried to hold her head steady, but she was cross-eyed with drugs.

She took two weak-legged steps back. "I got to talk to Venus, my counselor. She's at her bench until two." My aunt meant at Pershing Field, not our park. "Then I got to get to work by three-thirty, so I only got a minute, but let me tell you—your fucking mother, kid," she said dizzily as she shifted her weight from one foot to the other, trying to settle her eyeballs. As she spoke, Boy, at the table, nodded in agreement, not so much at anything specific she said, but nodding straight at me, head perfectly up and down, like there was something about the world me and him understood.

"I don't want to say it, but Miss Stuck-up got what she deserved," said my aunt. "Clay was the first one to see her scores. He seen them yesterday. She fucked up royally. The only thing she passed was arithmetic. All because she didn't study," my aunt said, her face red and twisted with false sympathy. "She was the smartest girl in her class every year. Year after year, all through Saint Paul's. Oh, so now, how much is two plus two. Duh! I could have passed that fucking test and I'm no arithmetic wiz." She fell back another step, her leg buckling outways at the knee like the joint was rubber and springs. "But she had time to study for that scumbag, though, didn't she." It had gotten to the point where I couldn't call him a scumbag, just average, but I didn't show my aunt. No way. "Huh, I'm sure *he* didn't fuck up royally. No, no, not the scumbag." I wanted to either sit her down or turn her around and give her a little shove toward Venus. Instead, she lurched toward me, like maybe Venus had psychically nudged her back my way.

Aunt Pat's bony fingers stretched out to show red knuckles, mountain ranges of veins, deep-bitten nails. Her nose was sharper and thinner than it normally was. Maybe that had something to do with snorting drugs. Her complexion, from sentence to sentence, breath to breath, and step to step, fluctuated between pink and yellow. Maybe it depended on her thyroid. "Now she's going to be in the Basic Skills, Clay says, with all the foreigners and niggers. Good for the Stuck-up. That's where I got to be in an hour, helping at the college registration with Clay. I got to get home and fixed up," she said. She put her hands on her hips and huffed like she hadn't had a day off in months. "You know, it hurts me to say this, but she did deserve it. She really did. You reap what you sow, Joey."

As though he hated to agree, but the lady had a point, truly, Boy's eyes were wide and his brows curled in a wave that matched his shoulder shrug. He pushed back his chair and stood. "Sorry about the news on your mom," he said, like there'd been a death in the family. He threw a wink to put me on pause. "I got to take a whiz, people."

Before stepping around the table, he messed with the tail of his shirt—a white Cuban or Mexican shirt that had been on the outside rack at Central Consignment for a month—and he patted himself on the hip. "Don't go away, little man," he said as he turned away, trying to point at me but missing. "Boy's got something for you."

Flo squeezed through the restaurant door as Boy went in. Bumping a plastic chair across the sidewalk, she pulled it to the table for me. "You want anything, Joey?" she asked. I reached for the menu, a single sheet on the same pink paper as the flier. Flo laughed. "That's not for you. That's for newcomers," she said. "We made it pink 'cause we figured they'd like that," she said, looking at my aunt. I laughed when they did. "Don't be scared of us, we won't bite you," said Flo. I didn't know who she was talking to.

Aunt Pat leaned both hands onto the table, like she was about to sit, but stopped halfway and stayed, midway between sitting and standing, her butt a turquoise balloon.

I stared at the menu anyway but couldn't read it, or could read it but couldn't focus my attention enough to make sense of the words. What was I doing here, wasting time?

"Don't look at that I said." With one hand she snatched the menu from me, with the other she wiped the table with a dish-cloth. "Get it together, would you, Joey?" laughed Aunt Pat.

"I said already about the prices. Just order, would you,

please, before we shut the grill," said Flo. "Two o'clock's when we start cleaning for our dinner crowd."

Flo laid a menu on the table, in front of Aunt Pat, then, as my aunt read, Flo scratched her nose with one white-painted fingernail, like she was real slick. My aunt was shaking her head and grinning, but I don't think she knew at what, just that she was supposed to. "Looka," said Flo. "Orange juice, $1.25. A fucking dollar twenty-five. Orange juice! You know what it costs us? A dime. My father was embarrassed. I said, 'These people don't know what things cost, Poppy.' Coffee. Eighty-five cents, that's a quarter more than we charge you. I think them people are nuts. I mean it. And they ain't rich. They dress like they're paupers. Excuse me, have you ever heard of an *ironing board*, lady?" said Flo.

My aunt, closer to the tabletop now—her elbows, not her palms, holding her up—smiled, smiled a little bit at Flo but mostly at me, something of that same sharing in the eyes, the same wanting to include me that had been in Boy's eyes minutes earlier.

"Some of them can be nice. I'm just saying," said Flo. "But a lot of them are very weird. Very, extremely weird."

"Don't make fun," teased my aunt, wobbling the table as she shifted her weight before standing straight and wobbling herself. "Joey's mother wants to be one of them."

"Really, Joey?"

Boy came back to the table, wiping his hands on his pants.

"I don't know. She got a new haircut. Big deal."

"Did you see the haircut?" my aunt asked Flo.

"Yeah, I thought it looked good."

"You're too kind, sweetie. Who do you know got a haircut like that? Come on. No one, I bet," said my aunt, anger pushing her toward coherence. "Fuck it. It ain't worth my health. You know me, Floey. I got enough headaches." She pushed her hands against the air, trying to keep away her tide of troubles. The force of the struggle knocked her off balance and she staggered back. "I got to get moving or I'm gonna miss Venus. She's hot shit, that one. Really, she's more a spiritualist than a counselor, but it would drive Clay crazy to know." Secretively, she said, "He's all

225

approval and disapproval, that guy. Even Joey can tell you," she said. Fortunately, neither of them looked to me for an answer. "He got me this gig at the college registration—it pays eight dollars a hour—but I'll give me and him no more than a month," she said with a giggle. She started weaving backwards, as though the sobriety line had been drawn with a Spirograph.

"Joey, tell your mother to get back to her roots. And I don't mean these roots either," she said, poking her scalp. "I mean her real roots, her community roots, her neighborhood roots. Her people's roots. Tell her fuck Buddy Resto and his dreams and schemes. Tell her fuck the Pioneer Cafe and their stupid radio station." She was still shuffling backwards, toward Pershing Field and Venus's bench. She was more than a storefront away, had to yell for us to hear. She paused to gain a quiet stage. "Tell her to use her head a little bit before she throws it all away," she said and smiled, pleased with herself and her magic moment.

"Sorry, gotta groove, and then, yo's, it's hi-ho, hi-ho, off to work I go. Got to do advisement. Auntie got kids to counsel and bills to pay," she said before spinning and hurling herself toward Venus.

"Your aunt's amazing. After what she's been through," said Flo. What's she been through? I wondered. Thirty-five years locked up with herself? "Let me get you boys something," said Flo. "Two Cokes, okay? It's all right, Boy. It's on me."

"Hey, thank you," said Boy, his face swelling with surprise. "Truly."

It was just me and Boy at the table. The sun had heated up the late afternoon enough that hints of steam rose from the wiped tabletop. Boy pulled a crunched pack of Pall Malls from his pants pocket. There were three left, but they were all broken, and over his shoulder, like she-loves-me/she-loves-me-not, he tossed them away and laughed at his luck. "Fucked up, isn't it?" he said, a smirk on his thin lips, like that little detail, busted-up smokes, deciphered by the likes of him and me, contained God's plan for mankind.

"Damn sure is," I said and he looked at me with a sad and glowing smile like he loved me.

"Hey, I'm with you, kid," he said. And this surprised me,

because I thought it was me going along with him. Boy observed me as I reached down and squeezed my ankle. "What happened to your head?" he asked.

"Oh, oh," I said and took a swipe at but didn't touch the bruise, afraid of the sting. I couldn't think of an explanation, but Boy bailed me out.

"Hey, those things happen, Joey. I got lots of things I don't want to share with no one," he said like a guy who'd never wound another living thing, at least not someone like me, family. "Anything happening with the murder? I hear they're gonna make an arrest."

"I don't know." It was the last thing I wanted to talk to Boy about.

"What about that girl you know, the black? Natasha."

"No," I said, gently touching my forehead, tickling the edge of the beginning-to-swell bruise, concentrating on it and my fingers more than the conversation. "They ain't gonna arrest her. She's out of it."

"No shit. You're kidding. So you mean the murderers are just walking these streets," he said, disgusted at what was becoming of this beloved neighborhood that had done him so much harm. "Oh, man, more than ever I got to do this, bro."

I lifted my head, paid attention.

Boy stood about five-six or five-seven, a little taller than me, but even though I was skinny, he probably weighed ten pounds less, 110, 115. He bought most of his clothes from C.H. Martins's Boys Section.

Flo brought out our two Cokes. "I won't take a penny for them," she said.

When she left, Boy said, "A good thing. I don't have a penny." He tapped his knuckles on the table. "I got something for you, man. I want to do you a favor like I did with Brian." Cold and blue as ice, his eyes narrowed. Finally, he was doing something important, enjoying the moment. "I can feel shit happening around me. That's what I'm good at," he said and squeezed his shoulders as he laughed. "You know how this neighborhood's going, bro."

I didn't know where Boy thought we were heading. I

227

leaned away, starting to back out of the deal, whatever the deal, but Boy leaned forward, hunched over the table. I didn't want to seem too scared.

Boy was wearing that Latin American consignment shop shirt—big white buttons, broad collar, some sort of embroidered pattern in a strip down the front from shoulder to tail—and worn blue jeans. The jeans were loose at the waist, but the butt and crotch were real tight, too small for a grown man, even Boy, so he kept his wallet slung over his waistband and hung his keys and penknife and black and white rabbit's foot from a belt loop.

"Joey, you notice how all shook up Brian looked the day after Uncle Mike died? You notice? He was here, inside the place with me. I said, 'What's a matter, bro?' He wouldn't talk—that's Brian, right?—but I could see something funny on his face. I said it again. 'What's a matter, bro? It ain't like you to worry.' Nothing ever worries Brian. I said to him, like I'm saying to you now, Joey, 'Yo, man, maybe I can do something.'" Boy turned a bit in his seat so that his one knee, the one crossed over the other, was now out from the table. He slid a hand behind his back, into his waistband. "It was my idea with Brian, like it is with you. Did he tell you?"

"No. I don't know what you mean, Boy," I said, frightened of whatever his hand was doing.

"I gave him a piece, yo. Sometimes the cops give me one to hold if they're looking to sell. No, truly. I'm serious, man. I still got another one at home. Shit, yo, Brian was surprised, too. He's like, 'What the fuck you giving me this for, Boy?'" Boy laughed at himself, at the way every once in awhile he could surprise people. "Shit," he said, shaking his head and grinning.

He reached his hand deeper into his waistband and I heard something unsnap. He kept his hand low and floated it under the table. His eyes started blinking as if they were burning, but I think more that it was overflowing joy. "I said to Brian, 'It's for you, bro. Just in case you should ever need it.' Brian holds it. He holds it right in view—anybody could have seen. 'We're all in danger, man,' I said. Brian's still staring and staring at it, all thoughtful and relaxed and shit. He shakes his head, then he says, 'All right, Boy. Maybe I can use it. It's good.' He says it real soft and low and nods his head. Brian's a deep dude. He says, 'It's good, thanks.' And that's all your brother says and all we ever talked about it. It was enough said. Cool, ain't it?" Boy smiled, wanted me to smile back. I stared at him. I must have stared like he was crazy. "Under the table, Joey," he said. I could feel his knees knocking like he had to pee again. "I got one for you, too. The same like Brian's. Hurry up, take it, bro."

I reached under. I held it in both hands. It felt like a gun, but I hoped it was a joke—maybe a steel dick that he'd bought at a porn shop or a cigarette lighter shaped like a gun, one he'd won at Central Arcade.

"What'd Brian say?" I asked, still holding the lopsided piece of metal under the table.

"Nothing hardly, like I said. You know, just 'All right, maybe I can use it, good, thanks.'"

"What'd he mean he could use it?"

"He said maybe. He didn't mean nothing, I don't think, except it would be good in case. That was my thinking, too. Why? What's up?" asked Boy. I hadn't responded like he'd wanted me to, like he felt he deserved, and he was losing patience. By his way of thinking, I was fucking up. "Brian, and you, too, yous is in that building a lot. Yo, Joey, put it away, huh? Don't just hold it there. Put it in your belt, man. Cover it."

I did. I slipped it under my basketball shirt, into the waistband of my shorts. "Is it loaded?" I asked.

"Naw," he said. He shifted in his seat. He squeezed his hand into his pants pocket and pulled something out. He stretched the little package toward me under the table. "Put it in your pocket. Don't put it in the gun, bro."

"What is it?"

"It's the magazine," he said. I didn't know what a magazine was. "The clip, man, you know. It's got the bullets. The pistol handle unlatches and you shove that thing in. You got six bullets, little ones. The gun's small but excellent, a Detronic .32, like Brian's."

"Boy, listen, man. Boy, hey. What do I want with a fucking gun?" I asked, sick with what Boy had done, what he'd set up.

"What do you want with a fucking gun for?" asked Boy.

229

Insulted that I wasn't thankful for the gift, he pushed himself back in the chair, thrusting himself away from me and the table, and he had to latch on to the table's lip to keep from toppling the chair. "Joey, see," he said, pleading with me one more time to see the light. "In case anything happens. You never know. Now you have one and Brian has one. Listen to Boy, Joey—you never know, yo. You never know."

I laughed at him.

"Yeah, Boy, I have a gun and Brian has a gun. That's fucking great."

"Fuck it then. I'm trying to do something nice for your family. This is my thanks? If you want to be a pussy about it, go ahead. Go ahead. I truly thought you'd appreciate it, like your brother, man. But you're a little punk, ain't you? You belong in HouseRAD, too. Listen, if you don't want it, give it to your uncle."

"My uncle?" My eyes ached. I shut them so they wouldn't explode like blood balloons.

"Yeah, yeah, that's right. Little Uncle Vic," he said. He shook his head, disgusted with my stupidity. I thought he was crazy—a gun for Uncle Vic? "Is your uncle in danger? Are we all in danger? That's what a gun is for, Joey. Fucking smarten up. You ain't a baby no more. It's time. Just take it with you, awright. God, I'm disappointed in you, Joey. I am. I truly am."

SEVEN

I T WAS TWO-THIRTY BY THE HEALTH AND BEAUTY
clock.

Far down the Hutton Street hill, across Palisade and
Ogden, out over the cliffs, above Hoboken, above the Hudson,
above the tip of the shimmering skyline, yellow rays streamed
through a pale blue haze, but directly overhead a huge fluff
cloud, more silvery than grey, blocked the sun. The air, briefly
warmed, cooled quickly beneath the cloud cover. The midsummer
shivers swept through me again.

With the gun inside my waistband, the magazine in my
back pocket, I walked past the Hutton lots. I could feel the
strength draining out of my body, but I wasn't as tired as I wanted to be. I wanted to be tired like when you can't even stay
awake, like when you can barely lift cement legs, like when your
eyeballs roll behind half-closed lids, like when your bed, warm
and soft and fresh with Mom's Lemon Scent Bleach, is the best
friend you ever had. But I tried and tried, and with each step I
got closer to the fatigue I wanted. By the time I passed the caged,
just-planted chestnut tree in front of Saint Paul's, I'd willed
myself pretty close. Like a drunk at daybreak, I staggered
toward the steps that led behind the church buildings, not knowing if I was acting or real, or if anyone was watching—truly hoping they were.

I turned down and into the passageway between the convent and church and sat against the stone wall, on the damp
ground alongside the staircase me and Brian had been on the
day before.

I felt the gun pressing into my hip. The Detronic, I
thought. Afraid to touch it directly, I touched it through my jer-

sey, the slippery material sliding back and forth against the handle, rippled with finger wraparounds. I started to cry. My fingers were trembling when I went to touch my bruise, to soothe it. "It's okay, it's okay. Aw, it's okay," I said as I petted it like I was petting a little pup.

But I was still crying, louder, this time with shaking and sobbing and tears rolling down my face when I took the magazine from my back pocket, held it in my hand. It was the size of a junior Kit Kat. It was plastic and heavy and the bullets wobbled when you moved it.

I felt that thing coming up my stomach again, up my throat, but this time, instead of pushing it down, I sucked it up, awful-tasting as it was, and it landed in my mouth like a baby brain, like an embryo. I spit it out, nearly gagging again on its acid taste and chewy feel. It flew from my lips and landed so hard and solid it bounced then rested, yellow-grey, melting in a diamond of sunlight.

I heard two nuns out on the balcony across the way. They had on white sandals and their light blue and white outfits, were dressed like the Blessed Mother. Their sleeves were rolled up and their heads uncovered, their brown hair held back by the same kind of plastic bands my mother had worn until her haircut. One was a little skinnier and lighter complexioned than the other, a Filipino. The Filipino was holding a wicker basket steady atop the balcony rail as the littler one took and hung whites from it—clothes and towels and a bedspread. From the yard behind the far hedge, a man's voice called, "Hello, Sisters," and they smiled and waved and said something back. He called again and they laughed but didn't answer.

They hung the stuff until the basket was empty—the bedspread the last piece—and the line was full. The Filipino nun tossed the wicker to the other one, who caught it by one handle and smiled. Chatting, they walked down an outside staircase and reenterd the convent from the ground floor.

I watched the big towels blow. I wiped my lips clean of the throw-up taste. My eyes fell shut and opened slowly, fell shut and opened. I nearly drifted into sleep but was too cold to. The way the parish buildings were all staggered back there, the breeze was irregular. One second the line would be still, the next a gust would wrap around the corner, so strong even the bedspread would whip. If I had that bedspread.

I could use it as mattress and pillow and sheet.

I put the cool magazine to the warm spot on my forehead and pressed it there the way a cornerman presses cold steel to a fighter's bruised eye. I took out the pistol—not worried or scared or trembling, only curious—and held it upside down in my hand, the handle up, the barrel pointing at me. I snapped open the handle's magazine release. The magazine dropped in perfect, like I'd done it a hundred times before. I snapped it shut and spun the pistol right side up.

"I'm gonna get the bedspread," I whispered.

I crept out, away from the church wall, into the sun. I held the gun against my thigh as I limped across the courtyard then hid against the convent wall. The smell was clean, of pine cleaner and hardwood.

I tiptoed up the convent's outside steps. I stood on the balcony, gun behind my back, and watched as the man in the next yard disappeared into his house. I switched the gun from my right hand to my left. I reached out my right hand and grabbed for the bedspread. Stupid. Even before I touched it, I realized, of course, that it was wet and colder than the air, but I couldn't stop the idea and I yanked the spread full force. The line jerked and rocked. The pole at the other end tipped toward me and the pulley squealed like an animal being slaughtered, the sound lessening real slow, echoing with each weighted bounce of the line. Still, there I was, standing with a pistol in my hand. I shoved the gun into my shorts and held the line with two hands, trying to steady it. The squealing slowly faded but would never stop.

Just get out, get out quick, I told myself. Like a spotlight on me, from between the convent and church the sun peeked from a silver cloud's wispy fringe. I was hopping down the staircase on one foot, crying for myself, when the convent phone rang out.

EIGHT

O N MY WAY HOME, I WALKED THROUGH THE PARK, half looking for, half looking out for Marcy, who I thought might still be there with Lanniqua, knowing I wanted to see her but that, the shape I was in, if I did the best thing would be to just maybe sit for a minute, on a bench far away, hidden and watching her. That would have been nice. But I didn't see any sign of her, and I couldn't take the time to do a search of the slope either, on the down side of the Cliff Walk, or out behind the Park House where they liked to get high. Instead, as I neared the end of the park, I saw Wilkinson and a tall black man in front of our house. I ended my hunting around for Marcy and limped along faster and faster.

It wasn't until I was already within three houses of them, and they'd spotted me, that I remembered about the gun and realized if I wasn't careful they'd see it. I passed the last tree before our house and absentmindedly touched it just below its new red X, my fingers dipping into a spongy ooze in the bark.

Luckily, the gun was on my right hip, where, turned the way I was, that side against the fences, it was less likely they'd notice.

"Hiya, Joey," said Wilkinson, dressed typically like a mail carrier. "Joey, meet Demetrius. Demetrius, this is Joey." He was tall, maybe six-three, wearing a Chicago White Sox baseball shirt, black permanent-press shorts, sandals. He had reddish little devil ears, something you'd serve on an hors d'oeuvre platter, and a stubbly neck that looked like he'd shaved himself with a carving knife. Just above both wrists were a pair of scars identical to one another, thin braided bracelets that reminded me of manacles and I was sure were there on purpose. "You guys know one another better than you think because I'm a talker around people I like," she said.

Demetrius gave a little snort, and I couldn't tell if this was part of his usual arrogant way of greeting people, or if he really hated me special and was disrespecting his girl for not. He smelled spicy-sweet, like candy root-beer barrels, and when he finally unglued his pink and brown lips to suck in some air, he showed polished white teeth. He turned and took a step back, off the sidewalk and just inside the gate, sideways, neither his front nor his back to me.

"So where you guys going to be moving?" Wilkinson asked, indicating the Sold sign wired to the fence. "I hear HouseRAD."

"How do I know? You think they tell me anything?" I asked, not knowing why I was acting so angry with my mom.

Demetrius gave off another snicker and a puff of air blew from his sticky lips. He did a half spin on the ball of one foot. Even with a foot on the porch's second step, Demetrius seemed stiff, like his muscles couldn't relax and his joints were ratcheted, not smooth. Neither of them made a path for me when I took a step forward.

"We were just looking for your mom," Wilkinson said. "Nobody's home."

"My mom's prob'ly working."

Tall weeds had pushed through the front yard's concrete— punks and snowflakes and tickle spears. They'd spread from the hill, crept down the alley, and were now even growing under the porch, poking through the grey sideboards. An infantry, they'd invaded and wanted to claim us.

"What happened to your head, man?" asked Demetrius. He had a deep voice, like he was practicing for the opera, and I'd expected an accent, either homeboy or Jamaican, but didn't notice either.

"I bunked it."

"You 'bunked it,'" he said and laughed, looked at Wilkinson, who smiled back at him. I felt like I might faint. "What happened to your ankle? You bunk that, too?"

"None of your business," I said.

"You better think of an answer fast, 'cause somebody gonna ask you," he said and he laughed again, not a snicker, a guffaw, almost a cough, three or four times that he couldn't stop.

"We want to know, Joey, can we look around the apartment?" Wilkinson asked.

"No," I said. "No, you can't."

"Joey," she said, like I was embarrassing her. "Come on." But I wasn't giving. "Your mom's at work?" she asked.

"I think so. I'm not even sure." I was afraid for the gun again. All of a sudden, it was hurting, digging hard into my hip bone.

"Because, look, there's some things she should know about the investigation. We're moving real fast now. I just got off the phone. And, you know, the information Lieutenant Resto's giving her may be misleading. Not intentionally or nothing."

"'Nuff said," said Demetrius, insisting. "'Nuff said, Rhonda."

"Things'a changed real quick. You know that. Natasha's out. We got the cables. I know you know that, too. They're being tested this hour. That's why we want to take a look at your apartment."

"Never mind him," said Demetrius. "Get the warrant."

"When's your mother coming home?"

"I don't know," I said. "College registration's today, too. She had to do that. Why do you want to search the apartment?" I shuffled my feet. The gun, under my red, white, and black jersey, was right in front of Demetrius. I turned. "What's there that you want?" I asked.

"I don't know what's there," she said, sucking and holding a deep breath that almost popped her bra. "We looking for anything to do with the crime." One hand on her hip, she tapped her foot. A tough job—trying to be funny for me, stern for Demetrius.

"Anything like what?"

"Joey, that's all I'm gonna say. Now you gonna help, or what?"

"Just get the search warrant, Rhonda, huh? Why you babying him?" asked Demetrius. "This ain't worth it." His "this" meaning me.

"Come on, Joey," she pleaded.

We both wanted to say the name Brian, to admit that's what it was about, but neither of us could.

"We just got to search the rooms. Ten minutes," she said.

236

"No," I said. She shut her eyes. She had long lashes and eyes that bulged under their lids. She shook her head and stepped back, her eyes still closed. I repeated myself, "Uh-uh." When she opened her eyes, she looked at me with a weary gaze. I was scared she was gonna tell me to fuck myself.

"After I saw you this morning I went up to your uncle's. He was all nervous about whatever you'd said to him. I called Community Relations to come and do one of their security things for his apartment. Prob'ly they'll come tomorrow."

"So what are you telling me for?"

Demetrius laughed at her. I understood why and I wished I hadn't said that, not so nasty anyway. She was trying to be nice. I could feel she was.

"What'd I tell you? He's just stonewalling to protect you-know-who," said Demetrius. He moved toward the gate to pass me. I turned sideways and the gun knocked against the fence. "Excuse me, please," Demetrius said, his face in mine, not satisfied with my hip turn. He stepped to the curb. Hands in his pockets, staring at his feet—not just to pass time, I don't think, but admiring his sandals, maybe his toes, too.

Wilkinson said, "Because I know you're worried about him, that's what I'm telling you for. What happened to your head?"

"I told you, I bunked it," I said, staring past her at Demetrius, hoping her eyes would choose me over him. They didn't. She stared up at our front window.

"Rhonda, I got other things I could be doing."

"I'm sorry, Wilkinson, but you can't come in," I said. She looked at me with agitation and worry. I knew I deserved them both.

I was on the landing, one hand on the door. "I'm going up. I'm sorry, but you can't come in."

"It's okay, Joey. Just be cool. This is going to be over soon." She was worried for me. She was a good person. I even thought that if it hadn't been for Demetrius, she might have tried to hug me. "It will. It really will, very soon." I pushed the door open. "Just be cool, okay? Joey, listen, all right? Joey, okay?"

"Yeah," I said.

NINE

I SHUT THE DOOR BEHIND ME AND CLIMBED THE stairs. It was clear to me. I had to do something, quick, to protect my Uncle Vic from Brian. He must have known, too, that an arrest was coming. I snatched the folded note my mom had left on the kitchen table. She was oblivious:

I messed up my test, Joey—flunked practically everything. Buddy talked to one of the Deans he sort of knows and they'll let me take the test again. Right now, 1:00, I'm going to. Maybe I'll do better.
You got a call this morning from Mr. Rodriguez. He's back. He's very convincing about the Wagon Train thing, Joey. Marcy called, too. She'll be up the park.
I've got to work tonight—four to ten. Then I got some apartment news I want to tell you about. Remember to check in on Uncle Vic.

That was the end of the note, or the first part of it. There was a PS written later—three-thirty. It was quarter past four as I read.

Yo, Joey, I just got a call from the college. Oh yeah! Oh yeah! I passed everything. But you got to do me a favor. Today's the last day of early registration when I can get my financial aid in on time. Go there for me and do it. It's downstairs from tutoring. Brian should be there. Or, if not, then Clay can help you. Thanks. I know you'll do it. I love you, my baby boy.
Pizza tonight?

I went into my room and tossed the gun onto the bed. I changed into some warmer clothes—long pants and a loose, hooded sweatshirt. I didn't want to keep carrying the damn Boy-gift around. More than anything, I was scared it'd go off and rip open my leg. But with all the snooping Wilkinson was doing, I was even more scared to leave it in the house. I lifted it from my bed, dropped it into the button-and-flap pocket of my cargo pants. I sat on the bed, went blank for a second. I got up. I went down the stairs, opened the doors, stood on the porch.

Next thing I remember, I was almost flattened by a beer truck as I crossed Journal Square, just half a block from HCCC. All I could recollect about the trip was the clapping of the gun against my thigh and a step count of 1,086.

Registration was happening on the ground floor of the building. A long time ago, it had been the lobby of a ritzy office building, gold-ceilinged, walls covered in marble paper, black witch-finger floor indicators above the elevators. But now the old barber shop, newsstand, shoemaker's, and coffee shop had been carved up. Their walls had been ripped down and only the structural beams remained in the otherwise open ground floor. The mob scene was like a crowd of immigrants in an Ellis Island clearing hall.

In one front corner, Student Activities, set up at something like a lemonade stand, was showing Jenny Jones to keep the seated students amused. In the other front corner was a coffee urn and donuts—a big mess, the stuff must have been out since morning. The entire room smelled from a huge stain of spilled coffee and the browned and hardened napkins that had been used to soak it up. The musty room was way too warm, and I sweated, could barely breathe in the heavier clothes I'd changed into.

I stepped deeper into the crowd. Running toward me, full of energy, was my Aunt Pat in black and green, the ghost of the White Race Past. I'd underestimated Venus.

My aunt had on green stockings and black ankle-strapped high-heeled shoes. She walked with a pained hitch and her legs were too muscular for the outfit. She clomped around the room like she was driving nails into the floor. Her black miniskirt was made out of a material that looked like leather but was more like paper, a skirt some kid would make in an arts-'n-crafts class. It scrunched up around her butt and hips. Above the skirt was some sort of half-tucked silk, or fake silk, kelly-green blouse, and with it hanging shapeless, unbuttoned three-quarters of the way to her gallbladder, you could barely tell her shoulders from her breasts from her fluffy waist. She looked like a roughed-up whorehouse bed.

"Hey, Joey," she called, wagging her hand, thumb against fingertips, in an ey-Italiano gesture. On her head she wore a Saint Patrick's tam, tipped to one side. She had no Irish blood in her, and we were in July, not March, but in this crowd, white was white. "Watchya doing here?" she asked, shoving toward me, shaking it all, though in pain, on her high-heeled shoes, a clipboard and a can of Lysol in one hand, an unlidded half-gallon coffee jug in the other.

"I got to do this for my mother," I said, holding up a blank registration form I'd picked up off the floor. "Where's Brian?"

"The fink never showed up. He was supposed to be here one o'clock. What's it now? Five?" she said. She turned and waved for me to follow her through the masses. "I'm here with just Clay. I tole you we're still mad because I had one lapse. Fuck him. Come on, we got to talk."

"So where *is* he? Brian."

"Maybe with Sonia. I don't know. They're busy on an apartment, you know," she said happily. The gun clattered against my thigh so hard and often I was afraid the safety had slipped off. "Come on, come on with me." She waited for me to catch up, reached out her coffee-holding hand and straightened a pinky for me to hold on to. She no longer seemed stoned, just high and nuts on a combination of caffeine, grandeur, others' crises, and whatever was in the pep talk from Venus. She bulled forward, the two of us held together by arched arms, like the dancers in *The Minuet*. "Excuse me, excuse me, sir. Excuse me, please. Ma'am, move the carriage out of the aisle, please. Fire code." She turned and winked. "I'm on a high. I love helping people. It's so rare. One of the deans, he got to be in his twenties still, he called me a savant."

"I got a gun," I said. Twenty people heard me, but my aunt didn't.

Rooms and stations had been formed partly by the floor outline of the old shops, partly by velvet ropes, and partly by portable half-walls that made a maze of the lobby.

"Excuse me, excuse me. Can you hear, sir? I said excuse me. Perhaps you don't understand our language."

She led me past a long row of faculty and staff tables. At one of them was Clay. He lifted his head from where he was signing for a blonde student opposite him. He smiled at me and waved, but him and my aunt ignored each other. In the after-glance, each grinned, Aunt Pat's grin, though, nasty and sly, like she knew what he didn't know she knew.

"I don't even want to talk about him," said Aunt Pat, refer-ring to Clay, as we cleared the crowd. "You ever notice he only registers the cute ones? I'm so pissed at him. He keeps secrets, Joey. I got to tell you something."

We passed between the structure beams of the old barber shop and into a back corner, what she called her office, a six-by-eight space protected by portable walls. Inside were two folding chairs facing each other, between them a third chair with its desk flap down.

"This is where I counsel," she said. "They only send me the pain-in-the-asses."

"Aunt Pat, do this for me, for my mom, awright?" I asked, one hand holding on to the gun on my thigh, the other showing the registration form.

"You're all sweaty." She pulled a handkerchief from inside her blouse. "Dab yourself. What are you doing with all those clothes on? You're dressed like it's November. It's the middle of summer."

"I was cold all day. Look, my mom passed the retest and she's got to get registered."

"Oh, good for her. She got to take it twice? Most people don't. I got something to tell you more important. Something I found."

"Aunt Pat, I got to find Brian."

"Joey, what's the matter?"

"I got a gun."

"So, that's what's a matter? Clay got a gun, too. Your mom's got a gun. She's had it since you were little."

"I mean right now."

"Are you gonna use it?"

"No. No way," I said, forcing myself to believe it.

"All right then."

"Forget it. You don't know where Brian is?"

"No. Maybe with Sonia, I already said. He stood Clay up. Clay put his reputation on Brian, you know." She sipped from her huge coffee jug.

"Yeah, look, I'm going."

"No, wait. What I found. Listen, I'm living with a killer. Clay killed Uncle Mike. I went home after I left Venus. There was a note from Brian in my makeup bag, where me and him exchange our notes. 'Go look behind the house. There's something awful there,' it said. Guess what? I got the murder weapon, Joey."

"Uncle Mike was strangled."

"I know it, I know it. I got the cable. That was the murder weapon. I got a mile of the shit. It must weigh two hundred pounds." She shook her head. Tears poured from her eyes. She dabbed them with the insides of her wrists. "What can I do, what can I do? I can't help it if I love the man."

I couldn't keep out the sounds of the hall, words foreign and English, crashing and rolling like waves at the beach. I had trouble listening to her through the roar.

"Where's the cable?" I asked, shaking the flip-desk between us like I was shaking her.

"Right behind the house. Behind Clay's. Between the kitchen and the garage in back." I pictured the spot—narrow and soggy and full of slugs. "Brian wrote he found it this morning."

"Oh, I got to get him. I got to get Brian. He's planning something evil, Aunt Pat. I don't want to say nothing else."

"No, Joey. First you got to help me get rid of that thing. I love him. Despite it all, Joey, I love Clay. I don't want him to go to jail. How could I ever live with me? He's my sweetie Clay."

I had to press my eyes with both hands to keep tears from bursting out. "I got to get him, I got to get him," I muttered.

"Come on, Joey. Don't fall apart on me. Be strong. God knows, Clay ain't perfect, but we got to do all we can for him. He's almost family. We got to move that big thing and dispose of it before it's too late."

I put my hand inside my pocket, on the gun—the safety hadn't come off, but I flipped it off—my finger on its trigger. And I shut Aunt Pat off. Whatever she did after I stood up—if she called me, if she grabbed on to me, if she cried, if she began a sing-along, if she stretched herself onto a cross—I ignored her. I hurried out, excusing my way through the buzzing crowd.

TEN

E VEN THOUGH THEY'RE SUPPOSED TO RUN EVERY
fifteen minutes, everybody knows you can never catch a
Palisade Avenue bus when you need one. But when I
pushed open the registration building's heavy glass doors, there
it was directly before me, its front door still open. No one sat next
to me, and I kept my hand on the gun and stared out the window
the whole trip. I stayed on the hot bus two blocks past my stop so
no one would see me along my walk home.

There was a new lock on the door to the downstairs apartment, a chain and small padlock. But locks weren't an obstacle.
I pulled out my little black gun and never hesitated. I held my
arm straight out, one hand behind my back. *Boom!* It took two
shots to blast apart the lock. The shots shivered the foyer and
rung like church bells. I put the gun back in my pocket, feeling
its heat through my pants. I entered the downstairs apartment
as if I owned it. The door to the hallway broom closet was open,
and I shuffled toward it, sliding my feet over the sandy floor like
someone was pushing me from behind. The spool of cable was
gone. Gone to Clay's.

The scratch marks that had been on the floor five hours
earlier were doubled. Some of them led to an alley-side window.

I trotted, unseen, hunched like Quasimodo, limping and
one hand pressing the gun to my thigh, through the park and
into HouseRAD, where I slowed to an out-of-breath walk. On
the other side of the first cross street, between me and the
Pioneer, two girls were walking toward me. It was Marcy and
Lanniqua. I panicked as I watched them come closer. I wanted
to disappear. Lanniqua waved first, then Marcy. I wanted to
tell Marcy, Don't judge me by this. This ain't me. This bruise

ain't nothing, this limp ain't real. I'm all fucked. Just let me pass, okay? Just for now. I don't mean nothing by it. I'll call you.

"We seen your mother in the new restaurant," said Lanniqua. Lanniqua was black, and she was as tall as me, an inch shorter than Marcy. Both of them dressed in the same skateboard style, though unless they'd done a lot of practicing in the past month, the best they could do on blades was roll down a hill. "She's with the guy who's a cop, a lieutenant or whatever," Lanniqua said. She had on a necklace—shark's teeth on a black cord. She played with it, moving the teeth around the loop. "Are they getting married or something?"

I muttered something—maybe there were words in it, maybe it was just grunts and shrugs—something that meant I didn't know.

Marcy's honey-brown hair was a bunch of loose, curly locks—some went up, some went down, some went sideways, and some, like New Year's Eve poppers, went all three. Her nose was growing—the skin across it shiny, a red pimple breaking the skin right on the bridge. Big nose, big lips, big boobs, great legs. And in the few weeks since I'd seen her, a sunny tint had soaked into her cocoa face.

"Look, boy, are you coming on the trip or not?" Lanniqua asked. She leaned an elbow onto Marcy's shoulder. "Marcy wants to know."

"Get away," scolded Marcy, the inside of her mouth as pink and tasty as bubble gum.

I stared at her. She was wearing a blank grey football jersey, large enough to cover a linebacker—her boobs pushing the shirt out at the chest seam—and cutoff jeans that came down just an inch below the jersey. For a minute, I wanted to start talking. I didn't know about what exactly. Wagon Train or next year in school or the year after, if she was gonna apply to college. Next week, next month, next year, 2001, 2010, it didn't matter.

"Joey, where's your head?" asked Lanniqua. "You gonna come with us? Come on, boy."

I looked straight at Marcy. "Don't ask me where I'm going," I said, but what I'd meant to say was *if* I'm going.

"Mr. Rodriguez tole you I'm going?" Marcy asked, just a whisper.

"Yeah, he said that. I know it," I said. I was getting all fucking upset.

"So go with us then. What's a matter?" asked Lanniqua, fiddling her shark's teeth again. "You got to call Mr. Rodriguez by tomorrow or you miss out. And you don't know what you're missing out on."

Marcy blushed. "Don't talk for me, Niqua," she said and smacked Lanniqua on the arm. I couldn't be sure if she was really pissed or joking.

"You never know what the future holds in store," Lanniqua said, laughing and ducking the next blow.

I stood there, feeling as if I was crying but no tears came. Marcy and Lanniqua finally caught on and were silent.

"I want to go. But I can't promise," I said in the wrong tone. It sounded like I thought if I went I'd be doing them a favor. "I didn't mean that. Everything's coming down, Marcy. I can't tell you about it now. I can't. But I will later. I promise I will. I really want to. I have your phone number written."

"Joey," she said, "what's a matter? I know you. Something's really a matter." She must have seen the confusion and terror and weirdness I felt. Her face lost its sun glow and her eyes went soft and more tender, tender as a statue's dark eyes twinkling over candles. She reached for my hand but wound up holding me on the wrist, her hand over my sweatshirt cuff. "What's a matter, Joey? Come on, man, something's really wrong." Her hold, though I knew it was gentle on me, loose, not even closed, seemed to be tightening, squeezing off the blood.

"Joey, I said you okay?"

"What's a matter?" asked Lanniqua. "Did you hurt your head, man?"

"I gotta go now. I gotta go," I said, slowly turning my wrist loose. "I'm gonna go on the Wagon Train, though," I said, trying to sound happy as I brushed past them and pushed down the block. "I want to go. I'm gonna call Mr. R."

As I limp-skipped down the block, though I was on my way to getting Brian, that's what I kept whispering: I'm gonna call

Mr. Rodriguez as soon as I can. I really am gonna call him. This is done.

Opera with a hip-hop drumbeat was playing from a boombox on one of three folding tables set up at the front of the Riviera's ground level. On the other two were unopened bottles of champagne, empty ice buckets, and dozens of plastic glasses. Behind the tables, against the wall, were six cases of beer, each one a different brand. New, too, since I'd been there a few hours earlier were a dozen plants the size of small trees that stood under track lights around the sidewalls. In the middle, under the skylight, a Ping-Pong table had been moved in, paddles and balls on it.

The elevator door opened as soon as I pressed the button. Even when I entered Brian and Sonia's apartment and the harbor breeze blew the door shut behind me, I could hear the tenor bellowing and the chugga-chugga of the electric drums.

Sonia and Brian were out. I was free to walk around. In the room where they'd been working was a mattress on the floor—the mattress that had been standing against the kitchen wall—messed over with tangled sheets and a summer blanket, under the blanket a half-hidden box of Oreos.

All their clothes were folded neatly against the wall in cardboard boxes—sturdy new ones, the kind you'd buy, not find. Other than the bed, the only thing in the room you'd call furniture was a tall, narrow mirror tipped into the corner between the boxes and the bed. In the corner where Brian had been cleaning were the things Sonia had brought back from Sears—two pillows, a quart of paint or stain, and a cluster of window shades.

I walked around the apartment. I felt like a stranger from another planet, a warden from Mars making sure every object could be recognized and named.

In the middle of the other section of the apartment, the long section to the kitchen's right, just past the still-foiled plants that separated the two areas, was a Persian rug, beat up but huge. At the end of the rug were a TV and stereo on the floor. Facing the TV were four beanbag chairs—C.H. Martins specials—a purple, a yellow, an aqua, and a black. Between the chairs and the TV, lying flat on the rug, was a legless marble tabletop. On it was a glossy magazine, Sonia's Spanish church missal, three cans of Pepsi, a beanbag ashtray, burnt incense, loose pot in a Ziploc. The windows along that side were opened, and the place smelled nice, of salt water and marihuana and strawberry.

Bang, bang. Two quick knocks pulled me into myself. It felt as if I'd gathered myself up and run inside, peeked through the blinds.

Someone had shut off the music.

I made sure I still had my gun.

"Brian, Brian. It's Mom. Brian, Sonia."

I stayed right where I was, faced the door.

"Brian, open up," called Resto. No answer, so he said, "I'm gonna break it in." All he had to do was lean. Another pair of hard knocks might even have done it.

Wilkinson's voice: "No you don't, man. If you don't have a warrant, you're not touching any door. You're not doing nothing."

"I'm his mother."

"Mrs. Scadutto, I'm sorry. I'm telling you, you cannot break that door down. Nobody's in there anyway. They'd answer if they was."

"Oh, Christ. Oh, Christ," cried my mom. "Marcy said Joey was coming here."

"Well, he's not here, nobody's here, and you can't break down the door. This is Brian and Sonia's apartment and they are over eighteen and, I'm sorry, you can't break into their apartment. And neither can we."

I heard another door open, shuffling footsteps. "Can someone tell us what's going on?" It must have been the grey-bearded twins.

"We're looking for my son," said my mom, her voice fast, out of breath.

"The guy who lives here?" said one, surprised.

"No, his brother," said Resto.

"Oh."

"We're looking for his little brother, a boy about fifteen," Wilkinson said. "Short, light brown hair. He was here earlier."

"Have you seen him?"

"Nope," said the second man. "Is he in trouble?"

"Oh, I can't believe this," said my mom. Through the door I could see her—fingertips rubbing her temples, Buddy's arm reaching behind her, the strangers' eyes on her like she was fucked up trash, a bad mom. I took a step toward the door, pressing the gun to my leg.

The furniture seemed to roll away from me, like it was tumbling out and I was floating down, dizzy and weightless, down through a clear, light space.

"We're trying to keep him out of trouble," said Wilkinson. "He's a good kid but he's just got himself all screwed up."

I got all goose-bumpy and shivered. I've got to call Mr. Rodriguez, I reminded myself.

"He's not dangerous," said Buddy.

"Yo," said Wilkinson. "He's a sweet kid, but he's very confused and he's fifteen and he's got a gun. Now, if that's not dangerous."

They laughed, the two strangers. I swear they laughed. "Well, we'll stay inside," said one, the first one who'd spoken. "If we see him how do we call you?"

"Just . . . I got a beeper. Well, just call 911 right away if you see him."

"We're not gonna see him," said the other one. "We're just gonna lock the door and watch movies. We don't need confronting no insane little teenager."

"Call your building supervisor. Tell him to cancel that party downstairs."

"Come on, let's go," complained Resto.

My mom cried.

"Look, do what I tell you. Call the super," ordered Wilkinson.

"Don't worry. Will do," said one of them. "The kid's one of those total wackouts, huh?"

ELEVEN

THE ELEVATOR HAD COME AND GONE, BUT I COULDN'T be sure no one had stayed behind, standing guard. My only way out of the apartment was to jump. I went to the sidewall of tall windows. I was two floors above the narrow back yard that, starting right at the base of the building, sloped down the hill toward Hoboken.

There were high weeds below me, and the ground, where I could see through the weeds, shimmered with green and clear and brown glass. Straight under the window, the first one in the long room, were three pallets stacked atop each other. Four windows over (also against the building but in the sunlight), more under the next apartment than Brian's, was a coffin-shaped stack of bricks, partly hidden under a dusty, sun-warmed tarp.

The apartment windows were the kind that didn't open at the top or bottom, opened only in their middle, where a three-foot-high pane swiveled downward on hinges. My second hard jerk pulled open the first window.

When I climbed onto the inside sill, I saw that there was no outside ledge, only a chipped seam where the mortar met the rust-coated metal frame. Standing on the sill, I faced the apartment, my back to the window. I put my left hand outside and grabbed on to the sharp brick edging. With my right hand, I held the gun in place. I lifted my left foot through and was barely able to get a toehold outside. I was sure that once I crouched and shifted my weight the hold would give. I turned both my feet sideways. I took my hand off the gun and held on to the sides of the framing with two hands as I slowly ducked and turned. I was half in and half out, my legs bowed to straddle the tipped-open window. I swung my head and body underneath the upper window and outside. The hold stayed.

I kept as much weight as I could on my back foot, the one still inside the apartment. I turned my outside foot so it was pointing away, heel against the building. My weight shifted forward, and when I tried to dig my heel into the building, the mortar crumbled and my foot slid down. For a second, just long enough to get my back foot through the window and clear, I held myself up with my hands, but quickly, in a finger snap, I fell toward the palettes, my back bouncing against the wall. I tried to kangaroo-hop off them, but the force of the fall smashed me through the rotted wood.

I was afraid the people in other apartments, hearing the crash, would discover me, so I stretched my arms out and splayed myself against the building like one of the vines already growing there. My hip ached and I was sure the bone in my ankle had cracked through, though the ache was gone, replaced by a cool then hot and wet feeling under the skin. The long pants and hooded sweatshirt had protected all of my body except the back of my head from cuts and bumps. In two throbbing spots, I could feel the back of my skull knotting up. With my cheeks pressed to the cool, rough bricks, I closed my eyes and caught my breath.

Back to the wall, I shuffled to the building's end. It must have been early in the evening, six or seven. Angling past the building's edge, the sun, orange in a grey sky, still strong and swinging like a pendulum over the Pulaski Skyway Bridge, hypnotized me. It lit the blooming blue and white wildflowers down the railroad cut, turned the whole of New York a gleaming golden red, eventually blinded me with a light that was warm and bright but gentle, not harsh. I closed my eyes. The sun felt great, like God. It soothed and nourished my face.

I smiled and pulled off my sweatshirt and rolled it up like a pillow. I boosted myself onto the stack of canvas-covered bricks, six feet long and just wide enough to lie upon with my hands folded across my belt buckle, the heavy pistol dangling over the side. The sun-soak nursed my bones.

I opened my eyes and shut them, opened and shut them again. With eyes closed to the sun, I watched the colors change inside my lids—swirling yellow and orange, silver, pink, marbly white. I drifted in the softly colored clouds.

251

The sounds I heard were far away, swishing sounds, railroad sounds, harbor sounds, seagulls, children playing, church bells, old sounds, old and gone.

The only thing that had kept my heart pounding and racing, that had kept me going at all, was my panic. As that drained off, my heartbeat settled to a slow drumming. I grew more worn and more weak, too worn and weak to keep my thoughts in the present, on what I had to do. I thought about tomorrow and on past it. Sometimes words told the tale, sometimes it was pictures. The more I thought, the more I dreamed. And the more I saw, the more I smiled, because what I saw was so confusing, so contradicting. Here, then there. Doing one thing, then another. With this person, then with that one. Imagining people I'd never even met, places I hadn't yet been to. I didn't know which of the pictures would turn out to happen, but any of them could have, just within a few days.

As the sun held my body down, it felt like a ghost rose up out of me and walked into tomorrow's scene—with Marcy, walking toward Mr. Rodriguez. Then I stepped through scenes further out—a month, a year, five years. Sex, college, marriage. A vacation. A daddy scene. Yeah, I said, a future. Sometime down the road.

I smiled with my eyes closed. It was something I'd always been afraid to do. And I watched myself stroll through all the things that could—that actually could—the things that could come to be.

I don't know for how long I lay there, breathing, imagining. I think maybe it was half an hour. I sat up on the bricks, my feet dangling down. I took the gun out of my pants pocket. The sun had slipped behind the building, but its last rays still lit the harbor and the southern tip of Manhattan.

I put the gun away. "Get this done with," I whispered. "You just gotta get this done with."

I didn't even bother to put my shirt back on. I knew what I'd do and I'd do it right away. Find Detective Wilkinson and turn Brian in before he hurt again.

Where the trees were thick and healthy, the park was darker, the high rectangular streetlamps, bright as prison lights and caged against stone throwers, already on. I passed under the first group of them, then stood midway through the park, on the concrete ring around the WWII Memorial. My hope was that the whole gang would be at our house.

But then, away, across Cobble Road, I could see Brian climbing Uncle Vic's porch. Banding his tiny ponytail with both hands, he kicked open the front door and entered. I began walking slowly, my eyes fixed on the building entrance. But the dread, after all of this, of being a minute too late sank deeper and deeper into me. My steps sped up and soon I was running toward the shrinking yellow light that fell from the doorway. I looked for the others, people I could bring with me, but the park, quickly sinking into evening, was deserted. Above me, ahead, Uncle Vic's bedroom light clicked on.

Barechested, I crossed the Cobble Road overpass. I swung myself around the front gate and up the outside steps. "Fuck this," I said. With some part of my body, a shoulder or a hip, I pushed through the first door. The inside one was held wide open with a rubber stop, and I could see straight up the stairs. Over the banging of a first-floor drum set, on the second or probably the third floor, Uncle Mike's old floor, there was an argument going on, wild screeches, women fighting one another and children wailing. It sounded like three languages.

Slowly, but two at a time, I climbed the steps, my eyes fixed on Uncle Vic's door. I heard more screaming from the upstairs, but now I heard Uncle Vic's booming voice, too. A second later his TV blared, drowning out his words. I kicked at the apartment door with my foot.

I heard a chair being shoved across the floor, something smashing against the refrigerator. "Who is it?" Brian yelled. "Who is it?" Nothing came from Uncle Vic. I kicked again but couldn't kick the door from its new lock. I blasted it, *boom*! Once, twice. *Boom*! "I gotta get this done. Damn it! Fuck!"

I kicked the door in, gun drawn. At the rear of the kitchen, one hand out like a cop halting traffic, the other reaching behind his back, Brian stood at the entrance to the bedroom hall. I aimed. "Joey!" he said. He dropped his front hand, slowly swung his back hand forward, a gun in his grip. "Waah!" I screamed as loud as I could. I fired and the bullet screamed back.

"Joey, don't! Joey, no, don't. Don't be crazy, man. No! Please don't! Joey!" He tried to run further back in the hall but I stepped deeper into the kitchen where I had an angle on the whole apartment. "Joey, stop! Stop it!" he said, this time like he was giving an order. *Boom*, I fired again. In his white boxers, holding a handful of photographs, Uncle Vic stepped from his bedroom. His mouth was opened wide but silent, his hands out, questioning, like I'd seen them a thousand times.

Brian raised his gun. His hand was waving from side to side as he tried to aim. He fired. I was out of bullets. I jerked the gun, snapped it in my hand like you would to lower down a thermometer. Brian fired again.

I staggered even though I hadn't felt the bullet, just a fire against my neck. The blood, warm and gloppy, poured onto my shoulder. I dropped the gun and reached to my neck with my hands. It felt like half my throat was gone and my head was plopped on one shoulder. I couldn't tell what was me and what wasn't, what had poured out and what was connected. It must have been veins and muscle, maybe chips of bone.

I was flying backward, down the stairs, bumping everything, legs, head, back, saying Don't panic.

On the floor it was better. Curled and resting like a baby, I could hear every breath.

Brian and Uncle Vic stared down from the doorway. There was a crowd around me, though at first I couldn't see them. Men and women holding children leaned over the upper-floor banisters. The ceiling seemed a mile away. The white lights were too bright. I saw even when my eyes were shut. It was much easier that way.

I tried to speak, to say It's over with, but I knew no words came up. To say It'll be better.

I felt my head being lifted in arms as soft and cool as a pillow. I opened my eyes. It was my mom holding me. She petted my chest with one hand, pressed a towel to my neck with the other. People were kneeling all around me. My mom and Resto and Wilkinson. I caught a glimpse of Marcy's face, swollen and red, before she buried it in Mr. Rodriguez's shoulder. It seemed like they were all touching me and touching each other, one way or another.

I felt so loved.

There I was in my mom's lap, soaking her jeans with the blood that leaked through her heavy towel. It didn't really hurt. It was okay, just stung a little and throbbed. It didn't hurt a lot, I wanted her to know. The blood was no big thing. I needed an ambulance, I knew, quick. It was the throbbing scared me. It felt like what was throbbing was me, but a part of me that had fallen out.

My mommy stopped petting my chest. Instead, she pressed down on it. She pressed then eased, pressed then eased, huh-phoo, huh-phoo. She was making my breaths for me. That's good, that's good, I wanted my mommy to know. That's good.

Medics barged in. They went on my other side, my mom still held me. They put something cold and metal to my neck. It felt like tongs.

While they clamped, my mom pressed down on my heart. I smiled and stared up, past her, at a light so bright it made me dizzy, even after I'd closed my eyes. "I'm right here," I whispered.

Photograph by Mark Speed

Joe Colicchio lives in Cranford, NJ, and teaches at a local community college. He and his wife have two sons.